Norwich 1144
A Jew's Tale

Norwich 1144
A Jew's Tale

A Novel

by
Bill Albert

Mousehold Press
6, Constitution Opening
Norwich, NR3 4BD
www.mousehold-press.co.uk

First published by Mousehold Press in 2014

ISBN 978-1-874739-74-6

Printed by Page Bros (Norwich)

For Saskia, Remmert, Maya, Saul and Charlotte

Acknowledgments

Right up front, I want to thank my wife, Gill. She has given me loving support in so many ways. It is difficult enough having to live with me, but she has had to put up with other William as well.

Thanks to my agent Lora Fountain, who has stood by me with great loyalty for over 20 years. Thanks also to Eric and Judy Homberger, Maya Albert, Saul Albert, Ada Raporport-Albert, Juliet Corbett and the Norwich Mice and Men Book Group for encouragement and valuable critical input. Jon Jackson did a fantastic text layout and cover and was endlessly patient with me.

Also by Bill Albert

And What About Rodríquez?

(Et Rodríquez alors?)

Desert Blues

Castle Garden

Desert Swing

Desert Requiem

Incident At Mirage Wells

http://billalbert.me.uk

Preface

Safed, Israel 1968

I was in a sixteenth century synagogue in Safed, a town 1000 metres above the Sea of Galilee. The rabbi, who looked as if he had been with the building since it was built, asked me where I lived. I told him I lived in Norwich, England. He looked alarmed, and then without missing a beat he turned and spat dryly over his shoulder three times. Having thereby ensured that the Evil Eye was placated, he told me the story of William of Norwich.

In March, 1144, the body of William, a 13-year old boy, was discovered in Thorpe Wood, near Norwich. His death was blamed on the small community of Jews in the city who were alleged to have killed him as part of a religious ceremony. Mob violence erupted against the Jews. About five years later, Thomas of Monmouth, a monk in the Cathedral Priory, wrote a book that helped to transform William into a local saint. This was the first documented accusation of ritual murder in Europe of a Christian child by Jews – what was to become known, in somewhat different circumstances, as the Blood Libel.

The story of William of Norwich has echoed down the centuries in a great many similar accusations and accompanying riots, pogroms and in wholesale genocide. As the rabbi in Safed demonstrated, the tale remains alive as a key event in the long history of Jewish persecution.

Do not consider it proof just because it is written in books, for a liar who will deceive with his tongue will not hesitate to do the same with his pen.

Moses Maimonides

1135 – 1204

Norwich
In The Year 1230

The End

Joseph the Fool is about to die, my death foretold by the baying of the mob in the street below. Fool I might seem to be, but still I comfort myself with the conceit that I, lifelong cripple with crooked back, feeble legs and wooden tongue, and so for all the world a fool, have managed to outlive all the learned, clever men I ever knew. All those men with their straight backs and their straight legs. All those men with their silken throats and clever words. So straight-backed and so straight-legged and so smooth of voice, so clever and now so dead, may they rest in peace.

William too. I outlived him, but that circumstance brings me no comfort. Although he is my abiding solace, he is also my abiding sorrow. My lovely William. My dearest friend. My saintly companion. Dead these many years. I take some comfort from the fact that he has long since found peace with God's Angels.

Moreover, William is remembered, he is venerated. Not so Joseph, an unseemly husk, a freak of body, a freak of an old age beyond understanding. I am thankful that no one is left alive who remembers when I returned, an apparent stranger, to the city of Norwich. I am thankful that no one remembers when I wasn't among them as a very old man. For the world now around me I have no childhood, no past. All my transgressions concealed. All my years as a respected scribe in a distant land unknown and unsung. Now little more than a drooling relic, an ancient fool who has always been there, slumped in the corner of the room. I am thankful for all of that lost history.

Walking on the cobbled streets, stumbling at every step, I hear the Gentiles shout, "Look at old Methuselah! Bloodsucker! Circumcised Devil! Murderer of our Lord!" Often the shouts are company to a rotting vegetable, soft decaying flesh against my soft decaying flesh. If my luck is truly raddled, I am slashed by a flint or bruised by a rounded stone. No matter the missile, always curses attend

Do the curses draw me into the fold of my brethren? Is a curse shared a curse diminished? Perhaps, but that assumes my putative brethren would deign to enfold me.

Jews. We have all had to face the good Norwich folk when we venture out on their streets in our pointy Jew hats. But for hats would we be noticed, singled out, reviled? Could there be a world without badges, with no clerical or knightly vestments, nothing to signal difference? No, my imagination cannot put flesh on such a world.

One hundred years old? I have heard it said that at seventy years a man is grey, if eighty years he must possess inordinate strength, a bowed back is carried at ninety but at one hundred! At one hundred years surely he has departed this world.

I look down and see that I have not yet departed. I feel all of those hundred years, especially as I struggle to stand from my bed, as I watch through a stranger's eyes at the shaking of my hands, at the meatless, skin-stretched thighs and the shrivelled bag and its lifeless companion hanging between them, that cursed and blessed root of so many of life's travails since my time began. And when that time ends today? Will the rain then fall and the waters rise covering the land? For Methuselah, but not for Joseph.

For me there has been a century of water - my tears, my saliva, my sweat, my urine. So much water, so many days, but when one day is the same as the last, who can be troubled to count them? Some of those days I remember, most I have forgotten, at least I suppose I have. Holes to dig, holes to fill in, holes to dig and on and on it winds out. Each day another hole. That's life, until the hole is dug that you fill with your emptied-dry mortal remains. Only then, and only if He is willing, will you find peace.

Will I find peace with no Lamech to recite Kaddish for me? With no family to sit shiva? But won't He be merciful to an old crippled man who has seen so much suffering of Israel in this foreign and terrible land?

May His great Name grow exalted and sanctified
In the world that He created as He willed.
May there be abundant peace from Heaven
May there be abundant peace for Joseph.
Amen.

Peace? Of course, peace. Even a fool wouldn't deny this as a blessing from on High. The way time is unwinding at this moment I would settle for a moth's breath worth of peace, even the fluttering touch of his night-soft wings.

Oh, now in the final moments, I long to see my William's smile, to hear his laughter, to feel his embrace, even as I know these miracles will not be visited upon me.

Instead it seems I will die as I have lived, not in peace or the embrace of love, but in a solitude of torment. No breath or flutter or warm arms to hold me, only angry voices swirling out the fire, as they have before and are now again, screaming for the blood of the Jews. All Jews. Any Jew.

Why is it happening yet again? The blessed Mark of the Covenant is why. The cursed Mark of Abraham is why. It singled me out at the beginning of my journey and now it comes once more to usher in my departure. I take no comfort in the fact that on this occasion it is not the contours of my verpus member that has provoked the trouble. My fate is sealed regardless of whose member it is that protrudes to stir the fires of Christian rage.

At present the offended member is said to belong to a five-year-old named Odard, the son of Benedict, the Jew who became a Christian. It is said he was taken away by Jews so as to be restored to the community. Of course, restoration meant the child had to be enjoined to the Covenant, and when he was found a few days later in tears, wandering by the river, his little cock bound in a sulphurous rag and still dripping blood, a hue and cry went up. That hue and that cry is now roaring out in the street below. Cut for cut. Blood for blood.

No matter that this house is made of stone, strong against the night's thieves and the furious clamouring of the mob. Or that the thick oak door is bound with iron bands and the windows shuttered hard. I sense that too soon all will be overwhelmed and they will come for me.

The single candle flickers, grotesque silhouettes dance and swirl across the beamed ceiling and the daub walls.

My ears have not served me well for some time, a blessing, muffling the murderous noise. Lying here on my straw pallet I reach out and lay my hand flat against the cold, rough wall. Vibrations from the mob's attack fill my fingers and travel up my arm. My sense of smell remains, and the stench of burning pitch is now stronger, having gathered itself to reach my eyrie under the eves.

I rise slowly. My limbs pain me for the effort. Steadying myself against the rounded top of a chest, I reach out for my crutches. I hold on for a moment and then shuffle two steps to the small window overlooking the street.

My sight has gone the way of my hearing, and below I can just make out blooms of waving fire, torches, filling up the night in the narrowness of Saddlegate. What I don't see, but can't stop myself imagining, are the bodies being torn and trampled underfoot. Too late these King's Jews sought shelter behind the Sheriff's arms in the Castle. To the Castle it is, for those not too old or too crippled, but a three-minute walk in the safety of daylight. What the poor unfortunates did not reckon with was how hatred can extend a familiar distance beyond survival.

Sounds of battering at the main door rush up the stairwell

13

and disrupt my reverie. I retreat to my pallet. I sit down heavily. I wait. Too soon the fine people of Norwich will be here, and the sleepless-night-time terror of so many years will be made real in bone and blood, my bone and my blood. Unbidden, from out of that darkness I hear the words of the Egyptian Rabbi. "Commune with your own heart on your bed and be still." I smile at memories of those happier times and am immediately overcome by a sudden and unexpected lack of fear. Its absence suckles me as if it was sweet mother's milk. I commune with my heart and am blessed for the moment by the stillness of calm acceptance.

The Escape

Icompose myself for a final prayer. Not having the courage to see Death enter the room, I bow my head, close my eyes and begin.

I lift my eyes to the mountains -- from where will my help come?

My help will come from the Lord, Maker of heaven and earth.

He will not let your foot falter; your guardian does not slumber.

Indeed, the Guardian....

"Grandfather!" a voice calls out.

I raise my head and open my eyes. In place of the Pale Horse and Rider, I see two tall, well-proportioned striplings of about sixteen or seventeen years, one dark, clothed in a stained linen shirt, the other fair haired and wearing a short leather apron. They seem familiar. I reach out for names. None comes. No doubt the failure of my eyes or the ill-lit room or my ill-lit memory.

"Grandfather," the fair one says once more, as they both advance across the room, gesturing to me. "You must come with us. Come now, quickly."

'Quickly' has not been within my grasp for many years. I begin to push myself from the pallet. I cannot move. All strength has abandoned me. Hands lay hold of my arms. With soft gentleness the two boys easily lift me to my feet. I stumble against them.

"Who...?" I ask.

"There is no time, Grandfather," one replies. "Let us assist you down the stairs. Now!"

Their strength is such that I do not resist as they half carry me towards the door. We emerge onto the landing. Here, away from the dim light of the candle, we are immediately enveloped in total darkness. The angry clamour from the street is suddenly amplified. Calm deserts me and fear assaults me anew. Finding a last shred of energy, I push myself backwards, away from the noise and the emptiness of the black void below.

"Not now, Grandfather. Please, give us your trust and we will bear you in safety away from this place."

I have no time to choose. I am lifted up, and we begin our descent. Each uneven stair jolts through my body. I close my eyes. When I open them we have arrived at the ground floor. Here the screaming of the mob is joined to the deep subterranean thunder of heavy objects being struck against the outer door. The acrid odour of smoke and murder tinges the air. Flickering torchlight from the street filtering in through the cracks in the shutters floods the empty room with a savage dance of shadows and light. All the others in the house have fled. I have been forgotten by everyone except the two young men. Who are they who would risk their lives for me?

A large plank of wood is dislodged from the buckling door and crashes to the floor. The success is immediately followed by howls of triumph. The assault on the door becomes more frenzied.

"Kill the Jews! Kill the Jews! Kill the Jews! For Christ and St. William!"

My William! His name, on the lips of a murderous rabble. If they but knew. However, I am the only one who knows, and that knowledge will not serve to shield me.

"The garden, now before our way is blocked."

"Kill the Jews!"

"My crutches. I cannot ...".

In response I am snatched up as if a child, cradled tightly

in strong arms and carried through the back of the house into the small walled garden. The night is cloudless and very cold. Moonlight illuminates the scene. The tumult of the street is muted briefly before a splintering crash announces that the front door has been finally breached. The lads dash across the garden to a low, studded wooden gate set into the flint wall. Behind us the ominous swell of outraged voices and heavy footfalls.

"It's stuck fast. It won't open!"

"We can't take the old man with us over the wall. Try it again. Push harder. Fast, they're coming!"

I have been set down on the ground, my back against a tree. The bark is rough through my nightshirt and against my tenderly-brittle bones. The mob is filling up the house, searching room by room for Jews to murder. It may be for the lack of a victim or victims that their fury has been directed onto more inanimate objects. I hear furniture being smashed. A shower of splintered wood, probably from damaged window shutters, rains down on our heads. It will not be long before their rampage has claimed all there is within the house, and they move to discover us trapped here in the garden.

I see my deliverers furiously butting their shoulders against the gate. When this doesn't succeed, they start to kick at it.

"No good. It probably hasn't been opened in years."

"In the garden!" someone yells from above and behind us. "The Jews are in the garden! In the garden!"

They glance behind them and then with an urgency fuelled by the spectre of an imminent and brutal death, they return to the attack.

As the first of the rioters emerges from the house, the old gate squeals against the onslaught and then, at last, with a deep cracking of wood, gives way, slamming resoundingly against the outside of the wall. Arms encircle me and they are pushing me hurriedly through the opening. Splinters of wood pierce my thin arms. Somehow they manage to shut the gate behind us. A thick broken tree branch, no doubt placed on the ground by Divine Providence, serves as a prop to secure the opening for a few vital moments, blocking the way of those giving chase.

With me clutched in their arms, the boys run and run through the moonlit streets. Behind us shouts and the heavy clatter of pursuit. Every few minutes they stop to pass me from one to the other. They run and run. Over their laboured breathing the mob can still be heard. Wait now. The sound has suddenly become more distant, as if those hunting us have veered off in a different direction. The boys stop to listen.

"I think we are free of them," says the one carrying me.

"We mustn't stop. No telling. Come now."

Our flight resumes, albeit at a slower pace. After another quarter of an hour or so we arrive at a rude shed. They push open the door, carry me in and lay me down on a pile of straw. There is the pungent stench of animals. Something large moves in the straw. It grunts, either a welcome or a warning.

"They will not look for you here, Grandfather."

There is barely suppressed hysteria in their laughter. I am too spent to join in with them or concern myself unduly why they laugh or with whom I am sharing my straw bed.

They leave me, promising to return in the morning and escort me to the safety of the Castle.

On The Run

"Grandfather? Grandfather? It is morning."

"Are you well?"

"He still sleeps."

I force open my eyes. The early morning lights up the pig-churned dirt of the yard in front of the shed. The two boys stand above me. The sun is low but directly behind them, haloing their faces so I cannot distinguish the fair one from the dark. Their hands are outstretched as if offering a benediction. What they are offering, more welcome than a benediction, is a large piece of black bread and a jug of milk.

"We have brought you food. Are you able to sit?"

I nod and push myself into a sitting position. Despite the sun, a hard frost tops the ridged soil outside. Two or three chickens peck at the earth. A grey pig, probably my companion from the previous night, forages in a shallow mud-filled ditch behind them. The air inside the shed sparkles with motes of dust.

I ache in places I have not until now been aware of, and I am bone cold. I readily attest that without a coat or even a blanket, all abandoned in the hurried escape of the previous evening, old bodies refuse to hold any warmth.

"He shivers. Please, Grandfather, take this."

A heavy blanket is laid across my shoulders. Milk is poured from the jug into a wooden bowl. I dip the bread and wait for it to soften in the milk, necessary for someone with tender gums and but few remaining teeth. It is most curious that they knew to bring me milk with the bread, my sole repast since well before their cords were cut.

"Do you have the strength to travel?"

19

Mouth full of milk-soaked bread, I shake my head. I am too fatigued to run any more. Even if it were possible, without my crutches I cannot move.

"We must take you from here very soon and deliver you to those who will offer you protection, a place where other Jews have found shelter."

"It will be difficult, all routes to the Castle have been blocked, and the Sheriff's men are too few or too cowardly to venture out into the streets."

"As we speak, men are searching throughout the city, looking to find The Old Jew, as they are calling you."

Old Jew! If they knew what I did all those years ago would I not be celebrated by the Gentiles and reviled by the Jews, instead of being hunted as an enemy of Christ? In truth, and against what Eleazar and other Jews never tired of repeating with vicious conviction, Christ has never been my enemy. Only some of his servants have assumed that role. For many years He was my refuge and I loved Him. I can freely confess to that now, for I feel certain that I will soon move beyond earthly disputations over Heaven.

"Please, Grandfather, we have a need for haste. Last night a great many eyes will have overlooked the streets and it cannot be long ere those unremarked observations are understood and joined together in a trail that will lead our pursuers here."

They bend down towards me and reach out their hands. I wave them away.

"No. I am sorry, but I can go no further. This old Jew is much too old, much too tired to travel further. Let it end here among the chickens and the pigs. Without my crutches I cannot walk. Even with them, if we, two boys and a hobbling cripple, were to be espied, as undoubtedly we would be, I would be soon taken and your young lives too would be forfeit. And for what purpose? To save a cripple of little value in this world, one who should have died a great many years since? Please, you have done enough for me without putting yourselves in further peril. Leave me here and save yourselves. Ha! But I forget. You will not have understood a word. There is no one who does, no one who wants to listen, no one...".

"But, of course, Grandfather. Every word. Why do you doubt?"

"Yes, every word."

Who are these boys who follow my toothless, cripple-lipped speech with such ease, something no one, except William, has ever accomplished at first meeting? If only the bright sun behind them did not continue to obscure their faces, much as the darkness did last night, I might know them.

I dip another piece of bread. When I look up from the bowl the two lads have disappeared. They have done what I asked of them. I tip the bowl to drink the last of the milk. Before I finish they are back pushing a large handcart, its high-boarded sides and wheels encrusted with farmyard muck.

"There is no need to walk, Grandfather. Come, your carriage awaits you."

"We go to a place not far distant from the Castle. We can stop there until the crowds lose interest or are scattered by the Sheriff's men."

I am lifted into the cart and covered with the blanket on top of which they pile a goodly quantity of pig-smeared straw. I am assured that this foul covering will deter closer scrutiny. That assurance does little to comfort me and nothing to make the stench easier to abide.

Followers of St. Francis

The two boys pull my crude and malodorous chariot through the streets. I can see nothing outside the cart's murky interior, but can hear the rise and fall of voices as we pass. Children shouting and laughing. The call of a drover urging on his charges. The sound of cow bells or goat bells. I am suddenly startled by the close-by and shrill voice of a woman hawker, crying out the virtues of her onions or perhaps it is her oysters. My defective hearing combined with the terrifying waves of street clamour make such fine distinctions impossible.

I have long since come to the realisation that in this world there is scant justice, even for the most virtuous. As virtue has eluded me, as I have eluded it, finding myself covered in animal excrement being trundled about in a farm cart comes as no great revelation.

The cart tilts and I am propelled backwards, banging my head against an unseen obstruction. We must be going up an incline. Somewhere near the Castle perhaps? If only I could see outside.

"We are now close, Grandfather," one of the boys says.

"Not much longer," says the other.

The noise of the crowds has lessened. We must have turned off the main roadway. We stop. I hear the rap of knuckles against wood.

"We are come, Friar, as we promised. Yes, we have brought the old Jew. Yes, he is safe."

Surely after all the effort they have made to rescue me they will not now deliver me into the hands of the friars. I have heard that these recent arrivals, with their street preaching, their begging and their strict adherence to poverty and the purity of Jesus, have crafted themselves as revivers of the True Church and the implacable enemies of non-believers.

The refuse is being removed from on top of me. The rug is taken away and I squint against the strong light. We are in a narrow alleyway. On one side there are houses, their first floors leaning outwards, as if bowing to the more substantial stone building across the wet and befouled alley. I see no one, but imagine curious, hostile eyes staring out at me from the overhanging windows.

I try to stand, but my legs, at the best of times untrustworthy and now numbed by having to sit akimbo for so long on the rough wooden floor of the cart, are unable to support me and I begin to collapse. I am saved from a fall and further bruising by the strong hands of my rescuers. They take me gently by my arms and then slide their arms under the legs, lift me in a sitting position from the cart and rush in through the open door of the flint-walled building. A short, stout, florid-faced man in a grey cassock swings the door closed behind us.

"Welcome, Rabbi Joseph," he says, beaming at me as if I were an old friend rediscovered. He speaks with a strong Italian lilt and carries a distinctly aquiline nose, which sits curiously in his rounded moon face. "Welcome to our humble community. May God be with you."

It is many years since anyone has called me Rabbi, and even then it was an honorific title bestowed in deference to my years.

I can but nod in reply, sitting as I am in the arms of the two boys, pieces of filthy straw raining down onto the floor. I ache terribly from the journey through the city and, despite the apparently friendly welcome, I can see no future for myself with this friar, or, for that, any friar or monk. The one time that I did glimpse such a future, I found at the last little but disappointment.

I look about the small, narrow room. The walls are crudely finished. There are two benches, one against the far wall, the other beside a table. A door gives out to a passageway probably leading to more rooms. The window onto the street is firmly shuttered. Shadows dance on the walls, thrown there by two smoking tapers that sit on the low table in the centre of the room.

"Please," says the friar, pointing, "You may set Rabbi Joseph down over there."

The boys carry me across and slowly lower me onto the long bench. It is only now that I notice there are two women and three small children crowded together at the other end of the bench. By their attire, Jews. They stare at me fearfully.

"Don't be afraid," I tell them, my hands flailing out a message, which together with the unmastered words and unmastered spittle erupting from my toothless gums serves only to magnify their alarm. They retreat further down the bench until they are in danger of tumbling to the floor. One of the smaller children buries its head in the arms of a woman, who I assume is his or her mother, and emits a piercing howl. This ignites an echoed response from the others and the room is quickly filled with the shrieks of terrified children. The noise brings the friar hurrying to her side.

"Oh, my dear woman," he says, "please quiet the children. At all costs we must avoid calling attention to ourselves. It would be dangerous if you were to be discovered, but you know that, do you not?"

Slowly the children are calmed. The friar leaves the room and returns soon after bearing bowls of porridge and several flat pieces of wood to use as spoons. He hands two bowls to the women and one to me.

"Here, Rabbi. I trust this will revive you somewhat. I apologise, that our vows of poverty and humility, as well as our true poverty, prevent us from offering a more generous table."

The porridge is tepid, heavy and tasteless. I eat.

"You are under the protection of the Order of Friars Minor. Some call us the Greyfriars. You have heard of the Greyfriars? Good, for we remain unknown by most. That is because we arrived in Norwich but four years since and there are still so few of us here. My brothers, there are three of them, are now out in the city, preaching to the people to observe the teachings of our blessed St. Francis, who taught us to follow our Lord Jesus Christ by not giving in to hatred and violence but instead to speak of peace and harmony, even with the Saracen or the Jew. These two gallant boys have been assisting us in this mission," he says, draping an arm over each one. "At great risk they have gone out to bring to us as many of your people as they can discover, to save them from the hatred of the poor deluded ones who now roam the streets with brands and clubs."

"Who are these...," I begin to ask.

He looks at me, struggling to comprehend. I repeat my questions two or three times.

"These boys?" the friar says, finishing my question, as most people are prone to do.

Is he being helpful? I prefer to believe that for him, as for others before him, at its core impatience governs their behaviour, for such actions extend beyond verbal interference. Doors are opened before me, chairs are set in place, food put on my plate, all without request. I have had to learn to tolerate being at the mercy of others' conception of what I might want and to tolerate it all with a complicit smile.

I smile at the eager friar.

"We don't know who they are. When the violence broke out in the city, having heard our council of peace they came offering to help. We asked no more. Do you understand? Yes?

So, my dear Rabbi, you may let yourself rest here without fear."

After a time I drift into sleep. I wake lying on the hard bench. Someone has covered me with a blanket and placed a straw-filled pillow under my head. The women and children have gone, as have the boys. Only the lone grey-clad friar remains. He sits at the table, his head bent over a thick book. His body rocks slowly back and forth as he reads, lips moving to capture the words from the page.

"Ah, my dear Rab Joseph," he calls when he notes that I have awoken. "Are you quite refreshed?"

He comes and sits by my side.

"You know, my most revered friend, judging by your years, if you do not take exception to my remarking upon it, you have survived as a Jew here in this Christian world for a very long time. If you are not too fatigued, perhaps you would be willing to enlighten me as to how you have fared so well, survived so long."

He smiles and settles back against the wall, waiting to be enlightened.

There is no reason why I should confide in this garrulous, long-nosed, round-faced friar, no reason to trust him with my life secrets. I have learned, through the most painful of lessons, that monks or friars or priests, no matter what colour their cassocks - black, white, or grey - are not to be trusted, especially by Jews. I have learned that secrets are secrets for good reason. I have learned that revealing any of your secrets puts your life in the untrustworthy hands of strangers. Even if they are not strangers but instead intimately known to you, even if they profess their blood-oath fidelity, in the end of all things and at the end of all times, everyone you might know is a stranger. Often I have felt a stranger to myself. But you, yes you, you are an unknown, a faceless, non-corporeal stranger. I am beyond the realm of concern as to your approbation or your condemnation, for I know you not, do not wish to know you, will never know you.

So, to the curious Franciscan I profess myself too stretched in years, too exhausted, too incoherent of speech to enlighten him further. But to you my unseen friend, I commend all my secrets, every last one. Do not fear that in the unfolding you will need listen to this stale, aged, querulous voice over-laden with bitterness, disappointments and regrets. No. If I can prevail, you will hear instead, as best I can conjure, a more tender voice, befitting the life I lived out in my more tender years. As for my secrets, they are yours, do with them what you will.

Thorpe Wood
In The Years 1131 - 1139

The Beginning

My beginning, my first memory, is an unadorned page of vellum, the unbroken whiteness of snow. It must have been cold, but that does not intrude. Of course, from this great distance I could amplify that memory, add to it details derived from a worldly consciousness that I did not then possess. If I am truthful, and I am almost always truthful, I see only an absence of colour and of understanding.

The whiteness tips sideways as I am lifted and pressed against softness. As I think back, the stench of animals joins, at once rancid and sweet, forcing itself upon me.

Understanding, albeit incomplete, only came much later.

I had been discovered in a field by Ederick, a hermit monk who resided deep in the tangled recesses of Thorpe Wood, which is perched on and runs back for about half a league from the high escarpment across the river from the city of Norwich.

Ederick stumbled upon me not a great distance from where William's body was to be found a few years later by the Lady Legarda, then by the forester Henry de Sprowston and then by the crowd from the city. Thomas told me there must be a Heavenly Equation to account for the locational congruence of these two events, but he was always too engaged in more important matters to move on to decipher the true meaning.

Ederick, one time a monk in the city's Cathedral Priory, was a large, carelessly put together man, his mouth inhabited by a few broken teeth, his skin dyed by soot and his hair and beard a single woven mat. He wore a long tattered coat of animal skins belted with a leather strap. His feet were shod in strips of hide.

"I was unable to find God," he told me. "Too many rules, not enough space or time to allow me to seek the truth of my Saviour. I felt a wrong bird among that flock of oh-so-more-pious-than-you Normans, always plotting my disgrace and damnation."

"No matter now, as here in the wilderness my battle against the Devil is truly joined. Every day, in the solitude of the wood I find it easier to combat the evil thoughts and vices spewed into the world and into consciousness of man by the Fallen Angel. Every day I find my soul closer to God, the same God who was looking after you, Joseph, my Little Jew that was."

I was a soul rescued for Christ and Baptised by Ederick. He had caught me early, when my only deficit was the Mark of Abraham. He believed with a burning certainty that I had a Great Purpose in the world, and he was to be the instrument for realising that Great Purpose.

"He must have guided my feet to take that path and guided my eyes to where you lay, swaddled and silent, waiting for Death. However, Death did not find you, instead Ederick found you. The Lord made me your Deliverer. It would be presumptuous of me to ask why this is so. But then as children were not Moses and Ishmael abandoned? Did they both not achieve greatness for the Lord? I am sure that in the fullness of time all will be revealed."

Ederick told me that when he plucked me from that field I had perhaps one or two years. Whilst he admitted to knowing little about children, he did at least know, even thin and small as I was and was to remain for a goodly time, that I was far too old to be in swaddling clothes.

"T'was a winding sheet," he proclaimed.

Ederick was immensely fond of proclaiming. Indeed, it was his preferred voice.

"As it is written in Ezekiel, 'Thou was't cast out in the open field, to the loathing of thy person, in the day that thou was't born'. Whoever set you there in the snow wished you a quiet death. Either that or the chance discovery by a kindly disposed stranger and the mercy of God. Whatever the reason, whatever the hope, you are an expositus, an abandoned one, chosen not to be chosen by the Chosen People," he said, laughing.

Such an event was exceeding rare. Ederick was not taken much with laughter, as his former vocation had imprinted upon him a prohibition against such boisterous frivolity. Life for him was serious and extremely painful. Denial of the flesh, indeed the mortification of the flesh, was his road to Salvation. He wished to experience the torment of his Saviour. Unfortunately, I was compelled to share in his joyful suffering.

He assured me that the regular beatings he administered, moderated in deference to my tender years, would save me from the everlasting torments that otherwise awaited me in the World To Come. If they did not, and that seemed to him the most likely outcome, as I was so slow to embrace my Saviour, then at least his blows would prepare me for what I had to endure.

So, when I stumbled, fell and failed to walk I was beaten. When I failed to speak so that he could comprehend, I was beaten. When I cried, I was beaten. And if I did nothing, I was beaten. After he had finished he would put down the willow switch and hug me tight, his whole body vibrating against me as if taken with the dance of St. Vitas. He would then weep and thank the Lord. Depending on how the mood took him, he might, in all weathers, strip naked and proceed to excoriate himself with a six-roped flail. I presume he did not want to deny himself the pleasure of the true penitent.

For me the pain never diminished, but after a time the thrashings lost their shock. They became the enshrouded capsule of my life in the woods and the path I followed to find the love of Christ.

Only many years later did I learn how I had come to be there, and even then there was no certainty as to the truth of that tale. Then, as far as Ederick could imagine, my plight had not been apparent to my father or mother until I became old enough for them to see that my inability to walk or speak beyond grunting and gurgling was not the usual transitory experience of the formative childhood years.

"They may have thought it kinder to put you out in the snow where death comes with the numbness of the senses and then a quiet sleep. After all, what use is a helpless cripple to those people who deny the divinity of Jesus Christ and his Resurrection?"

I was thankful that with Ederick I was safe in the loving arms of Jesus, the toll of pain being an insignificant price for that life-giving sanctuary. Of course, I quickly learned to hate and fear those mythical creatures, the accursed Jews, who had not only murdered the Son of God, but had attempted to do away with me, an embarrassment, an inconvenience, an innocent child.

I had no images to accompany the hate and fear. When I inquired of Ederick what manner of men they were, he told me they were in many ways as other men albeit their dress was often curious, they kept the company and council of their own kind and, that by lending money at interest, they ensnared and impoverished unwary Christians.

All his talk of money, interest, ensnarement, strange clothing meant little to the child I was, alone with Ederick in the Wood. Because of this, my education about the world lacked example I could see or touch. My world was in large part constructed from words of Scripture passed down to me through the agency of a troubled soul.

It wasn't that Ederick hated Jews, as much as he pitied them for their failure to embrace the One True Religion. Even in this failure there was advantage to be had for Christians. After all, as he never tired of explaining, Jews, scattered and homeless as they are, remained a living testament to the truth of Christ's coming and their enduring punishment for the denial of his Divine Paternity.

At the time I was inordinately pleased to hear of that punishment, the more the better for what I conjured were at one moment the horned devils he had described who tortured sinners in Gehenna and, in the next, the wicked sinners themselves.

What I then happily accepted as the truth, later, when I was finally thrown into the wider world, became a mystery to me, as I saw and heard of the slaughter of the Jews. Apparently their being a testament was also a mystery to the Soldiers of Christ on their sanctified quest and, as with many other Christians throughout the land, the good citizens of Norwich too remained ignorant that the Jews had been spared in order to offer witness to the certainty of Revelation.

In The Wood

Ederick and I lived in a lean-to made of branches roofed with woven reeds plastered with mud and bound with yet another layer of reeds. On the pounded dirt floor were our straw pallets covered in coney skins, a fire pit, two bowls and a wooden water bucket sealed with pitch. Although Ederick had abandoned the cloistered Benedictine life, he continued to follow the Holy Saint's admonition for frugal simplicity.

Our world was shadowed, closed in and always damp, even in those places where the sunlight lanced the thick canopy of oaks, blackthorn and hornbeam, blackberry bushes, lime trees and sycamores. Our shelter was as a cave within a cave. We were as dark as our world, soot blackened from the fire which burned day and night.

Ederick wove reed baskets and every few weeks he would take them down to a market close by the river. He returned with oats, sometimes a fish and if we were blessed by fortune, a loaf of dark bread. However, our principle repast was coneys, another delicacy, along with all animal flesh denied to the monks. The dish was prepared with wild garlic or fennel when we could find it. In the Autumn there were berries and mushrooms and horse radish, pignut and wild parsnip.

Our lean-to was not set in a clearing, so unless you stood directly in front of it, it was not visible. This was by design, all to further Ederick's need for the solitude he required to be as one with his God. Occasionally a horseman or wandering villain would venture near. On those occasions I would hide myself in a thicket to watch them pass. Rarely was there any contact.

Once a woodcutter was unfortunate enough to be espied

by Ederick on a Sunday. While the hermit usually spared no effort to stay out of sight, on this occasion he was overcome by religious impetuosity and stormed out from the undergrowth.

"How dare you desecrate the Lord's Sabbath," he bellowed, matted locks crashing around his face, his robe billowing to reveal his heavy, dirt-streaked legs.

The poor man let fall his bundle of wood. His face drew tight with fear.

"Do you know what God ordered Moses to do when the Israelites found a man gathering wood on the Sabbath? Do you?"

The man, even if he had known, was too dumbstruck to offer a reply.

"God ordered that he be stoned to death," Ederick continued, as he stooped, picked up a small flint and hurled it, catching the man on the cheek. The blow, which opened up a bloody gash, appeared to wake him from his terror-induced stupor, and before Ederick could follow his attack with further missiles, the man turned and fled splayfooted in among the trees. It was not until the following day that Ederick allowed himself to collect the offending man's bundle.

I asked why, when he did his best to remain hidden, he had shown himself to the woodcutter. Even though by then I had been with him for some time, Ederick still found it difficult to fathom my speech. When on this occasion he finally did, the question was met with rage.

"Would you rather I let such a trespass against the Holy Day stand? You remain a poor dumb beast for all my efforts! Baptised by these hands, wearing the Cross, but still at heart a Jew!"

Of course, beatings followed, a perfunctory one for me and then a more arduous one for himself.

"I too am guilty," he gasped, as he slammed the flail over his bared shoulder. "I should show mercy." Thwack! "I should pray for my enemies in the love of Christ." Thwack! "Before the sun sets I should make peace with my adversaries." Thwack!

"They know I am here," Ederick intoned, gathering his coat around his blood-specked nakedness. "Of course they know. They fear me, and now the stories will multiply as will the fear of encounter. So, Ederick will not be sought and not being sought will not be found."

He was an overzealous taskmaster, but when not in the grip of the Spirit he could show a less terrifying mien. At night he would encircle me with the warmth of his body so I would not suffer the cold. This maternal comforting, the first closeness of another I was to know, also helped quiet the violent jerks and stuttering of my body, otherwise so often overcome with its own devilish dancing.

From the age at which he determined I could understand, perhaps four or five years, Ederick compelled me to ingest a substantial daily helping of Latin Scripture, delivered by way of his measured recitation. I swallowed it whole and was thankful it did not involve a beating. In later years, stories of Jesus, his coming and his leaving, the lives of his Disciples, his Mother, the Holy Virgin, and the army of saints were to serve me well in ways I could not then have imagined.

Of all the gifts he bestowed, the most precious was his brutal insistence that I walk and speak, abilities of nature God had withheld, and which, to Ederick's pained, and for me painful, displeasure, I managed to resurrect only as crude parody.

The Beggar Maker

The visitors Ederick could not avoid or frighten off were a band of robbers, highwaymen and ransomers who lived somewhere at a distance from us in the Wood. Due to the nature of their employ they never held in the same spot for long. From time to time they came seeking Ederick's blessing, which he gave freely without asking questions of them.

"They do terrible things. This is true, but they are also God's children," he explained. "They seek my council and the comfort of our Lord Jesus Christ, and I cannot refuse them. As well, we share the Wood and it would not be to our advantage if they were to take against us."

When he heard them approaching, I was made to hide away out of sight. This suited me very well, for what I saw through the chinks in our lean-to's walls was a frightful, nightmarish sight. Bertram, their curiously well-spoken leader, was tall and skeletal, with a raised purple scar down one side of his face that continued across his throat, as if someone had attempted to behead him. Unlike his scurvy, famished-looking companions clad in rags, he wore ill-fitting garments, both men's and women's, of a superior stripe, no doubt purloined from unfortunate victims waylaid on the road. Ederick said they were merciless men, and we should never underestimate their potential for cruelty and violence.

I experienced this at first hand when at about six years of age I was caught off guard out in the open. It was a warm autumn day and the wood was drenched in sunlight and birdsong. I was picking blackberries, when suddenly the birds stopped their chatter. I had been told by Ederick that an abrupt quieting of the birds meant possible danger, but I had not heeded that instruction and so ignored the warning silence. Reaching

37

carefully into the bushes so as to avoid the thorns near a particularly large bunch of berries, I parted some branches and instead of ripe fruit, uncovered two terrifying faces grinning out at me. I screamed in alarm and fell backwards, losing my crutches and dropping helpless to the ground.

The owners of the faces came rushing out of the undergrowth. One of them, a short, thin man with a weasel face and lank yellow hair, bent down and scooped me up with casual ease. I was a puny child, with no weight to speak of.

"Look what we got us," he called to his equally short and equally thin companion.

The other glowered down at me, then shot out a crab-like hand and pinched one of my legs so hard I cried out for the pain.

"Not much meat on this one, Strummer my lad, not enough for a decent meal even. By his look and them skins he be wearing, and them cripple-turned legs, ain't no one going to want to be paying out coin for getting this one back to 'em. Reckon they might be paying to get him lost, better said."

"Right enough that is, Mendes, right enough. Guess we'll just have to bash in his skull and be done with it. What you say to that?"

"Seems only right. Put him out of his misery. Only kind turn to give the poor little soul. What good he be bringing to the world?"

With that I was upended and twirled violently through the air. I saw trees spin by. With each spin they got ever closer. I screamed and screamed. The two fiends laughed and laughed. The next thing I knew the laughing had stopped and my screaming was joined by that of another. A few seconds later I was flying through the air, landed hard and rolled up against a thorny bush.

"Away with your damned nonsense!"

It was their fearsome chief, Bertram, who had apparently struck one of the men senseless and was gripping the other by the ear and forcing him to walk around him in a circle, bent over away from the pain while he was being admonished.

"You've forgotten what we have to do to transform them and make them fit for begging, have you? Here you've found one who demands no such attention, one ready for the street, and the only thing you can think of is bashing his brains out. You're fortunate I don't bash your brains out, Mendes. That is supposing you had any brains."

"Yes!" sobbed the man who was staggering around Bertram trying to catch up to his captive ear. "We knowed that. We just be playing with him is all. We was going to bring him to you, we was."

"Of course, you were," said Bertram, letting go the man's ear and fetching him a boot in the seat of his trousers that sent him sprawling near to his unconscious friend.

"You boy," the scarred man said, with a tortured smile that puckered his scar so it too appeared to be smiling as well, "come to me now."

He frightened me more than the two who had tried to kill me.

"Oh, I see. Forgive me."

He bent over, picked up my crutches, brought them and set them down next to me. I made no effort to rise.

"Come now. I mean you no harm. You heard me say that you were not in need of turning. As I said to these fools, you're ready made for the task."

To my great relief this was when Ederick appeared, his massive frame crashing through the undergrowth. He emerged wild eyed and winded.

"I heard much screaming," he said, looking from me to Bertram to the two downed men who were rising unsteadily to their feet.

"Nothing to concern yourself with, Monk," said Bertram, with a hard finality. "You can leave us and go back to whatever of God's work you were doing. We will be taking this lost wildling crippled boy with us. He's got himself opportunities waiting for him down in the city."

Ederick stared fearfully at the scarred man. It was the first time I had seen the big man afraid of anything. I began to weep.

"You quiet yourself down, boy," ordered Bertram harshly, moving towards me.

I buried my head in my quivering hands. When a moment later I dared to raise my eyes, I saw that Ederick had interposed himself between me and the advancing highwayman.

"Don't be foolish, Monk. This is not your affair. Stand aside, else I will split you from crown to toe, cut off your fat head and pull your guts out through your severed neck."

In that small clearing, Ederick's fear was palpable. Fear or no, he refused to move.

"You will do what you must," he said calmly, "but this child is in my care and has been since a babe in arms. He is not yours, Beggar Maker, to take as you will."

There was a pause and then Bertram began to laugh, not a laugh of joy, but one whose hollow sounds echo out of the darkest night.

"So," he said, "God's Bear has got himself a cub. Imagine that. Are you then the father to this child? Is that why you've secreted yourself in the Wood? Doing penance for your sins? A scandal among the chaste ones? Is that how it is, Monk?"

"No," replied Ederick, "that is not how it is. I am not the boy's father. I am his mother and I am his father."

"Most curious," the scarred one said, leering at Ederick. "Father and mother. A miracle indeed. Well, father-mother, if that is in truth who you are, it was well calculated to keep him hidden. Damned well calculated and damned well done. All this time we've been coming here and never a sign. I'd have done similar in your place, what with so many dangerous folk wandering about unchecked in the Wood. I warn you that after today, you best keep him closer still, father, mother, monk. Closer still."

After the Beggar Maker's visit, Ederick explained to me the awful trade that had earned him that name. He also took me to a small cave not far from our lean–to and told me if ever the need arose I was to seek shelter there until he came to find me.

The encounter with Bertram left me completely traumatised. The ever-twitching motion of my body became so ungovernable that I could barely walk without stumbling and falling. My head shook so that speech was denied me entirely. I never left Ederick's side during the day, and at night I suffered from prodigiously vibrant nightmares peopled with Bertram and his men, their cruel mouths dripping blood and variously chasing after me or spitting me over a fire or pulling me apart limb by limb. I was rescued from this hell only when screaming I awoke to Ederick's soothing words and the comfort of his encircling arms. The sole benefit I enjoyed was that, in deference to my delicate condition, the soul-saving beatings ceased for a time.

It was many weeks before the nightmares retreated, taking with them the worst of the day-time fears. Nonetheless, I was never able to rid myself entirely of the spectre of that frightful afternoon in Thorpe Wood. Although they never returned to carry out their threats, a blood-soaked Bertram continued to linger in the shadows of my imagining both day and night, until many years later when, all too real, he would choose to emerge once again.

Abandoned

One day in winter, when I had more or less seven or eight years, Ederick failed to return from his regular sojourn to the river. By that evening I had fallen into a panic. I wept, prayed for his return and then wept again. I promised God that if He delivered him back to me I would truly give myself to Christ, I would embrace Ederick's beatings with the joyful and understanding heart of a committed penitent, something hitherto I had failed to do.

Alone at night for the first time, huddled close to the fire and staring out into the darkness and the thick swirls of snow, everything took on a sinister import. Sounds above on the thatch transformed into footfalls, the icy breeze pushing through the trees came to me as the whisperings of forest wraiths. And over and over again I heard Ederick's booming voice and his oft-repeated warning.

"You must not stray from here, boy," he had told me, sweeping a thick arm to take in the area about our shelter. "Mark you well what occurred with Bertram and his gang of cutthroats? Well, you are a small crippled child, and there are all manner of unseen dangers waiting for the young, weak and unwary, of which you combine all the three. There are bogs that will swallow you whole and leave nothing but rings of fetid air on the water to mark your passing. That herd of boars that pass by would like nothing better than to devour a soft-skinned boy lying helpless on the ground, and I need not remind you of how often I have had to gather you up and set you on your feet."

I heard them many a night, a wondrous and most terrifying snuffling, grunting chorus close by us in the woods. Ederick told me that they appeared in daylight but rarely. The one time I did see them was sufficient to convince me of the seriousness of his warning.

On a cold, wet morning, not long before Ederick vanished, we heard an unearthly screeching coming from a stand of trees above us. Truly, I thought, a soul suffering the full torments of Hades. Not waiting for my ungainly hobble, he snatched me up and made towards trees. The cries became more high pitched and urgent. As they did, Ederick stopped and then moved cautiously forward until, peering out from the cover of the undergrowth, we witnessed the last terrible moments in the life of a baby boar. It was being devoured by an immense, grey-bristled beast, as Ederick told me later, most likely the unfortunate's father. Only the small creature's head - eyes wide, mouth agape - remained to be swallowed.

When the monster Cronus finished his meal, he raised his bloodied snout and sniffed the air. I was positive his red eyes found mine behind our leafy screen. Before I could loose a cry, Ederick's hand closed over my mouth. Still holding me against him, he retreated one backward step at a time until we regained the safety of our shelter.

He told me that these beasts were surely the direct descendants of the swine from Gadara into which Jesus had cast the demons. I did not need to be convinced. The only difference I could see was that these animals had not had the decency to run themselves over a precipice.

For days afterwards, when I tried to sleep, I heard the pitiful cries and saw the beast's terrible face dripping with gore. Was it any wonder that I waited so long for Ederick's return before forcing myself to venture out?

In all my time with Ederick I had never gone further from our shelter than about ten or fifteen rods. To the North this was more or less where we had seen the boars. In the opposite direction was the rough path on which the woodcutter had fallen victim to Ederick's wrath and his sharp-edged flint. It was also near where I was almost taken by Bertram.

For three or four days I stayed in our hut, my well-founded fears of the boars, of scar-faced Bertram and his gang, of the death-quiet bogs and of the unknown world beyond the wood, all wrestling against mounting hunger and thirst. Each day the scales tipped more and more until in the end my rumbling belly and swelling tongue emerged victorious.

Surveying the hut and finding nothing I wanted, I braced my forked-stick crutches under my arms and struck out to the West, away from my nightmare boars, away, I hoped, from the murderous highwaymen and away from the hard comfort of certainty.

As I took my first step, the snow began to fall more heavily, coating trees, undergrowth and paths in a single white shroud. It was but a few seconds before our hut vanished in the swirling storm. A few minutes more and I too was lost, lost in the same white nothingness that had first greeted my arrival in Thorpe Wood.

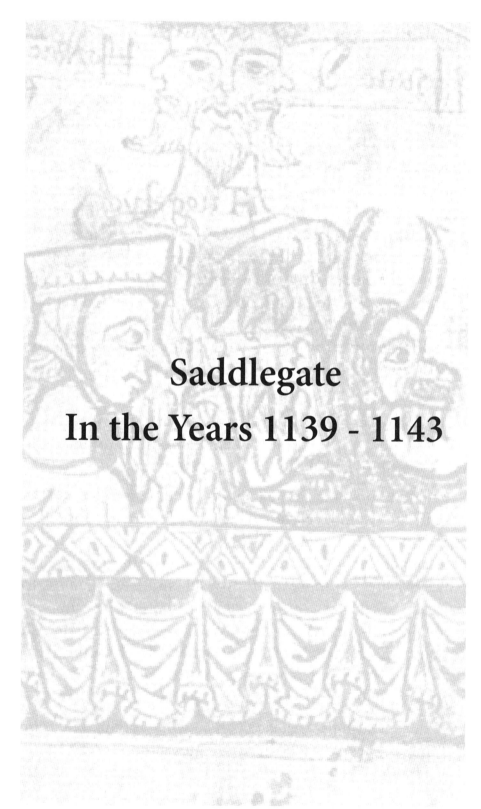

Saddlegate
In the Years 1139 - 1143

Saul Ibn Abraham

My journey through the wood was painfully slow. I was having to judge each step carefully, testing the snow with my sticks to confirm the footing. Often I was obliged to lean against a tree to rest before proceeding again with my finely calibrated movements. By the time I came to an incline leading down to a well-trodden path, the sky was darkening. With what I took for suitable caution, I began my descent when one of my sticks became entangled with a hidden root or stone beneath the snow. Forward momentum defeated my scrabbling efforts to free the stick and regain my balance. I slipped sideways and then plunged in a thumping roll toward the path, my progress only arrested when my head cracked painfully against a tree stump.

My last thought was of the baby boar disappearing into its father's bloody maw. Then I remember no more until a dark, hook-nosed face filled the space in front of mine.

Saul Ibn Abraham claimed he was a poet from Toledo in the Spanish kingdom of Navarre, the son of Abraham Ibn Ezra, a poet of great renown, as well as an astrologer, grammarian and scholar held in most high regard amongst the Jews. Whilst I owe my life and much more to Saul, and freely confess to my ears' woeful lack of tuning for poetry, neither I nor his reluctant hosts in Norwich, and possibly many other Jewish communities among which he passed, much appreciated his verse. On our first encounter, however, his deficiency in versifying skills was of absolutely no importance.

He was wearing a dark cloak and a white turban, but as he did not appear to have horns or a tail it did not occur to me that he might be a fearsome unbeliever, a murderer of our Lord – a Jew.

Ederick had spoken to me in English, leavened, when he recited the Holy Scripture, with Latin. These were the first words I now remember, but it was some time before they had meaning for me. It took much longer for my ruptured tongue to reproduce an almost passable semblance. Ederick struggled with understanding that semblance and would either finish what he took for my thoughts or beat me. Often he erred on the side of caution and did both. I expect he hoped the birch rod taken to the back of my legs would allow me to master my tongue. It did not. My tongue remained as stubbornly masterless as my legs.

So it was that my words meant as little to Saul as his, variously in Castilian, Arabic, Hebrew, meant to me. Together we had entered into that tower on the plains of Shinar.

After a time, he shook his head and mumbled a few soft words. I felt his fingers trace across my forehead. He pulled them back and turning his hand he showed me the blood. Once more I lost consciousness.

I awoke lying on a pallet on the floor near a flaming brazier set in the centre of a large room, the ceiling crossed with smoke-stained beams. The room was lit by candles and clouded with smoke. There were thick, multicoloured rugs strewn across the flagstone floor and a large table with wooden benches. All of this was new to me. I had never seen a table before nor rugs nor candles, and I felt warm in a manner I had not before experienced. Someone had dressed me in a white gown, and I lay under a soft blanket.

This was indeed a new world, at great distance from Edrick's one of straw, rough skins and dirt floors.

Of course, I did not realise at the time that I had been taken in by the Jews. If I had, I would have been more terrified than I was. You see, Ederick had raised me as a God-fearing Christian, one thankful to have been spared the tortures, in this world and the next, of being a Jew, that unspeakable fate ordained by my violated member.

The shock of the discovery, not too long after, of who my captors were, was blunted by their not having the expected horns and tails, but possibly more from the fact that being in the hands of Jews was but one of many, overlapping shocking discoveries – city smells and city noises, peculiar foods, a multitude of curious-looking people wearing curious-looking clothing, buildings of wood, churches of cut stone, a babble of unfamiliar languages and much more – that assailed the battered and half-wild, half-formed child, who from this distance appears sharply in my imagination, but at the same moment I find as little more than a stranger staggering across that crowded, untested stage.

Most unfamiliar and overpowering was the stench. Until I was first assailed by the malodorous reek of the City, the fact that I had been raised in the fresh air of Thorpe Wood did not occur to me. Norwich's narrow streets were fouled with all manner of waste, but above all it was the excreta thrown from the houses that occasioned the noxious odours, to say nothing of the clouds of heavy-bodied flies and summer mosquitoes. All was relieved only after a strong downpour, and then only if you did not reside in low-lying parts of the City, or when the winter ice captured the streets and a layer of snow made you forget for a time what lay in wait beneath.

However, that discovery and the others were only to be fully revealed some time later. What was perceived at my first waking moment was an enclosed space filled with a great many quarrelling people. In reality there were but three or four. It was the gesticulating shadows cast by the fire and the tallow candles, the raised, angry voices and, undoubtedly, my injuries, my fears and my unworldly eye that had so amply peopled the room.

Curiously, even though my eyes now fail me, the images

from that child's eye stay cleanly etched. It was meaning that remained closed to me, that is until I had mastered the tongues being spoken. Only then, when I could join the images to a command of what was being said, did that world come together as more than a dumb show of too many false understandings. Of course, even when finally unified, I was to find the world often insensible to any approximation of what might be called reason.

In order to spare others my false understandings, I prefer to recall the images of my early days joined to words given to me some time later by those who witnessed the events.

The quarrel to which I had awoken was about my deliverance to Eleazar's house.

"How could you risk bringing the child here?" Eleazar bellowed at Saul. "If he is discovered, there will surely be an outcry from the church and then the mob and then we will be forced to flee to the Castle for the King's protection. Either that or worse may befall us."

Eleazar, a squat, broad shouldered man with a heavy, stern silver beard, was unaccustomed to his word being challenged. Saul had not yet absorbed this stern lesson.

"But," countered the latter, throwing his hands up. "The boy is a Jew. Was I to abandon him there in the snow to die of his wounds? Is it not written that we must love all human beings who are of the Covenant? That it is our duty to save the life of a fellow Jew?"

"The token of the false messiah hung from the boy's neck. What manner of Jew displays such an unspeakable thing?"

"Flesh speaks louder than mere tokens, Rab Eleazar. Flesh does not deceive, and we have all seen the boy."

"Ah, but you knew nothing of this before you brought him here, did you? For all you knew this was a Christian child. For all we know now he may be a Christian child. A Christian child! Do you know what this could mean for all who reside here? I think not."

"Is it not written," countered Saul, "that a person must not stand by idly when a human life is in danger, even the life of a nonbeliever?"

"I have ever held that poets are fools and I remain to be disabused of that belief. Remember, we are told Gentiles are neither to be lifted out of a well nor drawn down into it."

He turned away from Saul and strode over to where I lay. I closed my eyes and feigned sleep. Whist I did not know what was being said, his hostility was clear, even to my unformed and addled mind.

At this juncture, Mordechai, a somewhat younger and more soft-spoken man, intervened. "What my brother means to say, is that you are a stranger to this hostile land, Rab Saul Ibn Abraham. Perhaps in your city of Toledo the interchange between Jew and Gentile lends itself more easily to following the Law as it is written, but here it is not so simple"

Eleazar turned from my pallet, walked over and stood toe to toe with Saul. Even though the latter was taller, in the jumble of flickering light and lashed by Eleazar's unbending diatribe, Saul appeared to shrink in stature.

"What the Poet doesn't grasp is that we are but few and we are scattered in small communities throughout the land, living at the pleasure of a Christian king and at the displeasure and suspicion of his subjects. If your folly of carrying the boy to us, the accursed murderers of Yeshu, becomes known by the monks or anyone who can stir the mob, the story will be told that we stole an innocent Christian boy and performed the circumcision so as to capture him as a Jew. Can you fathom what will follow? I think not, Poet. I think not."

Was this a prophecy, albeit 100 years too early? No matter. I seem always to be a victim, then as now, whether first hand or at some remove, of Abraham's knife.

Saul bowed his head for only a moment.

"I am an unexpected guest in your house, Rab Eleazar and I would be shamed and most greatly troubled if I were to bring misfortune to your door. But, let me ask you this. What would happen if the child had been found by others? What would they imagine had transpired to leave a boy showing both a crucifix and the Mark of the Covenant? I venture one does not need the imagination of this poor foolish wandering poet from Spain to tell that story, a story so much the worse to recount if he had perished in the snow."

Saul closed his eyes and began to sway back and forth,

"I was born under a heaven of bright stars
But my own star soon flickered and died
My mother then my father then my luck
Followed that star
Life is expectant, but no more than that
If the road was strewn with gold
My back would be unbending
My eyes sightless
If I baked bread
Each day would be Pesach
and I would be
An Egyptian first born
If my wine was …".

"Enough," Eleazar laughed, although not in a kindly manner. "For this, Poet, you expect the bounty of my table, shelter under my roof? Do such dissonant, vulgar lyrics, with no words for our blessed martyrs or the wisdom of the Sages, move the hearts of our brethren in Spain?"

"Perhaps," returned Saul, "you prefer the dark wailing more suited for this dreary clime?"

51

"Please, my brothers," Mordechai said, stepping between the two men. "This is not the time for a disputation on the merits of poetry. We must turn our thoughts to what to do with the child, and decide quickly before the serving girl returns."

The Gentile serving girl, the lowliest person in Eleazar's house, was also the most feared as she was, as all such serving girls, a potential conduit of damaging intelligence. The sudden, night-time arrival of a swarthy, turbaned stranger with a soot-black, badly injured child of uncertain provenance was just such intelligence.

As further discussion ensued, I slipped from feigned repose into an uneasy sleep.

Amongst The Jews Of Norwich

When hidden in the woods with Ederick I was black, head to toe, little more than a shadow against the trees and bushes in the day, fully invisible at night. In Eleazar's house I became scrubbed white but continued to remain hidden by the Jews' shame at my being what I was.

At first the bloodied head and bruised body gave the lie that the fall was responsible for my crooked body and garbled speech. It did not take many days before the truth was out.

Miriam was a healer, held in high esteem by not only the Jews, but by Christians as well. I was told that even the Bishop of Norwich had requested her assistance to cure his gout and other particular ailments acquired by such high personages.

She was dark-haired and rotund and to someone who had never more than espied the occasional woman from afar, of indeterminate years. A large mole to one side of her nose was what first caught my notice as I awoke to find her leaning over me applying a warm poultice to my head. It stank of fish. My attempt to pull away was met with a lopsided grin and firm pressure pinning me down.

"Lie still boy," a voice commanded.

It was the first time I heard English spoken since Ederick had left me.

"The mistress is only wanting to help you."

It was the serving girl, Aisly, standing at Miriam's shoulder. There was no sign of the disputational men.

I asked her to tell me where I was, but she could only stare at me, bewildered.

"Whatever strange tongue is this, mistress? Oh, and see

how the poor thing rolls his eyes and how he writhes like one possessed!"

I tried again, but my strange tongue, the one that lay behind my teeth, could fashion no words comprehensible to either woman.

Strong fingers probed my neck, chest, arms and hands, calves, feet and toes. My eyelids were peeled back, my mouth pried open.

Further examinations over the next few days led Miriam to announce that my injuries would mend, but that I would not.

"A helpless cripple and a gabbling idiot," was how Eleazar appraised that news. "Surely the woman who gave him life must have been impure."

"It is far more important to discover who the child's mother was than to concern ourselves whether or not prescribed ritual practice was followed," Miriam interjected, in a tone deep with impatience. "Where is she now? How did he come to be in Thorpe Wood and for how long has he been there? He appears to be at least five or six years of age, perhaps more. It is difficult to judge. So, how did he survive in that wilderness for all these years?"

Her list of sharp-edged questions momentarily silenced Eleazar.

"Well," Mordechai ventured hesitantly, "she must not have come from Norwich, for if she had, someone in the community would have remarked upon it. That suggests the woman may have been on the road to the city."

"Enough," Eleazar interrupted abruptly, glowering at his brother. "This discussion takes us nowhere. We must contend with what we have in front of us, and that is a cripple, who may or may not be a Jew."

The vehemence of his pronouncement ended the discussion.

"Whoever bore him and whatever the cause of his aliments," Eleazar continued, "it would have been kinder to have left him to perish in the snow."

"Remember," offered Saul, ever my defender, "that He sent the Angel Gabriel to guide the child Moses's hand to the glowing coals instead of the Pharaoh's crown, saving his life but rendering Moses slow of speech. We must not, Rab Eleazar, be hasty in passing judgement."

"You hold the foolish notion that this," Eleazar said, pointing a thick finger at me, "is another Moses?"

"I did make no such claim," replied Saul. "I am only saying the Holy One's ways are beyond our understanding. Besides, the boy understands. Look how he follows what is being said."

"A dog will follow sounds, but that does not denote comprehension any more than his barking should be mistaken for sensible speech."

At the time I had no idea of what they were saying, so Eleazar was correct. I was left unable even to bark in protest.

"I wager that given sufficient time and patience I can instruct the child to speak as well as anyone."

"Will you also straighten his limbs? Will you quiet his facial rictus? Will he be then offering sensible conversation or only mimicry? In short, Poet, are you to be a deliverer of the miracles so favoured by the Christians?"

As the Jews are so predisposed, their argument went back and forth, on and on and consisted of questions answered by yet more questions. The debate ended only when, sufficiently pricked by Eleazar's jibes, Saul Ibn Abraham of Toledo in Navarre agreed to become my tutor and my guardian.

With equal reluctance, Eleazar, despite his animosity towards both myself, for the danger a half Christian half Jew posed, and Saul, because of his argumentative nature and his offensive poetry, was obliged to shelter us in his house. As one of the community's most respected men he could not impose this onerous duty on others without forfeiting that respect.

Eleazar's house was in Saddlegate. I believe it was by far the largest house in the city. It comprised two small shops facing onto the street, an inner courtyard and a vegetable garden. On the first level was the hall and the solar where Eleazar, his wife and three children slept and above that, narrow and crowded under the eves, were cramped, low-ceilinged rooms used for storage. It was in the smaller of the two where Saul and I slept and where I was confined.

The room was even smaller than the shelter I had shared with Ederick. Saul could take little more than short strides in either direction and had to bend at the waist so as not to hit his head on the ceiling beams. The walls were made of bare boards. A pallet filled with straw served as our bed and a clay pot was there for our other needs. Light came from a very small, shuttered window at one end of the room. Without a fire, we had only thin blankets and the warmth of our bodies to see us through the winter nights. When Saul was not there, my companions were mice, rats and spiders.

Eleazar made it a condition of our residence that I remain hidden from view. Most of the time, especially during my first months in Saddlegate, Saul brought my food to the room, a wearisome diet of bread with pea and bean pottage. I longed for the taste of fresh roasted coney with garlic, the free air of the woods and even for the testing love of my lost Ederick.

"I tried to reason with him, but you cannot reason with an unreasonable man. He complains that a cripple, especially one so compromised as you are by your damaged body, together with the ambiguity of faith, if discovered is likely to bring disgrace or worse to him and to his family," Saul explained.

"Unfortunately, he is a man with a narrow view of life and of the world. As mendicants, my darling Gazelle," a name he used when we were alone, "we are obliged to embrace forbearance in the face of such ignorance."

Only when Eleazar was out on business or at prayer on Saturdays or when he relented and permitted me to be in the walled garden was I able to leave my room. When I did, most of the adults in the house ignored me, whether out of fear of me or fear of Eleazar's displeasure.

At first the other children in the house also shied away from the stumbling, garbled-voice creature that I was. Once they conquered their fears though, they taunted me, poked and hit at me with sticks as if I were a bear tethered in a pit. Like the bear, I was surrounded by jeering faces, my tethered legs making it impossible to escape the hard words and harder blows. Unlike the bear, I was not able to threaten my tormentors with teeth or claws or even a roar.

So, unless Saul or Mordechai or Miriam were there to shield me, I spent most of my time in the confines of our room perched on a barrel by the small window, with the shutters open even on the coldest day. Through the fog of self pity, I began to observe the flowing, incomprehensible dance of hats and shoulders on the street below. After the isolation of Thorpe Wood, the roaring, jostling crowds were at first terrifying, then fascinating and finally calming. It was a mystery, but one I soon embraced as I realised they could neither see me nor reach me. It was a safe place for a tormented bear.

Now all these years later, under the eves of another building this old bear, nearly blind, nearly deaf, had been likewise cornered until the two boys came to my aid.

For the next year or two, Saul and I were only apart when he journeyed to nearby Jewish settlements in King's Lynn, Beccles, Bungay, Thetford or Cambridge to bestow upon them his poetic vision and share his tales of fellow Jews in the Moorish lands.

Unlike Ederick, Saul was a very gentle, patient man. When we were alone he would sit me on his lap, stroke my head and sing sad tunes that, for all their lilting melancholy, always seemed infused with sunlight and warmth. On cold nights he would hold me in his arms and whisper his poetry in my ear to attempt to quiet my ever-trembling body.

Because of you my soul is sick,
perplexed and yearning.
Your eyes seeking out my heart
are like dew upon a parched land.
Draw me from the pit of destruction
that I go down to Hell

It was Saul who tutored me in languages, both spoken and written. To his surprise, and mine, I was an extraordinarily gifted student.

At first he sat me on his lap with a piece of slate upon which were chalked Hebrew letters. He sounded out each, tracing them with his thin finger.

"*Aleph, bet, gimmel, dalet,*" I said, repeating slowly after him.

"Astonishing," he exclaimed after he managed to tune his ear to my particular voice. "All accomplished without honey, nuts or raisins! Truly astonishing!"

He hugged me closer and planted a light kiss on my head as I sound-shaped each letter.

Soon he had me pairing *aleph* with *tav* and *bet* with *shin* and so on. As these were the first letters I had ever learned, I did not find them unusual, nor was I perturbed when Saul began to put them together and showed me that the words read from right to left.

Within a few weeks I had absorbed sufficient Hebrew to understand the words, as well as read and repeat, "When

Moses charged us with the Torah as the heritage of Jacob," a line that Saul told me stood for the entire Torah.

I found the book of Leviticus was a more severe task, but Saul was insistent.

"The Holy One," Saul intoned, "blessed be He, said: since sacrifices are pure and children are pure, let the pure begin studying purities."

Over the following months, as the harsh Winter gave way to Spring and Spring to Autumn, I added French and Latin, as well as some words of Castilian. The main difficulty was that although I could soon begin to piece together what Saul was saying, no one but he could with any facility disentangle my replies, and even he was not always clear as to what I said. I quite soon became skilled, fluent and wonderously incomprehensible in four languages.

"You expect me to believe this damp-spittle mumbling is any more than it sounds," Eleazar said, when after about a year or more of tuition Saul formally presented his pupil.

"You must give time for your ears to adjust to the lad's very particular voice."

"Must I? Please, Poet, don't test my patience."

"If you doubt his ability, then ask him to do something," replied Saul. "Anything."

Eleazar glared at Saul and then turned his stormy face to me.

"Bring me that goblet, the green glass goblet, from the table," he ordered in French, deliberately gazing in the opposite direction.

"You see," said Saul, as I carried the goblet to Eleazar. "Can you continue to doubt the boy's ability?"

The old man refused to take the goblet from my hand.

I say 'old man' because although I am now a great deal older than Eleazar was, and he was a vigorous, robust man, I can only see him all these years later through the eyes of my ten-year-old self.

"Walk to the door," Eleazar ordered, this time in Hebrew.

I had to ponder on those words a moment or two before swinging across the room on my crutches.

At that moment I was immensely proud of what I had achieved. It was the first time in my short life that I had experienced such feelings. I smiled at Saul. He nodded encouragement in return.

Eleazar looked ruefully at Saul and shook his head.

"You want for more?" asked Saul. "Here boy, read this out."

He handed me the parchment of the book of Leviticus.

Tracing the words with a trembling silver pointer, I began, "The Lord called to Moses and spoke to him from the Tent of Meeting, saying Speak to the Israelite people, …".

I stopped as laughter from Eleazar, Mordechai and two or three other men interrupted my reading.

"You laugh?" said Saul, his sharp-featured face suddenly flushed hot with indignation. "You laugh at the boy's reading of the Holy Text?"

"We laugh," said Mordechai, "because the sounds coming from the poor child are as of an ass braying."

"The quacking of a duck!" interjected another.

"Please, you must listen more closely," Saul pleaded. "Do not mock the boy."

"Listen to what?" Eleazar said. "Grunts and squeals? Do not insult us with low Spanish trickery, Poet. The boy is a fool, a simpleton, as anyone can see."

"More the fool it is who refuses to see what is plain to see," Saul responded with a bitterness I had not witnessed before.

"You accept my hospitality and call me a fool," Eleazar retorted, advancing towards my Poet, his face suffused with rage.

Saul did not flinch from the older man's threatening purpose.

"It is you, Rab Eleazar, who appropriates that …".

Frightened for my champion, I let go one of my crutches and grabbed at the sleeve of Eleazar's jacket.

"Please!" I said. "Please!"

He looked down at me, surprise and contempt chasing across his face. Raising his arm violently, he threw me to the stone floor.

Saul rushed over and knelt by my side, cradling me in his arms.

"My poor Gazelle, my dear, my darling boy. Are you injured?"

I shook my head, but could not hold back the tears brought on by fear, humiliation and pain. As it is written in Proverbs, pride brings destruction, and a haughty spirit prefigures a fall. That was a hard lesson to absorb for one so young, who still, even after more than a year, was so new to the curious and discomforting world of the Jews of Norwich.

It was this confrontation that, over the pleading of Miriam and Mordechai, led to Eleazar ordering our expulsion from the house in Saddlegate.

William

Upon awaking the following morning I found that Saul had gone and taken all his belongings. I should have been accustomed to being abandoned, but I had invested such trust in my Spanish Poet, and he had been so fervent in his caresses and his verses of love, that having him vanish without a word was unexpected. I took it very badly.

"I am sure he did it out of love," Miriam assured me, wiping my tears with a cloth. "Having to take to the road with an itinerant poet, especially a turbaned Jewish poet, especially in such uncertain and violent times, is not a life for any child, but for a child such as you, well...".

"I am convinced that he left as he did to spare you the distress of a long and painful farewell," ventured Mordechai.

"What is to become of me now?" I wailed.

They looked questioningly at each other. At the best of moments I defied comprehension and this was not the best of moments for me.

Reflecting on Saul's action some time later, I came to realise that by leaving as he did, it made it impossible for Eleazar to force me from his house. After all, putting a crippled child onto the streets would be a disgraceful act for a man so prominent in that small community. As Miriam said, his leaving was a gift of love.

So, I was allowed to remain in Saddlegate. Not wanted. Not welcomed. Allowed.

Without Saul to sing to me, to teach me, to laugh with me, to love me, life was a lonely place. Days were spent crouched on the barrel, peering out of my high window or, when I descended from my cell, trying to ignore the indifference of the adults and the taunts of the children. At least those children now kept a cautious distance from the crack of my crutches. For whilst my body and face continued to be racked by jerks and spasm, because of having to carry the growing weight of that body, my arms had become preternaturally strong for one so young, and with that strength I learned how to defend myself.

Miriam and Mordechai offered me some comfort, but it was not consistent, as unlike Saul, they both tended to defer to Eleazar. Neither could replace the love I had from Saul.

Then one day, about six months or so after Saul had left, William came to the house at Saddlegate, and my world was turned right side up.

"So that's what it looks like," someone said, as I was relieving myself, leaning against a wall in a secluded corner of the garden.

I was startled and tried to cover myself, only succeeding in befouling my hands and my feet.

It was a boy, about my age or a little older, with bright blue eyes and a tangle of straw-coloured hair. He was wearing a short leather apron and battered sandals, one with a broken strap which, as I was to discover, was always threatening to trip him up and often did.

My first impression was that his full mouth set in a pleasingly round face would be incapable of not smiling. As I got to know him, the impression was confirmed.

I stuffed myself back into my trousers and lurched away from the supporting wall, swayed to one side, my crutches falling to the ground

The boy reached out to steady me. He set me upright so I was once more back against the wall and then he bent down to retrieve my crutches.

"I'm sorry, I didn't mean to startle you, only I have heard you Jews were burdened with, well you know," he said, pointing at my crotch.

"Abraham," was all I could manage in reply.

To my surprise, he seemed to understand my answer and made no comment, as almost everyone else did, about my strangled speech.

"That's true. My Uncle Godwin says it's the Mark of Abraham, a curse he called it, to set the Jews apart, but I never fully believed him. Before now at least. Does it pain you?"

I shook my head.

"Well then, that is something to consider."

He took a few steps backwards and appraised me with a curious but friendly stare.

"So tell me what has happened to make you so terribly crippled as you are?"

"Nothing," I replied. "I was born to this state."

I could see he was concentrating intently to comprehend. However, I only had to repeat myself once more before he did.

"I am sorry for you then. Is it an affliction most difficult to endure? Do you not wish to be as other boys?"

"Yes," I replied. For although I had never known any other way to be, I did yearn, as was only natural, for the freedom of being unimpeded by twisted limbs and a screw-warped tongue. If nothing else such freedom would have allowed me to escape from my captivity in Eleazar's house. Truth to tell, where would I have escaped to even if the opportunity presented itself? There was no going back to Thorpe Wood and I would surely have found no safe haven in the Christian streets of the city.

"Who are you?" I asked.

"I would ask the same of you, but me, I am called William, apprenticed to Bigard the skinner. I come here to bring pieces of leather wanted by the Jew Eleazar. My master tells me it is to repair clothing left in pledge."

He moved closer to me and in a confiding whisper said, "My mother and my uncle have warned me about the peril that you Jews pose. When I ask them why, they say that your people practice a sin called Usury on Christians, and that it was you who crucified Our Lord Jesus Christ."

Besides the fact that Usury had something to do with money, neither of us had a clear understanding as to its meaning. As for crucifying Jesus, this was the tale that Ederick never wearied of relating, but I deemed it was probably safer not to say anything to William less I too became implicated in that crime.

He laughed. "I tell them that the Jews here have never been other than kind towards me.

"You see," he said, reaching under his apron and holding out a crumbled piece of gingerbread. "Just now, before we met, Miriam gave me this."

He broke off a piece and handed it to me.

"What about you? How are you called, and why have I never seen you before?"

"Most of the time I reside in a roof space above the solar. It is thought I should be kept away from curious eyes. Joseph, my baptised name is Joseph, but they, the Jews, refer to me only as 'the crippled one'. For them I have no name."

"I see, but don't understand. I thought that only Christians are given their names at baptism."

Perhaps I should not have tried to explain, as even Miriam and Mordechai had more than intimated that both my crippled body and my Christian past were to be kept secret, particularly

65

from the suspicious and dangerous Christians. However, this boy was so open-faced, so friendly, and I had had no one to speak to since my dear Poet had quitted Saddlegate, that out of loneliness I began to recount my time with Ederick. I never got beyond a few words when Eleazar suddenly appeared in the garden.

He stormed across to where we stood, grabbed me by the ear and administered a sharp blow to the back of my head.

"Why are you not where you belong?" he shouted, as he roughly pulled me away from my new-found friend.

He dragged me through the house, muttering threats I can no longer recall. I was bumped up the stairs and cast violently onto the floor of my room. Some time later, Miriam came in and placed my crutches against the wall.

"You must take more care, boy."

She leaned over and gently stroked my head and then she was gone. I was left alone. I raised myself up from the floor and assumed my seat on the upturned barrel by the window.

It took many hours before I could finally quiet my sobbing, for a truly Heavenly Light had shined into my hitherto sombre, dreary life, and before I could bask in its glow, it had been abruptly extinguished by the cruel hand of Eleazar.

Clandestine Meetings

A few days after our first meeting had ended so violently, William returned to Saddlegate.

"Eleazar has gone to Bungay to pay a visit to his cousin," said Miriam when she came to tell me William was waiting in the garden. "He won't return at least before tomorrow or perhaps the day after. We will maintain this as a secret between us. Yes?"

Fortunately for me, Eleazar was often called away on business, that is the lending of monies, or to see fellow Jews in one of the many communities near to Norwich. Without him the rules at Saddlegate were drawn far less strictly and I was permitted to descend from my under–roof cell. I continued to face the at-a-safe-distance teasing from most of the children and the hostile indifference of some adults as well. No matter. It was better than being locked away with my own company.

"I waited outside until I saw the old fellow and another man leaving and then climbed over," William explained, pointing to a thick vine gripping the flint wall. "Here, look at this. I have brought you some pieces of soft kid for your crutches."

Once again we were in Miriam's garden, known as such for the many cultivated beds of medicinal plants – angelica, wormwood, valerian, squill, monkshood and others – filling up that small space surrounded by high flint walls.

The fewer people who knew about our meeting the safer it would be for both of us, and so we hid ourselves behind some heavy-flowered bushes out of sight from those in the house.

"This should make it more comfortable for you," he said, as he carefully attached the leather with flat thongs to the top of my crutches.

"If Bigard had noticed I took this, he would have flayed me raw as a cow's hide, as this is the most costly of leathers. Fortunately, he was much in his cups this afternoon."

It was a sharply cold Autumn day. The wind was gusting, picking up red and yellow leaves, swirling them around us in small conical towers. We sat on the ground, close together for warmth. The urine stench of the tannery was very powerful on William, but I did not pull away. Even though we had known each other for a short time, I felt an immediate bond with this boy and wanted him close. It was as if I had always known him. He was the first person of my own age I thought could be a true friend to me. He had a reassuring, gentle nature, he was always kind and refrained from mocking me. And he made me laugh, so lifting my spirits. What was the odour of the tannery when compared to all that?

I can say without shame that mine was the innocent and immediate love of a lonely child, one who had suffered abandonment - my mother's, Ederick's and then Saul's – beatings, harsh words and taunts. I was an unwanted prisoner in the Jews' house and in my own twisted body. Is it surprising that all of these misfortunes piled on a twelve-year old child would bring me to dive head first into the crystal waters that William brought to me in that garden?

"That is a most dreadful story," he said after I had managed to relate something of the course of my life up until then.

He put a thin arm around my shoulders and to my chagrin I began to weep, from his touch, the softness in his voice and, of course, from my own childish self pity.

After a moment or two he let me go and leaning away he appraised me as if studying an exotic object.

"So are you a Christian or a Jew?" he said after a time, "From what you now said it is in a most uncertain state of affairs that you find yourself."

I shrugged. "Who would want to be a Jew? Because they," I said, pointing my crutch at the house, "believe me to be one of them? No, I don't want to be a Jew! I don't want…".

"Calm yourself, my little friend. Please, they might hear you and then what would that mean for my master's trade with the Jews? It is a very good trade, you know, and if it were to be lost he would indeed flay me until the skin came off. And you, what would they do to you?"

He turned and stared anxiously towards the house.

"I am a burden to be hidden away so as not to bring shame upon them. I would much prefer to be back in the Wood with the beatings and where at least I would have Ederick's stories of Our Lord and the Blessed Virgin to comfort me."

I had to repeat this several times, because even though William had a keen ear for my peculiar speech, trying to comprehend between my gasping sobs was beyond his reach.

Finally he said, "But you carry the Mark. How can you escape being a Jew?"

"I am not certain, but Ederick told me that some Jews have become true believers and I assume they also carried the Mark. Didn't Jesus himself carry the Mark? And surely he escaped."

He stared at me and then gave a toothsome smile.

"I never considered that, but come on, Joseph. Come on now," he said. "You must not be downhearted, for if you know where to look and how to look the world can be truly wondrous."

Getting to his feet, he reached a hand down to help up. "I must return to my master. When old Eleazar leaves another time I will come back to speak with you once more."

Giving a soft punch to my arm, William turned away, clambered up the vine and the rough flints, reached the top of the wall, waved to me and then dropped out of sight.

I now had something to look forward to and when a few days later Eleazar was again called away, somehow William discovered that and my friend returned to me.

It was warm for an October day and we sat under an apple tree, eating windfalls and talking of this and that, as children will. William was a cleverly accurate mimic, and to my delight he puffed out his chest, set his legs wide apart, planted a pinched frown across his face and became a convincing Eleazar, castigating me for eating the forbidden fruit of the garden with a Christian. He then whirled about and was transformed into his priestly uncle, a rollingly fat man with a squint.

"Stay away from the accursed Jews!" he said in a high, strained voice. "Stay away, stay away!"

For the first time I could recall, the dark foreboding that had been ever my life's companion was lifted, and I gave myself over to the unrestrained joy of laughter, something that should be any child's domain.

William smiled broadly at my response and, abandoning the assumed carapace of his uncle's pinched shell, sprang two neat cartwheels and rejoined me by the tree.

"Truly you have never been outside these walls?"

"No, they have said it would be dangerous for them and for me if I were discovered."

"Discovered? That has already happened, has it not?"

"Has it?" I said, suddenly alarmed.

Grinning, he pointed a dirty finger at his breast.

"If you wish, I can take you. There are so many things I could show you. The Market Place, where there is always the chance," he winked at me, "of coming upon some dainty that has fallen, unsuspectingly of course, from a barrow. Then there is the river, old Bigard's tannery, the Cathedral and the Monastery and the passages that run under the street called the Bedford and to which few are privy. Much more besides, Joseph. Wonders you could not imagine. When the old Jew is once more abroad, it would be a simple matter to secrete you out into the street. Then we…".

"Please, William, I don't know," I said abruptly, so frightened that the tremors to which my body was commonly afflicted magnified to the point where I contrived to shake myself insensible.

I woke, possibly seconds later, possibly minutes later, in William's arms, my head cradled against his bony chest, the stench of the tannery an unwelcome but reviving balm.

"Joseph? Joseph? What happened? Are you ill? Shall I call for Miriam?"

I shook my shaking head, my lips and chin wet with spittle, my trousers damp against my thighs. He propped me up against the trunk of the apple tree.

I do not recall more than the sensation of blinding fear that William's suggestion invoked, for you see I had never been out in a world any broader than our patch in the Wood or the Saddlegate house. There were, of course, terrors a plenty in these enclosed realms, but as these terrors had become commonplace they surrendered their ability to cut so deeply into my young flesh. 'Outside' on the other hand was an open maw of darkness, that William's very mention of venturing out into it put me in an overwhelming panic so powerful that I could see and feel the skin creeping painfully from my bones.

From my lofty perch gazing down at that one slice of the 'Outside' I had been able to hold such feelings at bay, knowing that I was an unseen presence to that jostling flow far below me. However, to be within it, without the safety of distance, touching against the crowd and being seen and perhaps taken to task by them for being a cripple or a Jew, or both, having all that as well as being obliged to negotiate the cobbles and the crush was all too much to contain for the pitiful child I was.

"I cannot, please," I finally managed to say, coughing up pieces of half-chewed apple. "I cannot go."

"What a curious creature you are, Little Joseph, curious in body, curious in the confusion of Christian and Jew and curious in your manner. More curiouser than anyone I have chanced to encounter. There is no cause to fear what is beyond these walls. You will come to no harm with me to guide you. It would be a lark, I can promise you, a real lark. Do you not want to get away from the Jews, from that room you've told me of, if only for an hour or two?"

"Yes…. No."

I began to tremble and felt myself slipping into another fit when William settled both hands softly on my shoulders. His touch instantly calmed my fears and my trembling body. I didn't comprehend at the time, but, of course, now I have come to know that his was a Saintly Touch.

He plucked another windfall and handed it to me. I held it but was still too dazed to attempt to resume eating.

"Come now, Joseph, we will speak of other matters. Will you tell me again the stories of your Spanish Jew poet? I would especially like to hear the one about the Moorish Prince and the caged nightingale. Please, Joseph."

I See You

y furtive garden meetings with William continued once, at times twice, a week, for some months. From this distance I can't say precisely how many, but the season was warmer and our innocent apple tree heavy with blossom when we met there for the last time.

We passed our brief encounters, brief because of the demands of his master and concern that we would be discovered by Eleazar, all too often with my bewailing the harsh treatment meted out by the Jews and William comforting me with caresses and assurances of my eventual deliverance. When the mood lightened I would tell and retell, at my friend's request and to his boundless delight, the fabulous tales I had heard from my Spanish Poet. In return William performed his mimicry for my delight or recounted his adventures in the City, which for its immediate proximity might have been as far distanced for me as Saul's sun-warmed, magical Spain.

Many times our conversations turned to the question of my true faith, which may appear to be an unlikely subject for young boys, but I was not able to play games or to do the other things most children do. Also, William seemed to find this to be a question of endless interest and concern. Perhaps it was because of his family's violent antipathy to the Jews, this being particularly true with regard to his uncle, the priest, who, according to William, never tired of preaching to him about the moral poison that his nephew would imbibe by consorting with those who had murdered Jesus Christ.

Of course, before I had been found by Saul, I was being instructed as a Christian and had accepted, as children will do, the truth of that formative instruction. Knowing nothing else, this is not to be wondered at. In his way I could see that

Ederick did love me and was concerned that I would be Saved. Repaying that love with the acceptance of Jesus and the Blessed Virgin, the Saints and all that went with them was a natural act for me. Then finding myself forced into the company of the Norwich Jews, who I felt only embraced me for their own protection, not as a fellow Jew, although Saul did embrace me both as a Jew and in other ways, not unlike Ederick had, I must admit to having been unsure as to where and with whom I belonged.

No matter, events were soon to transpire that would cause me to return to the bosom of the One True Religion. Whilst I now have ample cause to regret that return, at the time it suited me very well indeed.

That journey began not long after William and I were discovered by some of the children, who until then had apparently been either unaware of our assignations or too frightened to approach.

For some reason I was weeping, as I often did, and William was comforting me, as he often did. Perhaps I was so quick to tears because they were always followed by reassuring words and a warm embrace.

"Look at the cripple crying like a baby," jeered Samuel, one of the older children, who appeared at that moment from behind our special bush. He was accompanied by two others.

"In the stinking arms of the stinking skinner's boy," added David, Eleazar's youngest son.

I tried to stand, but before I could gather my crutches, William got to his feet and faced the three boys.

"Do you have nothing better to do than torment Joseph?"

"Why do you, Christian boy, why do you put your hands on the cripple?" David asked, a sneer playing on his rosebud lips.

"Filling his empty cripple's head with talk of your Jesus,"

Samuel said. "Talk of your Jesus in our garden."

We had been overheard as well as seen.

"You should not even be here, skinner's boy, you should not be in our garden with that stupid cripple."

"Stupid cripple?" retorted William "You are all so blind."

"Blind? We're not blind, skinner's boy," replied Samuel. "We can see clearly what you are at, can't we?"

The other two boys nodded vigorously in agreement.

"You're blind because you refuse to see Joseph," William said.

The three stared open mouthed at William.

Finally, Samuel said, "Oh, we can see him clearly enough. He's nothing more than a useless cripple, who can't even speak proper. It's you who is blind, rotten stinking skinner's boy, not us."

"I see well enough to see what you are," William said. "You are stupid boys blinded by ignorance and hatred and so, unable to see Joseph for what he really is."

"And what be that?" asked little David.

"You see a cripple and that is all you see. Someone to mock because he's different and because he frightens you. What you don't see is a gentle soul with more worth than any of you. You don't see Joseph, that's all," he said putting his arm across my shoulder. "You don't see Joseph."

It was upon hearing those words that my love for William rose above the comfort of soft words, the warmth of caresses and the joyousness of childish attachment. My love became a fire that neither circumstance nor time has extinguished. I have carried it with me from that moment and will carry it to the grave and beyond.

The boys were not so impressed, but finding no answer to

William, because undoubtedly they did not understand what he was telling them, they lapsed into abusive chanting.

"Skinner's boy! Stinking skinner's boy! Stinking skinner's boy!"

They advanced towards us, calling out and shaking their fists. William, slight and indomitable, stood his ground, and I joined him, crutches poised for any assault. None came. William's calm assurance or the threat of a blow from my crutches or both, served to dissuade them from moving from verbal to physical aggression.

"You won't be so clever skinner's boy or you either Cripple, when I tell my father what we seen here," David said over his shoulder as he retreated towards the house. "You wait and see."

The wait was not to be long.

The Thick Finger

"Your mind and your soul has been polluted, as has your body, by your time spent with that renegade monk, although I know you are not fully capable of understanding that fact. Now...".

Some weeks after Saul had been sent away, Eleazar's attitude towards me began to mellow somewhat. He no longer insisted on my remaining in the room all the time, and he even went so far as occasionally patting my head when he happened upon me. I was pleased to find that he was not a man devoid of gentleness or compassion, although these attributes did not extend to our general day-to-day intercourse, as he refused to believe, despite ample evidence to the contrary, that I was empowered with the comprehension of more than that of a small child.

We were sitting by the brazier in the hall. I don't know how or why these many years later I remember the weather at that time, but I do remember, as if I could still feel it and hear it, that a particularly violent storm was battering wind and rain against the shuttered windows. With light from the fire flickering across his dark face and smoke swirling in the room, Eleazar's countenance appeared menacing. This was not to be one of his softer moments.

"Now you may think I am not aware of your assignations with that boy, but I am and have been for quite some time. I was prepared to ignore this, despite my orders that such meetings were inappropriate. Miriam and Mordechai intervened on your behalf. They told me that no harm would come from them, that you were only children playing at children's games. Now I am informed that the skinner's boy has been speaking to you about love, even touching you and far worse, speaking to you about the false prophet Yehoshua, the deceiver, the bastard son of Joseph Pandera."

I gave him a questioning look.

"Yeshu, the magician, the self-proclaimed messiah they call Jesus," he said, as he turned and spat into the fire.

He waved away my attempt to respond.

"Nothing but harm can come from such talk, Joseph, for you and, more importantly, for us. Do you understand that?"

I could but nod. No argument from a twelve-year old could counter the forceful attack of such a towering grey beard, particularly one who was unwilling to decipher all but the occasional word that struggled from between my lips.

Of course, I knew by then the great contempt held by the Jews for their uncircumcised masters. Even Mordechai, the mildest of men, could be moved to passion on the subject.

In contrast to Saul's wine-inspired, sun-drenched poems of love, Mordechai, who was a teacher and the spiritual voice of the Norwich Jews, was often moved to recite darker, menacing verse imbued with calls for blood and vengeance against the followers of the cursed 'hanged one', the Christian oppressors.

For how long shall You be like a warrior who knows not how to deliver!

Make known the vengeance from the Gentiles for the blood of Your servants before our very eyes

Hasten the redemption and speed the vision.

For there is a day of vengeance in my heart and the year of my redemption comes near.

I did not grasp that this was the true meaning at first hearing, as I was too young and much of what he intoned was wrapped in cipher, with talk of wreaking vengeance on Edom or the vapour of Esau, drops of blood of the martyrs being counted one by one and splashed across God's garment to be avenged on the Day of Judgment and so on.

It was not unusual to hear more pointed curses hurled at the Gentiles, such as asking God to pour fury, thunder, destruction upon them, to break them, fill them with maggots and bitter waters, to trample them down, crush them, to make them disgusting and abominable. Needless to say, such vituperative comment was never even whispered where it might be overheard by a non–believer. Face to face with the Christian world, the Jews were modest and self effacing, which is hardly surprising, as their lives and livelihoods were held on loan from a Christian King.

'It is not that we pray only for the blessed martyrs slain or forced to slaughter their own children by the vile Christian knights on their way to despoil the holy places in Palestine," Mordechai tried to explain, "but we also pray for the destruction of false prophets, the destruction of all who follow them and all the enemies of Israel. It is only then that our final Redemption will come to pass."

It was not until a few years later and under the tutelage of Thomas that the true significance of these words and some of the Jews' other ritual observances, such as the Passover and the hanging of Haman at the Purim festival, were to be made clear to me. I was also to discover that what is posed as clarity can take a great many different shapes and shades, sometimes illuminating, sometimes obfuscating and sometimes serving only to do the bidding of he who carries the lamp.

But I get ahead of my story.

The shutters clattered noisily as Eleazar reached across and tapped a thick finger on my knee and did so repeatedly and with increasing force as he drove each point deeper and deeper into my flesh.

"From now on you will not visit with that boy." Tap. "I will

79

ensure that when he comes with his master's leather he will deposit it and leave this house immediately." Tap, tap. "If he attempts to climb the garden wall. Oh yes, Joseph I know about that too. Do you imagine that I do not have eyes and ears other than my own to inform me? If he climbs the wall again I will ensure his master is informed." Tap, tap, tap.

I had no answer.

"You will not be seen in his company again. That is all I have to say on this matter."

He lifted his weighty finger from my knee while continuing to stare fixedly at me, the flames from the fire, like those of the Devil's Kingdom, reflected in his dark eyes.

A great loss was being visited upon me. I could do nothing.

To Be A Jew Or Not To Be A Jew

Eleazar's admonishments were well founded, for not only did William and I talk about Jesus, for he was a pious boy and one taught closely and well by his Uncle Godwin, but I was increasingly open to the enticements of the Church as told through my friend's stories of the Lamb of God and His enfolding forgiveness, His resurrection and, of course, His magical curing of blindness, leprosy and other ailments. These stories, many of which I remembered from my earlier years with Ederick, albeit now stripped from the sting of the accompanying beatings, comforted me at a time when there was little of such spiritual comfort or hope offered to me by the Jews in Saddlegate.

What they offered me, as much if not more for their own safety than for mine, was shelter from the storm. I suppose I should not have wished for more. However, I did, for I witnessed the joyfulness of the other boys in the house and in the community, all of them much younger than I was, as they were taken through the observances required to become fully accepted as a Jew. I was not permitted to take part. So what manner of Jew was I? A Jew to everyone except the Jews?

"It is due to your deformities," explained Mordechai. "For it is said that idiots are not to be bound by the commandments or the punishments for transgression of the commandments. So it follows that there is no cause for you to be initiated into the study of Scripture or Mishnah. Do you not see?"

"I can read. Saul taught me to read."

It was a warm summer day and we were sitting in the garden under the shade of the apple tree I imagined belonged to William and me. I did not ponder on this at the time, but in later years when I had deepened my study of the Holy Book, it came to me that the monks were correct in their contention that the fruit forbidden in the Garden was neither the fig nor the pomegranate nor the grape, as many rabbis claimed, but rather the apple. After all, does not malum signify both apple and evil? Was it not under the apple tree that I was to gain from William the enlighteningly corrosive knowledge that was to lead to my having to flee the protective walls of the Saddlegate garden and find my way in the tortuous world outside? Was it not under the apple tree that I found myself castigated by Mordechai for my lack of knowledge? In this manner did that fruit and my attraction to it not signify both an addition and a subtraction from who I was, who I wanted to be and who I became? Enough! Such questions are best left to the endless rumination of monks and Talmudic scholars, not young, unformed boys or old fools.

Mordechai smiled with indulgence and cupped my chin in his hand.

"My poor crippled one, my poor child," he said. "You might read the words, but understanding is more than simple reading. It is only through speaking the sacred words aloud and through many repetitions and the proper instruction that you will come to a genuine knowledge."

Mordechai was gentle with me, but unlike William, he did not see me.

"I can speak the words. I can repeat the words. Did I not read aloud from the Book of Leviticus?"

"Did you understand what you read? Did others understand what you read? Was the meaning of ritual and prohibition and purity revealed to you?"

I had to own that he was right. The words were in the main but solitary notations drawn together as if randomly coloured beads on a necklace. Meaning or understanding did not follow until many years had passed.

Being marked out as an idiot, even by a person held up as a teacher and as well disposed towards me as Mordechai, meant that I was denied entry to the mysteries of the faith, but at that time, as importantly to me, I was denied the cakes, hardboiled eggs, raisins, nuts and other delicacies that accompanied the rites of passage to learning Torah and becoming a Jewish man.

I watched as Eleazar's young sons and those from other families came to the house enveloped in prayer shawls. Mordechai lifted them on to his lap and they were shown a tablet upon which Hebrew letters had been drawn. The boys were asked to read these forward and backward. When they had completed this task, Mordechai put a small drop of honey on each letter which the child was told to lick off. This treat was followed by the eating of cakes and hardboiled eggs upon which verses from the Holy Book had been inscribed.

"This is done so that the child's heart will be opened," Mordechai explained. "As it is written in Ezekiel, 'He said to me, "Mortal, eat what is offered to you; eat this scroll, and go speak to the House of Israel." So I opened my mouth, and He gave me the scroll to eat, as He said to me, "Mortal, feed your stomach and fill your belly with this scroll that I give you" I ate it, and it tasted as sweet as honey to me'. And for you, Joseph, the reason you cannot take part is in the next verse. Listen closely. 'Then He said to me, "Mortal go to the House of Israel and repeat My words to them. For you are sent, not to the people of unintelligible speech and difficult language, whose talk you cannot understand, but to the House of Israel."'.

I was too young to know that 'people of unintelligible speech' referred not to myself, but to nations other than Israel. Mordechai had simply used my lack of understanding to fool me, either to save the family from embarrassment or to save me from being mocked. I prefer to believe the latter, as I was fond of him, for unlike his severe older brother, Mordechai was a kind and gentle man. Whatever his motives, I remained excluded, an onlooker, a child kept in the shadows without a path to follow to The Light.

William, on the other hand, did offer me such a path and more as well.

"Have you not heard of the blessed St. Ethelbert?" asked William.

I shook my head.

"He was once long ago the king who ruled over all of the East. It is told that when his body was being taken to a nearby city to be buried, his head was severed and fell to the ground, where a blind beggar, not being able to see, stumbled over it, ..."

I began to laugh, as I pictured the scene of the ragged man's unseemly fall and the head rolling and bouncing along the road. For once William did not join in the laughter. As I have said, though he was full of mischief and a smile was either always on or near to his lips, he was at heart a most pious boy.

"This is not a topic for mirth, Joseph. Please, listen to what I have to tell you. Upon his foot touching the saint's fallen head the beggar immediately regained his sight. There were others. More miracles, more afflictions lifted from those who touched the relics of St. Ethelbert. Miracles, Joseph, just like the ones Jesus performed when he cured a man who couldn't walk or when he cast out demons from a boy who fell into fits or when he returned speech to a man who was mute and sight to the blind. Jesus said that everything is possible for those who believe in Him. So, if you were to be a Believer once again, as you tell me you were, by a pilgrimage to St. Ethelbert's shrine you too might find relief from the malady that convulses your body and twists your tongue, whether this is brought about by demons or some other cause."

When I asked where I might find this shrine, William said it was in a city called Hereford, far away to the West.

With such disheartening intelligence, the brief spark of hope that I might be freed from the ever-vexing tremors, that I might run and play as other boys, that I might not be the object of mockery and jest, that I might form words without effort and that they might be understood, all those wishes were extinguished. I could not leave Saddlegate, let alone undertake a long, arduous journey on what I had heard were difficult and lawless roads.

"Why do you hold out to me something that is so clearly beyond my reach?" I asked of William.

"It may not be so, Joseph. My uncle says…".

"William, you did not…," I interjected with alarm.

"I promised," he said holding out his hands to calm me. "I haven't said a word. Not one. I know very well of his hatred for the Jews, so would never speak to him of you or our friendship, as it would only serve to create trouble for me and for my master. My uncle has at times let his ill temper overcome his priestly instincts. What I was trying to tell you is that my Uncle Godwin has told me that some of the monks at the Priory have made a pilgrimage to St. Ethelbert's shrine and may do so again in a near time. If you were to go to them, told them you believed that Jesus was the Light of the World, the Son of God who came to redeem us, they may be willing to carry you with them when they next go."

His tale caught at me between laughter and tears, at the improbability of my escaping from Saddlegate, let alone finding monks disposed to accept me and take me with them.

Eating The Torah

It was not long after Eleazar ordered me not to see William, and carrying Mordechai's words of rejection still fresh in my mind, that I ate the Torah. I knew even then that it was a rash act. Now I see it as a childish act, but after all I was a child, and one living with a dismal present and an uncertain future.

That future appeared yet more precarious when Eleazar confronted William on the occasion of his next delivering Bigard's pieces of leather. To make his point more forcefully, I was summoned to witness the encounter.

"If you desire to continue coming here, I must insist that you obey me when I tell you not to meet in secret with this boy," the old man admonished William, pointing his thick tapping finger at me. "Not to meet at all with this unfortunate child. His mind is addled and must not be stirred with ideas that unsettle him further."

"I meant no harm," William countered, looking with humble mien down at his feet. "I was only speaking to him out of Christian charity for the burden he carries."

Wrapped in feigned sweetness, those words of diminishment cut at my heart. Did he not see me anymore? Had he ever really seen me, seen Joseph? I stared across the room at the boy I called my one true friend, the sole light in my otherwise dreary existence. Charity! Were his caresses no more than succour for a poor cripple, his offers of Jesus and of redemption empty promises? Was I now destined to be completely alone?

"I realise that you have acted out of kindness," said Eleazar, his voice losing the edge of anger, "but sometimes a kindness can be misplaced and end by harming those it seeks to help."

Eleazar's sudden softening of tone was calculated, not

heartfelt. He wanted to give William no cause to carry my story outside and in doing so inflame Gentile wrath against the Jews.

"I beg you, sir," pleaded William, "do not inform my master. I will do anything you order me to. At all costs I must keep my place."

"Then," said Eleazar, "I ask that you do not speak about this to anyone."

"You have my word, sir."

"Furthermore, you will come here only through this door," Eleazar said, indicating the shop entry, "not over the garden wall."

At this William's ruddy face lost the last traces of colour.

"Oh, of course," he spluttered. "The door, I will always come through the door."

I looked across the room, searching his face for a wink, a sly William smile, any sign of hope. He would not meet my eyes, but continued to stare down at the floor. Without another word or a backward glance, he placed the few pieces of leather wrapped in a sack on the large table in the hall, turned and walked out through the main door and for all I knew, out of my life forever.

I had expected nothing from Eleazar, and whilst Mordechai had marked me as an idiot, this had been offered with a degree of resignation and not a little affection, but William's betrayal of our friendship and his too easy agreement with Eleazar's demand to abandon me, this was most cruel and unexpected. However, on this occasion there were no tears. Instead I felt only numbness. This was followed moments later by a cold fury such as I had never known. It was directed at both William and Eleazar, so that when the later turned to admonish me once again, I did not quail but held fast against the anger in his eyes. Seeing this the old man hesitated, giving me enough time to pivot on my crutches, leave the hall, and ignoring his demands that I stop, make my way upstairs. I mark this as the day I turned my back on childhood and on indulging myself with tears of self pity. But for the deaths of two special friends, I was never to weep again.

I sat in my room on the barrel by the window, looking at the street and the people below without really seeing more than a lonely existence at Saddlegate stretching out before me until the end of my days. I remember that in a storm of agitation I had pushed my hands with such force onto the sides of my perch that splinters from the rough wood dug into my fingers. It was then, with the droplets of blood staining the floor, that I decided what I must do.

I waited until later that evening, after Miriam had brought me some bread and broth, together with a few words of reassurance, which did little to reassure or dissuade me from my purpose, that I stole as quietly as I could down the stairs. I thought that it would be safe, as I could hear no one moving in the house. I had also taken the precaution of fitting small pieces of William's leather to the bottom of my crutches so that I could move unheard, but it was very dark and on one or two occasions I staggered into the side walls and had to right myself before continuing my descent. At each false step I stopped and listened to see if anyone had been roused. I heard nothing except shutters creaking in the wind and the barking of street dogs somewhere in the distance.

After what seemed a very long time, but could not have been more than five or ten minutes, I reached the hall safely and then made my way to the rear of the house, near to the garden where the women did the cooking.

They had been preparing for a ceremony the following day at which two young boys were to begin their journey of learning Torah and becoming Jews. I had seen the eggs being cooked, smelled the cakes being baked, watched Miriam, under Mordechai's supervision, inscribing the verses.

Moonlight coming through the windows fell on two bowls that had been left near the stone oven. I lifted off the heavy pewter plates, set there to defeat the rats and mice, and found, as I expected, six honey cakes in one bowl and six roasted eggs in the other.

I proceeded to eat, as I knew was the custom, three of each. Mordechai had told me that by doing this children would be able to learn Torah and ward off the Prince of Forgetfulness.

"As it is written," Mordechai intoned, "the Lord said, I will raise up a prophet and I will put My words into his mouth and he will speak to them all that I command him. Jeremiah said much the same. The Lord put out His hand and touched my mouth and He said, herewith I put My words into your mouth. These words of our Lord are sweet as was the manna given to Israel in the desert."

I was thinking on what he had said as I finished eating the eggs and the cakes and sat down on the rug by the warmth of the stove. There I awaited to be filled with the Lord's words of sweetness and divine revelations of an open heart and to be reborn as a child of the Torah, as when the Jews were first given it at Mount Sinai.

I had imagined that once I had eaten the magical foods all this would happen and the Jews would finally be compelled to admit that I was truly and fully one of them, not simply a crippled orphan who happenstance had forced upon them. Then perhaps they would treat me with greater kindness, let me live in their world, rather than being shut away.

To my disappointment, mounting cramp in my stomach was all I experienced. Nothing more. No words from on high, no divine revelations or greater understanding of anything more than that the cakes were not sweet because the words of the Lord were written upon them, but rather due to the fact that they were filled with honey. The eggs too, despite having been inked with Holy Verses, were not adding to anything but a discomforting bloat in my belly.

Outside in the street the dogs continued to bark, the noise now moving closer to the house. I lay down on the rug, curled around the pain in my stomach and lulled by the warmth from the oven, fell into a restless sleep.

I awoke with the pain having travelled from my stomach to my ear, now grasped firmly in Miriam's strong hand.

"What have you done?" she was yelling at me, although it was clearly apparent what I had done.

"I am a Jew!" I yelled in joy, trying to twist out of her grip. "Now I am a Jew!"

The commotion woke the entire house. The hall was soon filled with more than a dozen frightened adults and children. They must have thought that they were under siege. However, once the cause of Miriam's shouting became known, fright turned to indignity, then outrage and finally to violent fury.

"He did what?"

"Sacrilege!"

"Out! Throw the cripple out!"

"Polluter!"

Lying on my back helpless, unable to free myself from Miriam's grasp, I was pummelled by slaps and kicks. I tasted blood, but protected by my new-found cloak of anger, I did not cry out or beg for mercy. Repeating over and over "I am a Jew! I am a Jew!, I coiled myself into a ball to protect my face. Still the blows landed singly and in flurries. Even the children joined in, shrieking with delight as they hammered their fists and feet into my arms, my legs, my back. I do not think they fully appreciated what I had done or why the adults were so incensed. For them it was sport, a safe opportunity to pay me back for all the times they had felt the sting of my crutches. The attack only ceased when, of all people, Eleazar intervened.

"Stop," he called out, as he dragged me, gasping and bloody, from the centre of the melee.

My relief for having been rescued was short-lived. Eleazar had a more enduring punishment in mind.

"You boy, have been a wretched source of defilement, first with that Gentile leather-worker boy and now this. Now this!" he said pointing at the eggshells and crumbs I had left scattered on the floor.

"I am a Jew," I replied softly. "Now I am a Jew."

Ignoring my declaration, he gestured to two of the men.

"Take this poor fool to the room. You are to leave his crutches down here and bar the door. He will remain so confined until we decide what is to be done with him. Go now."

Hard arms hoisted me up and roughly carried me from the hall. My banishment was accompanied by the children's catcalls and angry muttering from the adults.

Once again I was delivered to my room, this time transformed into a gaol, an unnecessary precaution since without my crutches I was trapped wherever I was.

I crawled across the floor and hoisted myself onto my barrel. I was still suffering from the effects of my overindulgence on ritual cakes and eggs, to which was added the physical pain occasioned by cuts and bruises and, more painful than the bleeding shins and the throbbing of my swollen eyes, a feeling of utter rejection and utter isolation. I knew beyond doubt that tomorrow would be a long time coming.

Out of Saddlegate

I awoke, as I always did, on my straw–filled pallet on the floor. It was very cold. My body ached, more than it always did, because of the beating I had endured the previous day. It was particularly difficult to open my swollen eyes. When I did and managed to focus, the first thing I saw was that one or more of the spiders had woven a thick web across the door to the room.

Having had to pass so many of my days in that room, I spent hours studying the wondrous creatures as they constructed their elaborate, intricate traps. I had been told by Ederick and by Saul that they had on occasion been called upon to do the Lord's work, their webs shielding the Christ child from Herod's soldiers and, in an earlier time, David's cave from King Saul. So, were the little weavers now protecting me? If so, from whom?

As I pondered these questions the door was thrown open, the complex lattice of silk torn asunder, and with it my meditation on the Divine Purpose of spiders. Aisly, the servant girl, came hesitantly into the room. She was looking over her shoulder, wide-eyed and frightened.

"Please come quickly," she whispered, placing my crutches on the floor and easing them across to me with her foot.

"Where?" I asked, as I swung myself upright.

"No time, no time. Come now."

I followed her out of the room and down the stairs. The girl kept turning around and gesturing at me to hurry, which I found difficult because the spasmodic twitching from which my body was never free had been worsened by the unmerciful pummelling to which I had been subjected. Every step on the uneven stair boards was painful and perilous. I expected that at any moment we would be discovered and this served to tense my tightly drawn muscles even more fiercely. It could not have been many minutes, but the short journey seemed to last for hours.

We finally arrived at the bottom of the stairs without mishap. The hall was empty.

"They have all left for their Saturday prayers," Aisly explained. "Please come quickly before anyone returns."

"Where am I to go?"

"Why, away from here, of course. Have no fear, William will be waiting for you outside in the street."

My friend had not abandoned me after all. That intelligence raised my spirits. However, the elation lasted but a few moments, as I contemplated with foreboding the prospect of venturing out into the street. Such a fear was to be expected, for since my arrival years before I had never set foot outside the house in Saddlegate. I was, of course, familiar with the street, but the familiarity was one of an observer secured at a safe distance from the riot of people and beasts that jostled and rumbled far below my high window. To have to become part of that dangerous spectacle was not a prospect that I welcomed. Yet, what choice did I have? I did not want to return to the prison cell my room had become only to contemplate the labours of my Holy spiders and to await further punishment and a life without the hope of ever again seeing my beloved William.

Aisly tugged at my arm, urging me towards the main door. Lost for the moment in the overwhelming conflict of having to make a life-defining choice, I stood firmly rooted, my crutches pushed hard at a resisting angle against the floor.

"Come child," she said, urgently. "If you do not leave now the opportunity will have passed and both you and I will have to endure the master's anger and may-haps worse."

"Will they not know you have helped me? Will you not

have to pay dear for what you have done?" I asked, although I have to confess I was far less concerned with her welfare than finding an excuse for not having to brave the chaos that boiled just a few paces on the other side of the door, let alone to face the thought of where I would find food and shelter outside the familiar confines of Saddlegate.

Tiring of my indecision, Aisly suddenly pulled the heavy door inwards and with a mighty effort dislodged my crutches and propelled me into the street. As I staggered, fighting to regain my balance on the wet cobbles, the door slammed shut behind me.

So it came about that I was tossed into the midst of the human river I had for many years espied safely from above. I remember that moment these many years later with the same disorienting clarity I experienced on the day. Every sense came under assault in the same instant; the fetid stench - so much more powerful near its source at street level - the jumble of shouting, voice babble and calling out, the axle-groan of carts, horses neighing, their hoofs clattering on the stones, the hurrying bodies shoving and bundling past too closely in the narrow defile of Saddlegate.

The whirl of that pushing, shouldering crowd and unfamiliar footing, mud seasoned by night soil and other waste spread over rounded cobbles, caused me to flail wildly. Before I could find purchase with my crutches someone ran hard into my back and I was thrown to the ground, my crutches kicked away into the passing tumult of legs. I sat there, stunned, unable to rise. No one appeared to notice me. I had escaped from the Jews only to find myself thrown aside, crushed and befouled in a pulsating Hell. Fortunately for me, my guardian angel was not far away.

"Joseph!" a voice called from somewhere out of the jostling mob. "Oh dear, are you injured? Here, give me your hand."

94

I may be describing a picture that was created for me by Thomas with my assistance some years later, but I am convinced that as I looked up to identify my benefactor, William's head emerged from the throng outlined in that yellow celestial glow so widely appropriated by the saints. No matter if there was or was not such a Heavenly Light, he delivered me up from the depths.

William got behind me, grabbed me under the arms and set me on my feet. Resting me against a wall, he waded back into the crowd and returned soon after holding my crutches.

"Come, let us…," he paused and examined me more closely. "What has happened to your face, Joseph?"

"I will explain later. For now take me from here before the old man or the others return. Please, William."

With him walking at my side to protect me from being upended we made our way down Saddlegate towards the marketplace.

I had made good my escape, but dazed, bruised, reeking from the stench of foul mud, caught up in the jolting flow of the street and with no direction home, I feared that my escape would turn out to be nothing more than a passing victory.

Norwich Priory In The Year 1143

Sanctuary

"Sanctuary," William said, grinning with impish delight at his own cleverness. "That is what we will do. Yes, sanctuary. They cannot refuse you that. They will not refuse you."

As he talked, William gripped my arm more tightly, steering me out of the path of an oncoming hay cart. We had just managed, with some difficulty, to negotiate the crush of people gathered close to the market. I had imagined that once I had ventured from the seclusion of the Saddlegate house I would be singled out and mocked as a Jew and a cripple. However, no one in the streets appeared to find my presence worthy of remark or ridicule. It must be said, this was many years before Jews were obliged to wear the conical hat that now marks us out for opprobrium. Further, to my surprise, being a cripple wasn't noteworthy either, as deformities of every variety were on display in Norwich – hunchbacks, blind beggars, lepers, men who had lost an arm or a leg. I particularly remember my horror at seeing a one-eyed old woman slumped in a rag heap at the corner of the market whose nose and ears appeared to have been roughly eaten away, stretching out a supplicating, fingerless hand towards us as we passed. What novelty did one more cripple add to this everyday scene? Strangely, this first close exposure to the sounds, sights and touch of the street left me feeling both revulsion at the cripples on display and reassurance that they were there. They allowed me a free passage without and later, when I had the opportunity to reflect, free passage within myself as well.

"A Jew?" I replied. "Why would the Christian monks take me in?"

"We will not tell them. You can say that you are an orphan, which is the truth. That you have been cruelly used by those who had posed as your protectors, which will explain the injuries to your face. Besides, how are they to know you as a Jew?"

I pointed downwards to what up until then had invariably announced the identity of my forbearers.

"Then you must keep yourself well concealed," William laughed. "It will not be difficult. I have heard that our cloistered Benedictine brothers place an inordinate value on their modesty."

We could see the Cathedral tower from the market, but it took us over half an hour to negotiate our way through the narrow streets before we arrived at the gates. Here more begging cripples congregated, and they were not prepared to extend a free passage of any variety. A legless man, stumps resting on a wheeled board, shouted angrily and advanced towards us, propelling himself with short sticks. His cry was taken up by two blind men who stood up and staggered in our direction, their eyeless faces swivelling one way and then another in search of the threat. They were joined by an old crone whose face was covered in suppurating reddish pustules.

"Away!" she screamed, spittle flying from her toothless mouth. "No alms, no alms!"

"Step quickly now, Joseph," William said. "Quickly!"

I needed no such urging. Pushing hard, I swung myself forward as I had never done before. Meanwhile, William fended off the legless man by kicking away one of his sticks, causing him to veer sideways into the path of the blind beggars. In the ensuing mayhem, which fortunately distracted the two men guarding the entry to the Cathedral grounds, we escaped through the gateway into the safety of the Cathedral's walled enclosure.

Our pace did not slow until we had passed out of view of our attackers. When we did stop, I was shaking so badly it was all I could do to remain upright. The wild boars, the Beggar Maker and the beating I had endured at Saddlegate were as nothing compared to the terror I felt at the assault from the nightmare Cathedral Gate Cripples. While I was left breathless by our encounter, William was rendered almost insensible with mirth.

"Did you see them, Joseph?" he said, doubled over in laughter, taking in a great lungful of air. "Oh what a wonderful lark it was."

Reading my thoughts, he explained that the beggars were guarding their treasured situation from what they had perceived as competition from an intruding cripple.

I had been so overwhelmed by the dislocation of passing through the city and then our contested admission into the environs of the Cathedral that it was only at that moment I became fully aware of the grand, celestial building in front of us. It was beyond imagining, if indeed I had ever paused to imagine such a phenomenon, which I had not. In a city of rude wooden buildings this monument of painted stone, inset with large windows of coloured glass, was a magical sight.

All that had transpired since I escaped from Saddlegate was put to one side as I stood mouth agape staring up at a vast stone wall growing out of the ground, reaching upwards as if to capture Heaven and down two long sides to claim the Earth. It was not a tower, but my first thought was of Ederick's story of the Tower of Babel, evidence for which I had already discovered in the confounding multiplicity of tongues spoken within a single dwelling.

Above the high, metal-studded door, and up to the roof line, a dozen or more men wearing leather aprons and pieces of white cloth covering their heads and necks, were clambering about in a web of wooden planks connected by ladders that crisscrossed the front of the building. People trying to enter the Cathedral were obliged to dash the last few yards so as to avoid the dust and fragments of stone that showered down.

William and I skirted the West Door and walked around the outside of the cloisters to the south end of the Cathedral near to the Priory. All along the side of the building we were assailed by the cacophony of noises thrown up by gangs of men, shouting to one another, dressing blocks of stone, unloading carts carrying uncut blocks and lengths of timber, winching all manner of materials up into the scaffolding. We eventually came to the South Door where we found a smaller, more modest entryway to the Cathedral, overlooked on either side by two narrow windows.

"Here, Joseph," my friend said, pointing to a large brass knocker in the shape of a lion's head, "you must alert the watchers with this. There is always a monk assigned to wait at those windows in order to permit entry to a person seeking sanctuary. Go ahead, use it."

I hesitated a moment or two, suddenly frightened as to exactly who or what awaited my summons on the other side of the door. Impatient, William waved a hand at me, urging me to act. Taking a deep breath, I closed my eyes, lifted the heavy arm of the device and slammed it down sharply against the door. The dull thud made by the knocker was answered almost immediately from within by a loud booming echo, the reverberation of which forced ice crystals through my bones. I turned to escape, but William, blocked the path.

"Joseph, you must not lose heart," he said. "Not when you have come so far."

We waited. No one came.

"Perhaps," I ventured, "the watchers are not watching or they are unable to hear over the noise going on out here."

Stepping forward, William grasped the knocker and brought it down once, twice and then a third time. Before the last echo

100

died away the door was violently thrown open and a tall, immensely fat, black-robed monk appeared, his face suffused with rage.

"What is this?" he shouted. "Do you boys think it is a game knocking so on Heaven's door? We are here to offer sanctuary, not to entertain the foolish games of children. Go on, away with you. Away!"

"Please, brother monk," said William, "we have come to ask for sanctuary for my crippled friend, an orphan who has been ill used and is in need of your protection."

The monk inspected me from head to toe.

"Has he been accused of a crime?"

"No, rather he is a victim, not a criminal."

"Can you not speak for yourself, boy?"

Fear had taken hold of my tongue. I could manage only a grabbled splutter.

"I see," said the monk. "I see, wait now…".

He swung his attention from William and looked at me more closely. Both anger and colour suddenly drained from his face. He then smiled broadly showing off a mouth decorated with a few broken, widely-spaced teeth. Bending down, he grabbed me by the shoulders, dislodging my crutches.

"Joseph? May the Lord and Blessed Saviour deliver us, it is indeed you! You have gained so much height I hardly credit you are the same as that child lost to me in the Wood."

"Ederick?"

I was lifted up without effort as if I was still that small child, not a stringy, splay–jointed and weighty lad of almost 14 years. He proceeded to gather me in the folds of his cassock. He carried a sweetish, smoky odour that I later discovered was that of incense from the censer used during the offices in the Cathedral.

"Brother Edgar," he corrected. "Since I have returned to my brethren I am called Brother Edgar. Come in now, Joseph, and your friend with you. Come in. Come in."

In that moment I was reunited with my father and my mother, a most curious role to ascribe to a Benedictine monk.

Brother Edgar

"Please believe that I would never have abandoned you, my son. You see, I fell and broke my leg and was carried to the infirmary here in the Priory. While the leg was mending," he lifted the hem of his cassock and exposed a livid gash below his knee, "I contracted a fever. By the time I recovered and made my way back to our shelter, you had disappeared. I asked after you in the City and to folk who abide near to the Wood, but to no avail. I am truly sorry, my dear Joseph. What more could I have done?"

Except for the shattered teeth, this beardless, smiling, neatly robed and tonsured monk was as unrecognisable to me as I was to him. Even the wild abandon of his gaze was gone. It had been replaced by a demeanour of beatific calm.

Brother Edgar led us up a narrow spiral staircase to the small room overlooking the South Door. The stone walls had been freshly plastered and were unadorned. Except for a stool by the window, the room was empty. The Spring warmth had failed to penetrate. The air was chilly and damp, holding a faint odour of sweet incense that had drifted up from the Cathedral altar.

The monk nodded towards the stool. Exhausted by our journey through the city, the dash into the Cathedral grounds and, finally, the torturous climb up the stone stairs, I did not hesitate to accept his invitation. William stood beside me, his hand resting protectively on my shoulder.

"I prayed for you, my son. Every day. I lit candles and asked Our Lord to protect you or, if the worst had befallen you, and I assumed it had, that He welcome you into His Heavenly Kingdom."

"I thought you wanted nothing to do with those in the

Priory. Did you not tell me they all plotted against you?"

"Ah, yes, I did that, Joseph. But during my time recovering in the infirmary I had a vision of our Father calling me to resume my true vocation of praising him, not alone but in the company of my brothers. That vision and the conversations I had with the Prior made me understand that I must open my heart, the heart that had so hardened against others in my self–imposed exile, and receive and execute the admonitions of my loving Father. As it is laid down in the Rule, only 'by the toil of obedience thou mayest return to Him from whom by the sloth of disobedience thou hast gone away.' Poor sinner that I had become, and still am, I had gone not only away in body, but also, and more importantly, astray in spirit from the Lord. No longer, Joseph. I have returned with a true heart and proclaimed to our Lord God my faults of pride and anger and impatience, the whispering of the Evil One. It is only by renouncing my pretensions of the individual road to salvation and submitting to the most excellent arms of obedience that I am now finally able to battle for Christ the Lord, the true King. I have left the highway of regret, Joseph, for the Holy Highway of life everlasting."

As he spoke, leaning forward close to me, I could see in his eyes the fervour he had carried in Thorpe Wood rekindled. It was at that moment that I knew my Ederick was still alive.

As William had suggested, to avoid the possibility of having my request for sanctuary refused, I did not recount to Brother Edgar the years with the Jews in Saddlegate. Instead I wove for him a tale of having been rescued from the Wood by a goatherd living hard by the hamlet of Thorpe.

"At first I was well treated by him and his wife. However, after some little time the poor woman was taken by the ague. After that the man's temper soured and he turned against me. At the least provocation he took to beating me. In the end, yesterday in fact, as you can see," I touched the bruises on my face, "I had to flee, and as fortune would have it, I chanced upon this boy who told me that as a crippled, abused orphan I could ask for sanctuary from the monks at the Cathedral Priory."

"I fear your friend has not understood," he said. "The 37 days of sanctuary are offered only to those under accusation for a crime and, if I am to understand correctly, you have not been so accused."

"No, I have not been accused of anything. I am sorry to have imposed upon you, Ederick."

I gathered my crutches and began to push myself up from the stool. William's hand tightened on my shoulder.

"Come now, Joseph," said Brother Edgar. "Be of stout heart. Sanctuary is not our sole recourse. Firstly, you are our guest, and as such I must send for Prior Turbe to greet you in the proper manner. You will wait here please."

Gathering his robes around him, Brother Edgar hurried from the room.

"I can see you are in secure hands, Joseph. Now I must get back to Bigard before he misses me. I'll return, if I am able, to see how you are faring. Be of good cheer and put your trust in God."

He bent and kissed me on the forehead.

"William, please do not leave me."

"Be not fearful, Joseph," he said, squeezing my arm. "You are reunited with your friend and soon with Christ the Lord."

Then, before I could plead further, he crossed the room and disappeared through the doorway. I listened to his sandals tap tapping on the stone stairs, waiting for him to stumble over the ever–dangling strap. He managed to descend without incident. The sound grew progressively fainter until it was no more. The shouts of the builders intruded again, filling the void left by the exit of my dearest friend. It was the last time I was to see him alive.

The Priory

Prior Turbe was a short, slight figure. At least he seemed so standing next to the towering, bulky Brother Edgar. A sharp–nosed face with milky blue eyes peered out at me from the too-ample folds of his cassock. In addition to Edgar, three other monks accompanied the Prior. They stood in silence behind him, heads covered by their cowls, eyes cast downward.

"So, Brother Edgar," he said, in a deeply sonorous voice that belied his diminutive stature, "this is the foundling you so often have told me of. Curious he is, indeed."

He walked across the room to where I sat. I was alarmed by his steady, piercing stare. It was as if he saw through me, knew everything I had experienced or would experience. Close to I was forced to observe the yellow sores that decorated his thin lips as they parted in a smile completely foreign to the sinister gravity of his demeanour. These signs of normal human frailty for one so exalted helped somewhat to ease my fears.

"Welcome, my boy. We are pleased to receive you into our house, for as our Lord said, 'I was a stranger and you took me in.' So it is with those of the household of faith, which Brother Edgar assures me you are, as he rescued you from both the snow and the Hebrews. Praise be to our Lord Jesus for your deliverance to our family in Christ. Let us pray together and so avoid the deception of the Fallen One."

It occurred to me then, and many times since, that Christians never tire of proclaiming their faith loudly and in the view of all, while we Jews keep our rituals as a guarded secret from outsiders. Christians see almost everyone as of the Faith, at the very least potential Christians. We see almost all non-Jews as potential, if not actual, enemies.

Thomas told me it was too obvious a question to demand an answer. Then he proceeded to answer it.

"Christianity is the one true religion, Joseph. Christ wanted to bring everyone to the Lord. The Jews, well, the Jews want God for themselves alone."

At the Prior's bidding, the monks fell to their knees and began to recite a prayer. Many times I had heard Ederick often make use of it. When they had finished, one of the monks handed the Prior a water jug and an empty wooden bowl. He reached down, took my hands and first turned the palms upwards and then down as he poured the water over them. When he had done, two of the monks kneeled at my feet and began to wash them. I attempted to keep still, but could not. My feet, indeed my entire body, went into violent spasms. The more I attempted to control the movement, the worse it became, and soon the entire party was soaked with the holy liquid. They threw their arms up in alarm and retreated hurriedly.

"I'm very sorry," I stammered, my fear forcing the white foam of spittle from my mouth.

The monks looked at me aghast and then for reassurance to Prior Turbe, to whom they gestured, their fingers skipping in the air.

"Speak," he said. "It is permitted."

"Is this not a sign of the Devil?" asked one, who I later discovered was called Brother Jocelin, the monk in charge of the building work in the Cathedral.

"The boy is surely possessed," offered another. "See how his limbs twist and how his face contorts."

They all made the sign of the cross, even Brother Edgar. I assumed the latter did this more out of reflex than conviction, for he came immediately to my defence.

"The child is not cursed nor is he possessed," Brother Edgar

107

retorted. "He was always so, more when frightened, which he clearly is now. I have known him since a babe. He is, in truth, a holy innocent."

"You may be proved correct," said the Prior, "but then again perhaps not."

"What is to be done with him?" inquired one of the other monks.

"Yes," the Prior replied, picking with thoughtful detachment at the edge of his scabrous lips. "Indeed, as you say, what is to be done with him? What are we to do with him?"

I was yet again the subject of disputation, neither Jew nor Christian prepared to embrace me without question. My subsequent behaviour was to show their reluctance to have been well founded.

"Is his place not with the other cripples at the gate?" asked Brother Jocelin.

Appearing both sad and contemplative, Prior Turbe shook his head slowly from side to side. From below in the Cathedral the reverberative sound of chanting reached the watchers' cell.

"Not a generous sentiment for one so pious, Brother. God has put the unfortunate child in our care."

"An oblate?" asked another of the monks.

"No," the Prior replied. "The boy has no one to sponsor him to that. No, we will be obliged to bring him in as one abandoned."

"But reflect," countered Brother Jocelin, "did Brother Edgar not say how he came looking for sanctuary? He was not abandoned, but rather he has run away."

The Prior pondered this argument for a long minute.

"This is true, my Brother. Nonetheless, he came into our world through Brother Edgar's intervention after being cast aside by his mother. Being discovered so, he was indeed an expositus and even if taken in by strangers, he remains an expositus. We must remember that St. Gregorius was such, and he rose to the highest of God's callings here on earth."

"It will be a blessing upon our community to take him in," added Brother Edgar. "From when I found him lying in the snow, wrapped tight in the armour of his swaddling clothes, I have held that he was left there for me to discover because he was to serve some Greater Purpose. Now he has returned to me, to us, to our Priory, I sense a Divine Confirmation of this Purpose has been delivered."

"What," asked Brother Jocelin, a twist of disbelief playing across his face, "would this Purpose be?"

"That has not been revealed, Brother. In time I have no doubt it will be revealed."

The other monks tittered at this, cupping their hands over their mouths in order to protect their modesty. As William had said, this was a virtue strictly demanded of them by the Rule of St. Benedict.

"You mock me, Brother Prior."

"I intend no such offence, either to you or the boy," Prior Turbe said, but like the others he found it difficult to hold back a smile. "However, he need not fulfil your expectations of Divine Purpose. It is enough he has come to us for protection and that we will afford him with gladdened Christian hearts."

So, I was admitted to the Priory as an expositus, the first one to be brought into the Cathedral. I was something new in a world highly regulated by ritual and because of this a world that valued conformity and the expected, neither of which I carried. For this I became a curiosity to the brothers. My youth, being a cripple and having been born a Jew enhanced my novelty and, unfortunately, my susceptibility to the taunts and oft times worse, particularly from the oblates and novices with whom I was obliged to live.

Worthy Vessels Of God

"Look at this," crowed Marcus, as he grasped my Hebraic appendage in his soft-skinned hand.

I had been at the Priory for but two days. I was not experiencing a propitious introduction to the monastic life.

Marcus was a dark haired, stocky boy of about thirteen or fourteen years. He was the son of a wealthy Norman family. His parents had recently succumbed to a pestilence raging to the north of the city. His paternal uncle, Simon de Novers, had then moved to take control of his brother's castle and estates and consigned Marcus as an oblate to the Priory. De Novers claimed this was to shield his nephew from the illness. Marcus was convinced his motives were less charitable. Whatever the actual cause, Marcus was vengefully unhappy about his new situation. In my form and heritage a painted bird among crows, I was an easy target for the rage he carried, even if such rage, whether held in check or let loose on the world, infringed the most basic tenets of the Rule. Did he not give way to anger and desire revenge? Yet, like myself, Marcus had not been there long, and we were yet to be put to study of the Rule.

I had great strength in my arms, but Marcus was taller, heavier and much stronger. Further, he had taken me unawares, pinning my arms behind me whilst I had my heavy novice robes hoisted around my waist so that I could relieve myself in the reredorter.

If only William had been there. It had been just a few days since he had left me. I thought about him constantly. I longed for his loving smile, his assurance, his touch, and especially at that moment, for his protection.

I was alone, exposed and helpless in my crippled Jewishness.

Four or five other novices moved in closer to gaze upon the cursed member, the revered member, a branded member I could not escape.

I inquired of Thomas as to why if Jesus himself carried the Mark of Abraham, as had his disciples, it had become such a badge of shame among his followers.

"It is precisely because Christ was circumcised that True Believers need not submit to this ritual, now only observed by the Jew and the Saracen. His circumcision prefigured His final sacrifice on the Cross, a sacrifice for all of mankind. As the blessed St. Ambrose has told us, 'Because Christ suffered the rabbi's knife, there is no longer need for the blood of each man child to be shed.'"

Such a measured, if mysterious, explanation, and many others that I have heard over the years, was of no concern to the young men clustered around me, pointing and laughing at my Jewish shame.

I was saved further humiliation by the arrival of Brother Jerome, the Master of Novices. A short, stout man with a rounded, brightly speckled face that appeared to present a jovial mien, he was in practice a hardened shell, an exacting and oft-times harsh guide to the Rule.

As he hurried across the straw-strewn floor, Marcus let go of me and of mine, yanked down my robe and patted me on the back in a proprietary, fraternal manner.

"I am growing weary of having to admonish you about transgressing the Rule of Silence. Especially in this place. You know that you are not to love speaking, not to speak useless words that provoke laughter, especially boisterous laughter."

"We were…," began Marcus, his excuse cut short as Brother Jerome raised a finger to his thick lips.

Silence.

Silence, one of St. Benedict's Rules that as the weft running through the warp, wove the whole Holy Cloth that was the life of the Priory.

Silence.

I will take heed of my ways, that I sin not with my tongue: I have set a guard to my mouth, I was dumb and was humbled, and kept silence even from good things.

Silence.

In much talk thou shalt not escape sin.

Silence.

It belongeth to the master to speak and to teach; it becometh the disciple to be silent and to listen.

Silence. The most critical instruction. No conversing in cloisters, the choir, the refectory or the dormitory and with particular prohibition in the reredorter, where the opportunity was greatest for acts of indiscretion and worse, for lewdness and carnal sins. With certain exceptions - chanting and the public reading from Scripture during meals and some essential verbal exchange while at work - monks and novices were to communicate only through hand signs. Too much talk could lead to gossip and gossip to impure thoughts and impure thoughts to disobedience and an inability to follow the Path and to do battle for Christ the Lord, the true King.

If not for those signs, something my palsied hands refused to master, not speaking would have admirably suited my corkscrewed tongue. As it was, neither the permitted finger-waggling dumb show nor vocalised common discourse was readily open to me. I was, therefore, given dispensation, when all other manner of communication proved futile and no disturbance or offence might be caused, to speak and, to a more limited degree, be spoken to. I soon discovered that when not overseen by others, most of the monks quite freely flouted the Rule and would converse.

Having spent most of my days and nights at Saddlegate alone in my upstairs cell, being now forced to sleep in a long, narrow dormitory with fifteen novices was at first unsettling. It was made more so by the teasing I suffered when they were awake and when they were asleep by the snoring, sobbing and the screams induced by nocturnal visitations of devils and saints experienced by my ever-cold, ever-hungry, ever-exhausted fellows.

Hunger and tiredness were constant companions for both novices and monks. We had to get up in the middle of the night to sit behind the monks in the choir as the Night Office of Vigils was celebrated. It was only through the fear of Brother Jerome and the eye-watering spark given by the chewing of peppercorns, that we were able to stay awake. Vigils was followed at dawn by Lauds of the Dead and a few hours later by the Prime, then Terce, Mass, Sext, None, Vespers and finally Compline. Given that we were sustained in this endless round of Offices by only meagre meals, consisting primarily of pulmenta and black bread, sometimes a bit of fish, sometimes pittances of cheese or fruit, but never meat, the latter strictly prohibited by the Rule, it is hardly surprising that both monks and novices were prey to night-time phantoms.

Whilst life at the Priory was testing, especially in those first few weeks before the novices lost interest in tormenting me, before I was able to grow accustomed to the strict regime and before I began to absorb with an open heart the Novice Master's exacting lessons on the Rule, I found great solace and spiritual comfort in the eight daily Offices. During these times, and they took up much of the day and the night, I could escape unwanted attention and immerse myself in the gliding rhythms of the monks' chanting as it rose up, together with the sweet odour of incense, to the roof beams far above the stone floor of the nave and from there up to Heaven.

As each day passed, I discovered that my Christian faith grew more tenacious. It had been mother-milk imbibed during my formative years under Ederick's exacting love, reinforced in talks with dearest, sanctified William and given blatant counterpoint by my lonely existence on the margins with the Jews in Saddlegate. For once in my short life I had found a place and a purpose. I was a well-prepared vessel for the Heavenly Demands of St. Benedict's Rule.

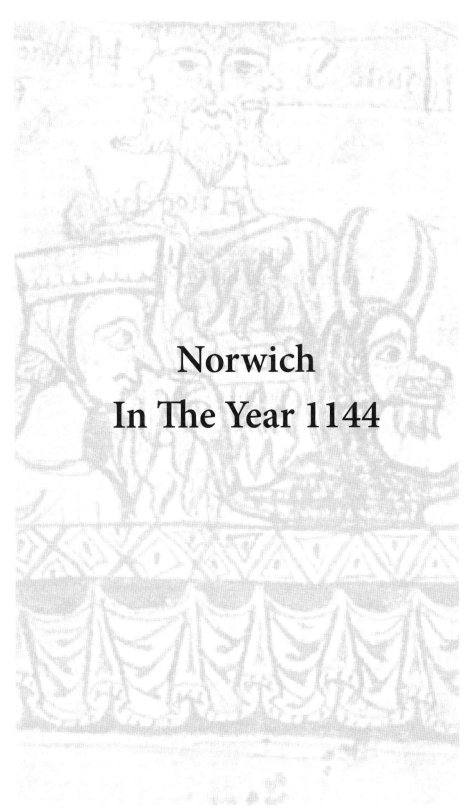

Norwich
In The Year 1144

Godwin

I remember hearing the dull but loud thwack of the tabula that hung outside the Chapter House. It was struck to mark the hour instead of the customary bells, silenced until Easter Day. It was a frantic, festive time in the Cathedral and throughout the City. A time of additional Offices. A time of processions and joyful celebrations. "Christ is Risen!" The Resurrection and the end of Lent. Our souls were devoted beyond measure to the former, our bodies were beyond being thankful for the latter.

I was leaving the choir after Prime, when a monk whose name I cannot recall - mostly they appear in my memory as shadow-hooded faces - came to me and gestured that I should follow him. He led me to Prior Turbe's room, a sparely appointed cell up a narrow staircase off the cloisters.

The Prior was sitting on a high stool behind a table. He indicated a bench opposite. I sat.

"How are you, Joseph?"

I nodded and smiled.

"Very good. Very good, my son. Brother Jerome tells me you have been a most devoted student in your first months. I am pleased to learn of this, for the monastic road can be very difficult, very stony and one not to be travelled by everyone."

"Now, it is not our custom," the Prior continued, "to allow novices or indeed our brothers to see visitors or have any contact outside these walls. As it is said, just as the oyster is safe within its shell yet is prey to crabs and diverse enemies when it emerges, so the monk is safe within the confines of the Priory, but if he wanders out he is exposed to the snares of Godlessness and Evil. However, we are this day faced with a dilemma and are hoping that you may be able to assist in resolving it for our brother priest, Godwin Sturt."

He pointed, and it was only then that I noticed a squat, bulky figure in a dark robe sitting in the shadows in the far corner of the room. He was staring at me with undisguised hostility. I had heard a great deal from William about his Uncle Godwin, the priest. Although I had renounced my ancestral identity by entering the Priory, with his visceral, violent antipathy towards Jews, for all I knew even converted Jews, he was someone I had no desire to encounter. Of course, at that moment I had no choice.

The fat priest grunted as he rose heavily and came across the room. He stood above me, his breathing laboured, his double chins wobbling. From the shadow of his breath, he had recently dined on a roasted fowl.

"So, this is the Jew," he said after a long pause, his squint eye roving. "The Jew."

Compared to the Prior, Godwin's French was roughened, uncomfortable on his Saxon tongue.

"Please, brother priest," Prior Turbe said, "he is now one of us. He has accepted Jesus as his Saviour and has proved himself, despite his crippled body and curious manner of speech, to be a devoted student of the Rule. A Jew no longer. He is our brother in Christ."

"Of course," said the priest, patting me softly on the back. "You must excuse me for such an unintended slander. When I tell you the reason I have come you will better understand why I am so exercised by the least association with those accursed people. As I explained to Prior Turbe, I know from my nephew that you are, better said, were, a Jew who lived with the Jew Eleazar at a house in Saddlegate. He told he this after bringing you to the Sanctuary Gate."

"Well," added the Prior, "it appears that the priest's nephew is missing. He feels that as you were the last to see him you may be able to assist in discovering his whereabouts."

I could but nod dumbly at the news my friend had disappeared. Did he imagine once I was safe inside the Priory there was no longer need to withhold the truth from his uncle or the Jews? Fearing for his safety, I had begged him not to return to Saddlegate.

"The Jews are bound to place the blame on you when they find I have gone," I told him. "Then who knows what they will do. They may appear peaceful people, compliant people, but as I found to my cost, they can be harsh and brutal."

I had raised the hem of my tunic and displayed for him the purple-green bruises inflicted by the boots and fists of the outraged Jews.

"Please, William, please promise me you will not go back there."

"You must not worry, my dearest," he replied, grinning and reaching over to tousle my hair. "It might be they will be pleased you are gone. After all, as you know, they have not been kind to you, have they?"

"That is true, but as you know, they feared my presence being known to Christians."

He laughed. "I will be mindful of what you say, Joseph my dear one."

I had hope he had, but knowing William I suspected his good-natured trust would have prevailed over my warnings. Now I feared for the price he may have paid for his lack of caution.

"William visited my house with a man my wife did not know," Godwin said. "This man said William's mother, my wife's sister, had agreed to the boy being taken to serve in the kitchen of the Archdeacon. Being suspicious of this unknown man, my wife sent our youngest daughter to follow them. Her instincts were borne out, for they did not go to the Cathedral but to the house of Eleazar the Jew. He, that is the boy, has not been seen since. Not at his master's house or his mother's house or in the Archdeacon's kitchen.

"What do you know of these Jews?" asked the Prior. "Go on, my son, you may speak."

"There is more to tell," Godwin interjected. "More that proves without doubt the guilt of the Jews."

The Prior indicated with a wave that Godwin should continue.

"My wife had a dream, a vision, on the Holy Palm Sunday recently passed. She saw herself in the Market Place surrounded by fiendish Jews who, wielding clubs, broke her leg and detached it with force. This was surely a warning about what was going to happen to someone close to her."

"They did not approve," I began. "They didn't ...".

Godwin obviously could not understand what I was saying and looked at the prior for an explanation.

"I think he said the Jews did not something, ... but then my comprehension failed," the Prior said. "I'm afraid my ear remains uncertain as to our Joseph's meaning. Let us call for Brother Edgar. He was the one who took in the lad when he was a foundling and tutored him in the Faith."

He rang a small hand bell on the table. A monk appeared a few moments later and was sent to find Brother Edgar, who arrived in the Prior's room not long after.

Looking at me with incredulity as he repeated what I said, Brother Edgar translated. "He says that the Jews in Saddlegate did not approve of the friendship between them and that William was admonished by the Jew Eleazar and warned that he must not have further contact with Joseph. Joseph, are you saying? They beat you because you ate the Torah and after that William helped you escape?"

119

"Yes, hard boiled eggs and biscuits with verses. I was hungry and wanted to be...".

"I don't understand," he said, shaking his great tonsured head. "I also don't understand why you told me a completely different story when you came seeking sanctuary. Why did you lie to me, Joseph?"

"William said it would be best not to say that I was a Jew or even that I had lived with the Jews. It was more likely that the monks would take me in if they believed I was a simple Christian who had suffered mistreatment. I also did not want the Jews to discover where I had escaped to. I did not want to be found."

"I am very disappointed in you, Joseph," Edgar said, after having deciphered my words to the others. "Very disappointed. You need not have lied to me. The Church would never abandon you. Neither would I. Never."

"What do you expect from a Jew!" Godwin spat out, his heavy jowls shaking with indignation.

"Forbearance, my brothers," said Prior Turbe, picking thoughtfully at his crusted lips. "He was a frightened cripple, a wounded child. So, whatever story is true, he came to us in need and we opened our door to him and he has committed himself to a new life with Jesus. Besides, at the moment we need to discover what has happened to Priest Godwin's young nephew."

As if a Divine Response had been offered to the Prior's question, a few minutes later an out-of-breath monk hurried in to announce that the body of a young boy had been discovered in Thorpe Wood.

The Synod

Shuffling of leather sandals on stone, the sweetly rancid smell of tallow mixed with perfume of incense, shadows flickering across the freshly rendered walls of the nave, whispered voices. Then a stunned silence.

"I accuse the Jews, the enemies and murderers of Our Lord, the enemies of all true Christians, of the shedding of the blood of my nephew, a pure boy who never did harm to anyone, but was a paragon of virtuous deeds and thoughts."

A few days before the Synod met, word reached our cloistered world that a great concourse of people had been to view the body in Thorpe Wood and on their return to the city had set up a hue and cry against the Jews. However, it was only after Godwin, together with William's brother and cousin, came back from the Wood that I learned what I had feared.

"It grieves me to tell you," Prior Turbe said, as he sat with me in the cloister garden, "but the priest Godwin has this day, not more than an hour since, informed me that the boy who was discovered is indeed, as suspected, his nephew, your friend William."

Godwin paused and looked out over the congregation of churchmen who crowded into the Cathedral nave - a congress of right-side-up bats, black–robed shoulder to black-robed shoulder. He took a deep, shuddering breath. Tears rolled down his over-fleshed cheeks.

The Prior draped his bony arm across my shoulder. His hand, soft as butter, held mine. I sobbed, uncontrolled, my whole being wracked with monumental spasms. Tears streamed across my face. I struggled for breath. My arms and legs joined in an individual four-part, spasmodic and twisted dance macabre. The Prior tightened his hold.

I have continued to grieve for my dearest William from that moment until now, when after these uncountable years of emptiness I long to join him, but know this old, sin-filled Jew will find no seat among the host of angels with whom he resides.

Then, before he was raised up and venerated, his body lay far distant from the company of angels, beaten, bruised, unwashed and hastily buried without ceremony by the forester who had first found him. To ascertain his identity, a few days later he was disinterred by his uncle and then returned to a shallow, unconsecrated grave.

"The truth of the deed is well rehearsed," Godwin continued, his voice quivering. "This dear pure soul, this martyred child lies without a Christian burial in the wood where he was found, his wounds evidencing the cruel nature of his demise. I come before you today, at the gathering of this Holy Synod, to plead for justice and ask you, my brethren in Christ, to call the Jews to account as is prescribed in law."

Sitting behind Godwin, I had a privileged view of his audience. All the upturned faces registered shock at his report of William's murder and a palpably joyous, eager agreement with the priest's excoriating of the Jews. It was a story they were ready to hear. A story they swallowed whole as if it was a sweet, boneless fish. I too was more than ready to corroborate the story, for had I not suffered sustained cruelty at the hands of the Jews in Saddlegate and heard so often their vicious hatred of Christians? Moreover, had I not heard their warnings to William himself? Indeed I had, and all of this I recounted in ripe detail to Prior Turbe and to Godwin Strut and to anyone who would listen.

In The Book, Thomas embellished the account I relate here, which by my dying word is the true account, an account the monk illuminated so to speak, as was his custom. However, there is no great or meaningful distinction between the two stories, and there is no harm in illumination. I like to think of Thomas's method as akin to what we did at our copying tables in the library or what was done by the men in the workshop of the Cathedral's master painter. Thomas added layers of colour to fill in the outline, as the workmen did, to the frescos of Bishop Herbert de Losinga then being completed in the aisle of the South Nave. Thomas quite rightly made William's story more arresting, more vibrant, more a story to befit God's chosen, that is to befit a saint.

Despite Godwin's passionate entreaties, despite the approbation from members of the Synod, despite calls for retribution by the Norwich mob, despite Bishop Eborard's demands that the Jews be summoned to answer the charges of brutal murder laid against them, the Jews refused to appear.

It was only after the Synod had ended that the Sheriff was persuaded to bring a number of prominent Jews, including, I was told, Eleazar, before the Bishop to answer the accusations made by Godwin. I had not been asked to attend, which saved me from having to face the Jews, although I am convinced they would not have recognised me, draped as I was in the protective, cripple-masking folds of my cassock.

"Of course, they denied it," reported the priest. "Of course they refused to submit to trial by ordeal. Cowards! Liars! Before anything could de done the Sheriff spirited them away to the Castle, beyond the reach of the Bishop's authority."

I was at one with Godwin in his fury at their refusal and at their retreat. Of course they had killed my friend. Who else would have put a crown of thorns upon his head and pierced his sides? Who else would have placed the barbed gag of teasel in his soft mouth? Who else had a reason to do such a barbarous thing to an innocent Christian child? The Jews! Who else but the Jews.

"You must not, my Lord, let them take refuge behind the Sheriff," insisted the leather-faced Prior Dom Aimar, a visitor from St Pancras in Lewes, who was passing through the city on his way to his Cluniac order's cell at Castle Acre. His mouth was too small to host the profusion of yellowish teeth that jutted out between his lips, giving him the visage of a large brown rat and adding a wet, sibilant hiss to his speech.

The Bishop spread his palms in supplicant agreement. "I agree, my dear brother, but they are, as he says, the King's Jews, and he is the King's representative. What would you have me do?"

"Ecclesiastical justice!" Prior Aimar insisted. "Surely, even the King would not, could not, deny a bishop's right to demand such a thing."

"Trial by ordeal," Godwin said. "Is this not the customary way to proceed? Water or fire and the truth will soon out."

Together with the Prior Turbe and Brother Edgar, he being there to translate for me, the senior churchmen had met in a grand anteroom in the Bishop's Palace. The Palace was thronged with workmen and although they had quitted the anteroom, the sounds of hammering and their shouts could still be heard. The Palace was less austere than the Priory. As in the Cathedral, the rendered stone was being illuminated with murals of Christ and the Holy Mother.

It was extremely unusual for a novice to be invited to attend such august company. I was there on Godwin's urging. He was anxious for me to repeat my story to the Bishop and Prior Aimar.

"What more proof do you require, my Lord Bishop?" Godwin asked, after I had finished my account of what had passed at Saddlegate. "Christian conscience cannot be satisfied until the Jews are made to answer for their deeds. Until they are all eliminated. Finished. Driven out."

The Bishop glanced at Prior Turbe, who nodded his assent. Nonetheless, the former continued to appear uncertain, looking down at his feet, turning his staff around and around in his hands.

"Yes," he said finally, "I feel as every God-fearing man must at this terrible crime, most terrible crime. Jews indeed."

His voice trailed off.

"As we are all aware," he continued after a distracted moment, "these are precarious times, lawless times. The King is fighting many battles to protect his throne and what with the Earl of Essex closing on Cambridge and Hugh Bigod here in Norfolk changing his loyalty once more, to mention nothing of risings in other parts of the kingdom, as well as in Normandy, we must take care that we are not seen as defying King Stephen, tying our fortunes to that of his enemies. Precarious. Yes, decidedly so. The Jews are his. We must show allegiance or no one will invest us with their trust. The King's Jews. Any king's Jews. Yes, a dangerous thing to contemplate. Now they are truly out of our reach in the Castle, there is nothing more to be done."

Prior Aimar

Some may say, some said at the time, that is before the role I played was forgotten, obscured by years and deaths and decrepitude and layers of passing events, that but for my offering an account of what transpired at Saddlegate, William would not have become venerated as a Christian martyr and the Norwich Jews would have been spared the persecution and death visited upon them.

If not for my testimony, it might be claimed that Thomas would not have been moved to write the Book and Godwin's accusations against the Jews would have evaporated as thin water on sun-hot stones. Perhaps. I would like to flatter myself that it is so, that I was of such moment in raising William to Jesus's Heavenly Choir. I would also like to be convinced that it was not true, for being given such a prominent voice in this story is a weighty and pain-filled burden to carry, especially for one who struggles simply to carry himself through the unremitting cruelties of this world.

It is true that the timid Bishop was initially unwilling to do more than bluster. Further, the attempts of Godwin and William's mother to rouse the city against the Jews met with only a half-hearted response that endured but a few days. Even weighing in my words of injudicious witness, if William's body had remained in the shallow grave in Thorpe Wood then his death may have soon been forgotten, at least by those who had not known and loved him.

It was the timely intervention of Prior Aimar that made the crucial difference and helped launch William on his saintly journey. If praise or condemnation is to be laid at anyone's door, it is at his, not mine.

While the Bishop and Prior Turbe were talking in the far

corner of the room, a smiling Prior Aimar approached me.

"How would you care to accompany me to Lewes, my son?" he asked me in a low voice, resting his hand on my arm. I shivered as the coldness of Priory stone seeped from his pale fingers though the thick fabric of my novice's cassock.

When I didn't reply he turned to Brother Edgar.

"Of course, Brother, you too would be welcome. I can understand that the boy needs such assistance as you might offer. Oh, I see by your look, that my request leaves you puzzled."

"As it does me," said Prior Turbe, who overhearing the conversation crossed the room.

He was joined by the Bishop, as well as Godwin. The Cluniac prior finding himself cornered, let go of my arm and, as if to call down Divine Intervention, bowed his head and made the sign of the cross.

"You must forgive me, your Grace," he said, ignoring the others and addressing himself to Bishop Eborard, "I did not intend such presumption, but if you would allow the boy to come with me as witness, then I would be willing to carry the remains of his martyred friend to our Priory. This would relieve you of the need to defy the Sheriff. You see, in Lewes we need only the bones and the witness against the Jews. We have no need, as you have, to persecute those responsible."

"It will also place valuable relics at your disposal," Prior Turbe said, deep gravel rolling in his voice.

"Well," replied Aimar, "there is that consideration, of course."

"The Jews," shouted Godwin, his face a hot scarlet. "What about the Jews? Are they to escape their crime? Is my nephew to remain unavenged?"

He was so exercised that his French deserted him and he reverted to English.

He turned to the Bishop, opening his thick arms wide in a pleading gesture.

"Please, your Grace. This is not right. They must be punished. The Jews...".

The Bishop gestured at him to be silent. I could see that the old man was losing patience with the one-note priest.

"As I was saying," continued Aimar. "We have recently had to assume heavy debt at the Priory and more building is having to be carried out at our sister cell at Castle Acre. It would greatly assist us in our holy work if more pilgrims were to find their way to Lewes, for I have no doubt that miracles will attend one martyred so young and in such a fashion."

"Have you failed to mark what is going on here at this very moment in our Cathedral?" asked the Bishop. "Are we not besieged by masons, carpenters, painters and all that attends with them? Please, Brother Prior, you are not alone in seeking a way to pay for God's work."

"Of course, Your Grace. I see that you have built a magnificent edifice, a stunning testament to our Lord. As I said, I am only trying to help you in resolving the vexed impasse with the Sheriff and the King's Jews."

At this, Prior Turbe motioned to the Bishop and both men retreated to the other side of the room. They were soon engaged in a heated, albeit whispered, conversation.

Prior Aimar leaned close to me. "I am sure you will find Lewes to your liking," he lisped. "Most importantly, your dear friend will be elevated to a high station. He will be venerated in a proper manner. They are without doubt good men here in Norwich, but it appears they are not prepared to embrace the martyrdom of the boy as it should be embraced. You see that, don't you, my son?"

"This boy," said Brother Edgar, "is recently arrived at our

house. He is at the beginning of his novitiate. His journey to us has been troubled. I do not believe that another long journey and yet another new start would be suitable, especially for one so terribly afflicted as he is."

Before Aimar could reply, the Bishop and Prior Turbe returned.

"Your offer is generous," said the Bishop. "We know it is made in the best interests of the Church. However, on reflection we feel that it would not be wise to accept. After all, the boy was a local child and although we cannot, at least at this time, take action against the Jews, both the Prior and I agree that it would be more prudent to bring his mortal remains to the Cathedral for an appropriate burial. If, as some maintain, the lad has been a victim of the Jews, if he has in truth been martyred for the Faith, then we are certain that the miracles that follow such events will soon manifest themselves. Of course, we also desire to keep our dear Joseph close. He has not been with us long, but the Prior informs me that he is dearly loved by all."

While their language was polite and pious, I could not help but hear marketplace haggling. No words of love or appreciation for the boy who lay violated and twice buried in Thorpe Wood. Even Godwin was more concerned with igniting a crusade against the Jews than mourning for his nephew. For the others the real William, my William, whom they had never known and would never know, was reduced to little more than a collection of valuable bones.

Coming To Rest

Clods of damp earth clung to William's body when the monks finally unwrapped his Holy Remains. Ripe corruption rose, as did a swarm of black flies from out the folds of the winding sheet in which he had been carried on a bier from Thorpe Wood to the Cathedral. The monks buried their faces in the side of their cowls. One stepped to the side and was ill, dark liquid spilling in a rush from his mouth onto the stones of the monks' choir where William's body had been taken after Mass.

William was laid out as he had been first discovered among a pile of leaves in Thorpe Wood, naked from the waist down, but for his worn out sandals with the torn strap on one side. I cannot now remember whether it was the left sandal or the right one. Over the many years I tried to remember, picturing William, moving my focus from this face, trailing my remembering gaze down this body to his feet. Each time the errant strap appears, but each time on a different sandal. At times both straps seemed to be flapping loose, at other times both are neatly fixed. So it is when one has to scramble for a detailed memory. The harder you press your thoughts upon it, the more it flickers insubstantially.

I puzzled at the time both why the lack of trousers and why no one found this a peculiar circumstance. During that April in the year 1144, the more immediate question for everyone was who had murdered him and why. The most immediate and convenient, as well as most probable, answer was that Jews had killed him. They had done so because he was a Christian child, and that's the kind of thing that Jews did. Also, was it not Easter when Our Lord was crucified through the connivance of the Jews? Besides the bloodthirsty nature of the Hebrew, as evinced by their belief that sacrificial blood makes atonement for the soul, as well as the slaughter of their own children during the Holy Crusade, who else would want to do such a terrible thing?

As I watched the monks washing William's brutalised corpse, I heard the voices of Eleazar and Mordechai cursing their Christian masters in blood.

Bile, maggots, rotting flesh, adulterers, defiled women...

More than capable of murdering a child were people of such low worth.

Swallow them, lop them off, make them bleed, murder them, smite them, crush them.

My poor William!

Destroy them with bereavement and sword from without, and fear within.

Jews! Jews! Jews!

The cry started by a few people that crowded behind and around the bier as it was brought into the nave, was quickly amplified with more voices added to the call for immediate vengeance against the enemies of Christ. The demand reverberated loudly inside the Cathedral until some time later when it was drowned out by the uplifting sound of Mass being sung, singing that swelled out so sweetly because the monks were obliged to devote most of their time to Benedictine silence. Unleashed from that duty, it was as if a dam of emotion had been suddenly breached.

The body was placed with gentle ceremony on the cold washing slab. It was immediately surrounded by black-hooded monks. William's budding manhood, strangely engorged in death, was exposed to all, a disconcerting sight for the cloistered, Rule-chaste brethren. There were marks of a beating on the discoloured skin of his head, his torso and his thin, hairless legs. His right hand had been badly mangled.

It appeared as if he had been pecked at by birds or gnawed by rats. Crowned with a forest wreath, twigs and brambles festooned his hair. This crown was matched by the light new-Spring green of softly blistered flesh on his chest and lower extremities. Although his eyes had been closed, for which I was thankful, the bones in his face stood out sharply through waxy skin, disrupting any suggestion of peaceful repose. This was not to be wondered at. William had been vilely treated and lay dead in the midst of the damp Wood for more than 30 days.

He was still recognisably William, but not my William. My William had been laughter and knowing grace. My William had sported an ever-changing grin. My William had been everything that was worthy, gentle and boisterously irreverent in life. No more. The new William was a frozen mask captured on a dry stalk, to be taken up by the monks and many common folk in the city and beyond as a dead receptacle of pious reverence and hoped-for miracles.

"No, Joseph. No. Please, this cannot be said," protested Brother Thomas. "You must be misremembering. The shock, perhaps. The grief. You do agree, do you not, that William was martyred for the Faith? Good. Then it follows that he must have been in death as in life, free from corruption. It is said, must be said, must be written, that not only was there no bodily corruption, but that the air was perfumed with sweet odours of sanctity. Sweet odours, Joseph. Sweet perfume. Mark that well. Those destined for sainthood give off the holy scent of the Garden as it was before Eve gave into temptation."

How could I deny Thomas? The truth would have denied William, although if I had insisted on my story, Thomas and the others would have ignored my account. Nonetheless, I was not going to deny William.

So, no corruption and only sweet odours attended. This was true even as a wriggling nest of bone-white monks' fingers swarmed across his body with vinegar-soaked rags. Finally, those fingers moved in more measured concert and wrapped William in a white linen shroud. Only his dear face remained visible when they lifted him up and, with due reverence, placed his freshly cocooned body in the stone sarcophagus, setting down the latter in the monks' cemetery behind the Chapter House and near the narrow entryway to the cloister. William had come home.

Speaking To William

It was a month or two after William had been brought to the Cathedral, celebrated and then interred. I was on the grass in the centre of the monks' cemetery resting on my crutches, head bowed, saying a quiet prayer for my friend. House martins swooped close overhead to and from their mud nests set in the niches above the stone walls. The early morning sun caught the edge of the tomb, bestowing a celestial benediction. I felt his arms warming me against the cold of the dawn. I felt his soft breath touching me with his love. I saw his round face animated with joy, not the rigid mask of death of the stranger that had been captured in a cold stone sepulchre.

As I often did when alone with William before the gates were open for the pilgrims, I began to relate to him the events of the previous day. Because the Rule dictated silence, I spoke inside myself, even though he was one of the few people who could understand my spoken words. I told him how some of the other novices continued to torment me, stumbling in front of me so I would lose my balance or sticking out their legs as I passed to trip me or twisting their faces to mock my twisted speech. When Brother Jerome wasn't near, they whispered about the Jew Cripple and how he was an abomination who would soon be cast out into the street where he belonged. Anger flared and I wanted to retaliate, smashing their shins or their mocking faces with my crutches. However, I had imbibed the Doctrine and the Word. I turned away and instead of meeting evil with evil, I prayed for a peaceful deliverance from the abuse I suffered. I prayed to the Blessed Jesus. I prayed to God. I even prayed to William. Up to that point all my prayers remained stubbornly unanswered. I was a good Christian, a good Benedictine, and so I suffered this rejection in silence.

Suddenly, a weighty hand dropped on my shoulder. I turned

and found Brother Edgar staring down, as I was, at the double-headed red rose growing near William's tomb. It had appeared a few weeks after the burial. Some claimed it was proof of William's sanctity. The doubters pressed for more convincing, transformative miracles. So the debate raged among the monks as to William's true status. To my surprise, my Edgar had sided with the sceptical ones.

He looked around the graveyard to see if anyone could overhear us. Assuring himself that no prying eyes were in view or ears bent in listening, Edgar whispered to me.

"He was a pleasant lad, Joseph. I could see that. Not a saintly lad though. Not saintly. There was absolutely nothing in his poor, short life to indicate he had been chosen for such a lofty position."

"What about his death?" I asked. "Martyred by the Jews. Does this not weigh in the balance?"

"Can we be certain of this tale, Joseph? I fear not. His uncle, the priest Godwin, has not only a hatred for them, which I understand for they are a most defiling and perfidious people, perfectly capable of such a deed, but from the beginning he has had his mind fixed on owning a family martyr. It raises him up. Him as well as his son and William's brother too. A martyr raises them all. Do you not mark that he has been the first and the most insistent in championing William? This is telling of his purpose. You must see that, Joseph."

I saw that. I saw that William raised me up as well. Was that more important to me than my devotion to William? It was not. Further, I had my well-justified suspicions about the Jews of Saddlegate. Even the Bishop, the most sceptical of the claims made for William's being one of the Blessed, believed the Jews may have murdered him, although he stopped short of maintaining that such an act meant that this necessarily bestowed saintliness.

"Murder is murder," Bishop Eborard had declared, "but not all those murdered, even if they are dispatched by non-believers, can be said to have been martyred. Martyrdom demands a much higher test of faith and of sacrilegious intent."

"Miracles?" asked Edgar. "Where are the promised miracles, Joseph? The Bishop allowed the boy to be brought here in the event he was murdered for the Faith. You remember what he said? Miracles, Joseph, miracles. There must be miracles. There have been no miracles. None."

I pointed at the rose. Surely its sudden appearance was a sign. Edgar shook his head and smiled sympathetically.

"I know you want this for your friend. Nonetheless, a flower is hardly sufficient. Also, you know what the others say, don't you? They say that if the boy was a genuine martyr, if he had been murdered by the Jews in order to mock the Faith, then you, Joseph, you who have spent almost every day since he has been with us praying at his tomb, you who were so close to him in life and so attentive to his memory in death, you would surely have been cured of your affliction."

"I have never prayed, as the pilgrims do, for cure. I have sought only spiritual comfort from being in his presence."

"No matter, Joseph. No matter. The proximity to a true saint, the close familiarity with a genuine saint should be enough in itself. Not asking might even be seen as a more effective way of calling down Divine Intercession."

"Do you recall what you said to me when you called yourself Ederick and again when I first came to the Priory?"

He inclined his head and questioned me with a raised, shaggy eyebrow.

"You told me that you had found me there in the snow, that your feet were guided to that particular spot in the Wood by the Lord because I was destined for some Great Purpose, a

Greater Purpose. Remember that?"

Brother Edgar appeared bemused.

"Well, you did say that, and William is beyond denial that Greater Purpose. Can you not see that? Surely a Greater Purpose that my journey has brought me here, now to bear witness to the truth of his life and his divine sacrifice."

"I am sorry if my words misled you, Joseph," he said pointing to the tomb, "but I doubt this poor boy is why I found you in the snow or why we were so fortunate to be reunited in God's House."

"Perhaps there is a need to wait for more time to pass," I ventured, feeling my faith in William's sanctity beginning to crumble.

"Perhaps, Joseph, perhaps," he kindly replied. "For your sake, I would like to believe, but as do the Bishop and many of the other brothers, I harbour doubts about whether there was anything more than evil intent to explain his demise."

Such doubts were not shared by the ever-growing number of pilgrims. They pressed in against William's tomb, touching the sarcophagus and praying for relief from sickness and from deformity and from ill fortune. As was commonplace, they were not dissuaded by continued sickness, continued deformity or continued ill fortune. It was not William's fault, they reasoned or were so informed by the monks, but their own failings for not being deserving or not praying with sufficient dedication or humility.

Edgar looked up. I followed his gaze and we watched the martins flap-wing dive and dart across the graveyard hunting their insect breakfast. After a time he lifted his hand and patted me fondly on the back. He must have felt my anguish. After all, he was the closest I had come to having a real father, or for that matter a real mother. Without a word or a gesture, obeying a higher calling, at least I believed so, we both turned our eyes from the birds and stared down at William's rose. It was a magnificently beautiful rose with a perfect conformation and a colour of deepest blood red, the symbol of Christ's Passion.

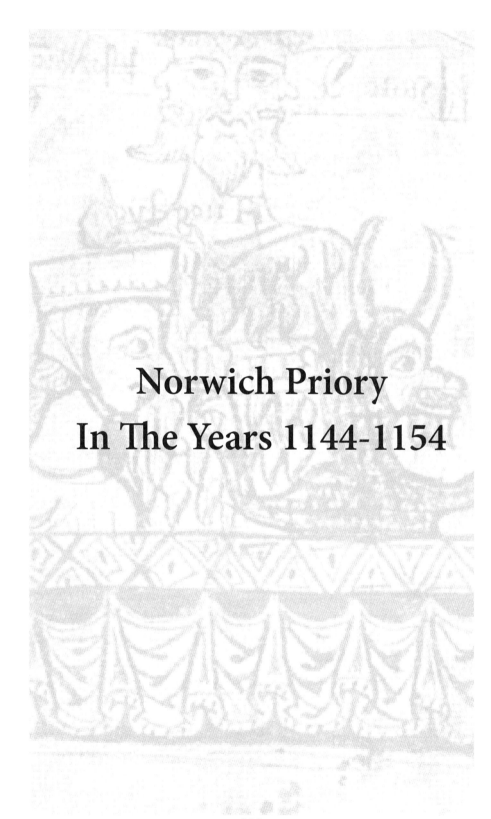

Norwich Priory
In The Years 1144-1154

William Fades

espite the miracle of the rose, a miracle that many of the brothers refused to acknowledge as such, within six months or so after he had been laid to rest in the monks' cemetery William's Passion had begun to fade from the memory of most, except for the wretched pilgrims and those of us in the Priory who fervently believed in his martyrdom. I remained constant in my attendance at his tomb. Every day I went to pray for and to speak with him. A few others came as well, including Godwin, whose attacks on William's murderers were not only undiminished, but increased in vehemence as recognition of his saintliness diminished. The fat priest was often accompanied by his son, Alexander, together with Robert, William's brother, who was later to become a monk and one of his famous sibling's most prominent hierophants.

"Have you not duties to attend?" Godwin asked, pushing his bulk against me while I prayed at my station next to William's tomb.

Usually I visited William in the morning directly after Matins, when no one but the monks were allowed in the grounds and I could be more or less alone with my friend. That day, however, I had come later, after the last few pilgrims had been ushered out but before Compline, when the gate to the cemetery was shut to outsiders. Unfortunately, Godwin and the two boys, who when the opportunity arose, jealously guarded William from what they believed was my contaminating presence, had yet to quit the Precinct.

"Yes, boy," interjected Robert, moving closer. "You must have Offices to perform. If you value your cripple's life you should go from this place now."

140

When I did not reply, he grabbed my arm and pulled me towards him. I staggered but managed to brace my crutches and remain upright. Unlike his brother, Robert was darkly taciturn and unkind. He put his mouth too close to my ear.

"You know do you not that you are a living rebuke to my dear brother?" he said. "Having you, a crippled Jew, here, shaking and blubbering near his tomb magnifies that rebuke."

Alexander, who was only about sixteen years old, but already exhibiting his father's gross proportions and hateful disposition, laughed. "He thinks that just because they allowed him the novice robe that makes him better than he is. He thinks that having known our William for a short time makes him better than he is. He thinks that...".

"You should be on your knees praying in the chapel for forgiveness for what happened to my nephew," Godwin said, "not coming out here in the pretence of pious contemplation and innocence, not assuming the mantle of a martyr's perfection, as if you and he shared anything of value before our Lord Jesus. I know what Prior Turbe said. One of us, he said. A brother in Christ, he said. Do you know what I say? I say you are not my brother. I say under that robe, behind that wooden cross around your cripples' neck, behind the shadows of your dissembling, you are what you have always been. I hold you responsible. Yes, you, with your falseness of faith, with your delusions of friendship. What manner of friendship leads to a shallow grave in the woods?"

He pointed at William's tomb and then turned an accusing finger at me.

"A Jews' friendship. Only a Jews' friendship, a mendacious friendship, a calculating friendship. That's what killed poor William. If not for his assisting you to escape from the other Jews, he would still be alive. Go, now! Leave our kinsman in peace!"

He pushed me roughly. I flailed my crutches seeking a hold that was not there. A second or two later I lay sprawled on the ground, my robe twisted under me, my mouth pressed into the grass in front of a stone marker. I was immediately undone by a rude cacophony of emotions, as fear, confusion, pain, loss, anger, guilt and humiliation raced through my soul. My body pained me too, but that pain was but a fleeting moment compared to the slow poison released by my turning inwards the many barbs of Godwin's assault.

Did the priest speak the truth? Had I not entertained similar thoughts about the risks William took, the dangers he faced because of me? Yes, of course I had. Godwin's seeds of hate had, therefore, found within me a well-prepared soil to take root, to grow, to develop dark flowers with black stems and pustulous blossoms.

Fortunately, these flowers did not bloom for longer than it took me to lift my eyes, gaze on the glory of William's rose and remember a passage from the Song of Solomon I had read with Brother Jerome just the previous day.

My beloved is unto me as a cluster of camphire in the vineyards of Engedi. I am the rose of Sharon and the lily of the valleys.

Yes, I knew that William, my beloved friend, loved me and I him. I knew that Godwin's hatred and that of the others could never erase that love, no matter their curses or blows. Our love was beyond the reach of their malevolence, as it was beyond their understanding. It was a love that endured and grew after death, William's death and now, these many years later, my own, which will no doubt soon arrive.

Having reached out to gather my crutches, I planted them in front of me and, throwing my weight forward upon them, I levered myself up from the grass. The priest and the two boys watched my efforts with indifference. In their eyes I was a harmless worm safely crushed under heel.

I wondered why I found enemies with those whom I shared the fervent belief in William's Grace, while in those with whom I felt the closest ties, such as Brother Edgar or the Bishop, the former who treated me with affection and respect, the latter who was unaware of my existence, were in the camp of the deniers.

Marcus

A year passed and then another. One year was more or less as the last had been. There was little choice. Mostly I treasured that security. Each minute of each day was marked out by the routine of Offices, contemplating the Rule, prayers, meals, studying in the library and, of course, my morning conversations with William. The prescribed arc of time was broken on occasion by Feast Days, albeit these too came and went in a familiar pattern, or by the distraction of some major or minor disaster.

One cold winter's day a large black pig ran into the calefactory and bowled over two monks who were warming themselves by the fire. A great commotion ensued as a gaggle of black robed figures gathered together and attacked the brute, who managed to upend a few other hapless monks as it made its escape. Some said that Satan had turned himself into the pig so as to invade and defile our sanctuary. Others held it was only a pig. Whether pig or Satan, it made for a refreshing change.

More serious were the unforeseen fatalities and crippling injuries. Workmen were the most frequent victims, dropping from scaffolding or being maimed by falling masonry. I recall the three workmen who were crushed by a fall of stone and timber, occasioned by high winds. When I happened upon the scene I could see no bodies, only a pile of rubble out of which seeped a slowly expanding pool of blood. All sound had been consumed by the sudden calamity. A dozen or so monks stood around, a fine white dust settling gently on their black robes. They were too stunned to attempt a rescue, which in any case would have been too late.

Then there was the death of Brother Stephen, an aged monk and the Cathedral Dean, who was discovered hanging naked from a low roof beam in the reredorter, his pale, mole-encrusted and hairless belly distended, unshod feet pointing straight down towards the floor. Suicide being a mortal sin, he was denied a place in the monk's cemetery. The poor man's body had to be carried away in the darkness by some undisclosed persons and disposed of in some undisclosed place outside the Cathedral grounds.

I am ashamed to reveal yet another secret. I had welcomed such ghastly events, even if only to a degree, although at the time, as a most devout Benedictine, I would not admit this to myself. Marcus, whose commitment to the Rule was, at best tenuous, did not entertain similar restraint.

"All down his legs and all over the floor. Shit. All over with shit. What a sight! What a stink. Worse than it usually is in the reredorter and that is worse than a pigsty. The mad monk was just covered in shit. Shit, shit, shit." Marcus said with a broad grin, rolling the word over and over on his tongue with undisguised relish. "If you hurry, you might just see before they cut him down."

I cast around the dormitory to see if anyone was nearby who might overhear. The room was empty, but nonetheless, out of my perpetual fear of transgressing, I motioned to him to be quiet. This only succeeded in encouraging him.

"Shit, shit and more shit!" he proclaimed loudly, reaching over and clapping me firmly by the arm.

Frightened that we would be discovered, I pulled away from him. I dropped a crutch and stumbled as his hand fell from my arm. Neither speaking nor touching was permitted and our friendship was taken up with both.

"It is true, my crippled friend, that I speak useless words, that I too much enjoy laughter. It is a fact beyond dispute that the longer I am confined within these holy walls with the holy monks, the more I see that it is our beloved St. Benedict and his precepts, not my damnable uncle, that are my true goaler. All those pleasures that are denied, talking, drinking, eating, the other, Ah, Joseph the other! I assume you know nothing of this, do you, you poor misshapen husk? Please spare me that disapproving look."

At this time most of the young men with whom I had started my journey had completed their novitiate and had been brought into the Order. Of that group, only Marcus and I remained outside the Secret. In my case, I imagined at first that I was excluded due to my physical inadequacy or the taint of heritage, or both. The reason was, however, more prosaic. At fifteen, although my precise age could not be ascertained, I was simply too young for the cassock, the scapular and the tonsure. Marcus too had not yet reached seventeen years, although his outspoken blasphemy was destined to keep him forever on the outside, despite his uncle being a generous benefactor of the Cathedral. At the same time, it was only the depth of his uncle's purse, and as I was to learn, that depth was illusory, that allowed him to remain for the few years that he did.

When I first entered the Priory, he had been my most dedicated tormentor. By that time he had become my most dedicated companion and special friend. To begin with the attachment was of his own desire and design, for not only did I always carry the cripple's fear of rejection, I would have preferred to maintain distance from someone who was increasingly flouting the Rule, in perpetual conflict with Brother Jerome, as well as the Prior, and, therefore, by his unruly ways, a dangerous person with whom to be associated.

Nonetheless, gradually his rough affection won me. He did not have William's gentle hand, but I learned to welcome his embrace and the affection in his bright green eyes. The spiritual love of Jesus was wondrous, but with William and with Saul I had tasted the warmth of worldly caresses and, although I knew it was a sin, Marcus, not by any measure a scholarly

146

boy, convinced me that Jesus would not have frowned on our familiarity.

"Jesus touched all He came in contact with," Marcus explained. "In the spirit and in the flesh, He celebrated friendship. Did Our Lord not have a Beloved Disciple, a special friend? Well, you are my special friend, Joseph, and I am yours."

I did not fully understand what drew Marcus to the deformed me, but I never questioned it. He carried the strength of a bear and took it upon himself to love me and to be my protector. That was enough to hold the balance against the perilous nature of our friendship and to forestall, on my part, more searching enquiry.

"I am not here for the love of Jesus, my dearest, my crooked-back Jew, albeit I do love Him, as we all love Him. I am here because my uncle wanted me gone from the world and did not have the courage to do what needed to be done."

He drew a fine noble Norman thumb across his fine noble Norman throat.

I asked William to intervene on Marcus's behalf, to show him the way to forgiveness and a trusting heart.

"Please, Joseph. Save your prayers. Your dead friend cannot soften my uncle's heart nor mine."

In this Marcus proved to be perfectly correct.

News Of Murder And Riot

Brother Stephen, who had been at the Priory for so many years that no one, including Brother Stephen, could remember when he had not been there, was a close confident of Bishop Eborard. Perhaps their intimate bond was forged because they came from the same village in Normandy. Also as Dean, the old monk attended all clerical offices with the Bishop. Even when not officiating, the two men were almost never apart. You could often see them strolling in the Cathedral grounds, black-cowled heads pressed together, lost in forbidden conversation. Brother Stephen's gruesome demise affected the Bishop so badly he was never again able to celebrate Mass and within a week or two, without explanation or farewell, he gave up his position and retired to a monastery in France.

His departure was quietly welcomed, as to celebrate would not have been in keeping with the Holy Rule, by those of us - a few good and true monks, Godwin and his family and, of course, myself - who supported the claims for William's martyrdom, claims that Bishop Eborard had resisted. We were further heartened when Prior Turbe was elevated to the Bishop's Throne. He was strong and clear in his advocacy for William and in the belief that the Jews were guilty of his murder. Unfortunately, without new miracles to evidence William's divinity, the flow of pilgrims dried to a trickle and the new bishop's support alone proved futile in reviving his fortunes. To make matters more difficult, Brother Elias was elected as the new Prior by his fellow monks and he, as had the old bishop, refused to credit William as a true saint. It appeared that William was destined to be forgotten.

At the very moment that I began to lose faith in seeing William's preferment, news came that rekindled my belief in

Divine Intervention, as well as opened a sliver of doubt as to the veracity of my own witness.

It was a cloudless, windless afternoon, ripples of sensually-perfumed heat rose from the freshly turned earth in the garden. Balanced on my crutches, I was weeding the vegetable beds. I was not proficient at the task, but even cripples were obliged to perform such physical chores, the last of the three basic elements of Benedictine daily regime after liturgical observance and spiritual reading. I was deep in contemplation of the joy and wonder of God's gift of such a completely perfect day, that I had not noticed Marcus until he almost toppled me with an urgent pulling at my sleeve. He motioned me to follow him. He did not speak until we were near the stone wall on the far side of the garden, well out of the hearing of the monks bent diligently at their work.

"Great intelligence has come, Joseph," he said low and breathlessly. "He is murdered. The moneylender Jew is killed. The Usurer is dead. Your friend is avenged at last. Rejoice!"

"What are you saying, Marcus? What Jew murdered?"

"I have not yet gained his name. It is said he is the chief of the Jews, the most important one in the city. Dead as dead he is. Are you not filled with joy at this? I thought you would be. I was most assured you would. Is this not what you've wanted? I have also heard word that they are rising in the streets against the other Jews, putting them to the sword and the torch, chasing them out of the city. Does that not make today miraculous!"

My first touch of pleasure at the news was fleeting. Yes, I wanted William to be celebrated. Yes, I knew such celebration relied on his being martyred for the Faith. Yes, I knew that the Jews were the perfect and most likely, indeed the actual, instigators of this crime. Yes, despite the disdain and brutality he exhibited towards me, I also believed Godwin's account of the events that transpired before William disappeared into the Saddlegate house. Had I not too suffered violence at the hands of the Jews in that very house? Had they not threatened William there? While all of these facts were written in blood, being still an unworldly child I had never contemplated them leading to murder and riot. I wanted only veneration for my William. He would surely not have welcomed blood on his gentle hands, even the blood of those who had murdered him. Would their blood then be on my hands as well?

I tried to comfort myself with the thought that my voice had not been the most strident in putting forward the Jews as William's murderers. I had not volunteered my tale before I was asked to do so by Godwin and Prior Turbe, and then it was only to add credence to the priest's accusations. Of more telling import was the story offered by Liviva, Godwin's wife, about William being led to Saddlegate by the man purporting to be an agent of the Archdeacon, added to her vision in which she lost her leg in the Market Place to a swarm of vicious Jews. It was she and William's family who were to blame for murder and riot, not me.

Eleazar

Eleazar's body was found in a wood near Holt, a town to the north of Norwich. It was said that his throat had been slit, virtually severing his head from his neck. All his clothing had been stripped from him, and the naked corpse bore the black and blood-red signs of a vicious beating. As he had lain on the ground for several days, feral beasts further ravaged the body, while crows or other wild fowl had pecked out the eyes, leaving empty, blood-encrusted sockets. I cannot attest to the full accuracy of this account, as it was delivered by Marcus, who appeared to take unholy pleasure in describing each violation and indignity visited upon the stern-bearded patriarch, as if he had been there to inflict them by his own hand.

"I would wager, if we could do such, that my dear uncle had a hand in the murder," Marcus claimed with more than a hint of pride in his voice. "Where the old man's body was discovered is not far from his estate at Swanton Novers. I also know that he was most heavily in debt to the usurious Jew and, even before he abandoned me to the monks, that was more than two years since, he complained that he was being pressed without quarter for payment he could not meet. So, it appears two debts are now finally settled."

"How so?" I asked.

"Why, is it not as obvious as your own sweet Jew nose? One debt of gold owed to the Jew and the other debt for a life taken, that of the boy William, your martyred friend. Is there not Divine Justice at work here, Joseph? Little William brutally killed and left half naked in the woods, food for scavenging animals, which, as we know, did not feast on his blessed body as they did on that of the Godforsaken Jew, who you yourself have implicated in the lad's murder."

I may have persuaded myself that Eleazar's murder should not be brought to me, but, if others were to adopt Marcus's narrative, I would be unable to escape blame or a celebrated status. Fortunately, I was safely hidden under the cowl and behind the walls of the Cathedral, so neither blame nor status would single me out for wider opprobrium or celebrity.

While I lived in Saddlegate Eleazar had harassed me constantly, decried my abilities, ridiculed my all too numerous inabilities and, with scant mercy, punished me for any real or perceived transgression. I feared him so deeply that I feared hating him in the event he sensed my enmity and made my life more intolerable. Nonetheless, when I learned that he was the Jew who had been murdered it gave me no pleasure.

Curiously, the first memories of Eleazar that followed on the news of his death were the times when he had tousled my hair with his hand, not when he used that same hand to beat me. My initial soft-glowed recollections lasted but a moment before a new fear pushed them abruptly aside.

If there had been no hesitation in murdering in such an open and brutal manner a King's Jew as prominent as Eleazar, one protected by gold, by position and by the Sheriff, and if the mob were burning out and slaughtering the remaining Jews in the city, how much longer would it be before the flames of contagion reached out to engulf me, someone who, although a most pious, observant Benedictine novice, was often singled out as "The Jew Cripple". The sobriquet was for most, although not all, in the Priory whispered with barbed affection.

I did not relate my fears to Marcus or, when I was able to speak with him, to Brother Jerome, who, as master of the novices, assumed the role of our spiritual guide. I said only that I bore no malice toward Eleazar and rather, was saddened to learn of his death. Both appeared surprised by my reaction, as were the other novices who were taking part in a rare open-voiced discussion in the Chapter House, a discussion occasioned by the dramatic events then unfolding in the city.

"Now if you were reading these happenings through the blood-soaked Testament of your former brethren," Brother Jerome said, "rather than the Gospels, your feelings might be completely different. But I am pleased to say, my dear Joseph, you appear to have become a good Benedictine, a true Christian."

Brother Jerome's charitable assessment was never shared by members of William's family, especially Godwin, who because of their hatred of Jews and jealousy of my closeness to William, took any and every opportunity, when not overseen or overheard by others in the Priory, to make known to me their hostility and loathing.

As an example, and one directly related to Eleazar's murder, two days before the news arrived from Holt, Godwin and Robert had come upon me while I was on my knees in a side chapel. It was unusually quiet in the nave, no Offices being celebrated, the ever-present workmen absent. I heard the two coming for a minute or so before they arrived, the sound of their sandals slapping on the floor getting closer and reverberating loudly up and back from the high roof of the nave and against rendered stone walls. The noise ceased abruptly when they drew level with the chapel. Not wanting to break from my prayers, I remained bent in supplication, ignoring what I immediately recognised as the priest's heavily laboured breathing and the unfriendly eyes I knew were being brought to bear upon my back.

"Do you believe yourself truly secure here in God's House?" the priest asked me in an almost jovial tone. "Safe from the storms that might rage outside the walls?"

Still on my knees, I turned to look up from the calm landscape of my meditation. I nodded assent, the palms of my hands still pressed together in prayer. I had discovered that holding them in that manner suppressed their otherwise constant shudder and shake. Brother Edgar told me that this indicated my vocation was in God-given tune with my unfortunate condition.

After two years I found his belief to be true. I had settled with considerable comfort of mind into life in the Priory. God was good and I learned that loving Him yielded its own reward in a quiet certitude, gratefully appreciated by a love-abandoned, storm-tossed orphan. I had found a place of acceptance. So I imagined.

"Well my fine cripple, my fine crippled Jew that was, I think you may soon come to see that your assumption of safety does not hold. I think you may soon come to understand the real blood and bone limitations of that assumption. I think that you may soon come to see that a time of Holy Cleansing will be upon the land and those who deny Our Lord will feel a Godly Wrath."

At the time he and Robert had interrupted me at prayer, I assumed it was simply another instance of their ongoing abuse, abuse that I had learned to bear without rancour, as directed by the Blessed St. Benedict. However, after hearing of Eleazar's murder, the true purpose of this visit assumed a more sinister import than previous confrontations and made it more difficult for me to maintain my usual Benedict-like equanimity. Had he known what was going to take place? If so, how had he known? Was he in some manner implicated in Eleazar's death? Was I too marked out to be a victim of a domestic Crusade? One question chased the next, but I found no answer even many years later when I was to return to that brief encounter with a clearer understanding of its true meaning.

Thomas

The Norwich Jews, of whom only a few had fallen to the mob, most managing to find shelter in the Castle, reached the same view of what had happened in the woods near to Holt as did Marcus, and some time later, when able to exit unmolested from behind the Sheriff's protection, they too laid the blame for Eleazar's murder at the hands of Simon de Novers and his esquires and demanded temporal justice from King Stephen.

Such justice was never forthcoming. The King was otherwise engaged in fierce and costly battles with the Empress Matilda, and Bishop Turbe took up a vigorous defense of the knight, who controlled his manor as a fief from the selfsame bishop.

The Bishop argued that not only was Simon de Novers innocent of the crime, but also that until the Jews had purged themselves of William's murder, Christians should not be compelled to answer accusations as to the murder of a Jew. As they had two years before, the Jews proved unwilling to answer the charge.

This refusal revived bitter memories of my friend's brutal murder and led to the popular uprising against the Jews, while rekindling the belief in the Divine Truth of William's martyrdom, a belief that, judging by the steady fall in the number of pilgrims visiting his grave, as well as opposition and indifference within the Priory, had all but disappeared by that time.

"Mark, you," Bishop Turbe said to me as we watched the tangled crowd of the anguished and the ragged pass through the cemetery gate to press themselves up against William's sarcophagus, weeping, beating their chests and imploring his intervention, "while many of our Holy Brothers demur, these simple children of the Lord are prepared to travel far and suffer hardship to testify to the Truth of the blessed child's sanctity. I have no doubt that very soon this Truth will be proclaimed by all."

Unfortunately this did not come to pass. Just as the violence against the Jews quickly came to an end, short lived too was the renewed enthusiasm for the healing power of William's bones. Except for myself, a few constant monks and a small number of devoted pilgrims, within about six months his grave site was as quiet and peaceful and unattended as it had been before Eleazar's murder. Even Godwin and his son and his nephew seem to have given up on the fight for his recognition and their visits became more and more infrequent.

The sparrows, robins, swallows and other small birds that had quitted the graveyard because of the pandemonium attending the holy crush of pilgrims, returned to spread their wings and their songs and, although like these simple creatures, I also welcomed the tranquility, I grieved for the fading of respect and reverence due to William. This state of affairs only began to be rectified five or six years after William's death with the arrival at the Cathedral Priory of Brother Thomas.

He came to us from a monastery in Monmouth in Wales. He was an intense, clever, learned man. A forcefully devout man. An ambitious man, an unheard of and dubious quality for a cloistered monk. At first sight these character traits were masked by his bowed legs, diminutive stature and a heavy, bulbous head, completely bald but for a thin tonsure line of ginger fringe. Such a personage was more to be expected as a court jester than a monk, and behind his back less charitable brothers called him 'The Dwarf', sometimes 'The Holy Dwarf'.

By the time of his arrival, I had shed the novice gown and become a tonsured monk, full-hearted in the commitment to my new vocation. It was an easier, less confusing road to follow after Marcus had been finally asked to leave, his uncle's money not weighing in the balance against his nephew's too obvious failings. I did miss him mightily at first, but adhering to the Rule was demanding and immersing myself in its rigour numbed the pain of Marcus not being with me.

Against all my shortcomings, of which I had a great many, it was decided that my contribution to the community would be as a scribe.

"By undertaking a task which will test you beyond what you believe you can achieve," explained Brother Cartusium, the armarius, "you will find the purity of the Holy Spirit concealed in your damaged body."

More than anyone else who spent their days copying manuscripts, I had to enforce upon myself the most exacting concentration. Even with my right arm braced in a shallow wooden trough, devised to fit by one of the more inventive of the Cathedral's workmen, I still had to give exclusive attention to the work, lest through uninvited spasm I spoiled the parchment. Although I question whether I found either the Lord or the Spirit in the work, it did give me greater mastery over the hitherto unfettered gyrations of my hands and arms, and I discovered I was able to produce an excellent script. Furthermore, being a scribe meant I could avoid for a goodly time during the day the stone coldness of the Priory in winter by availing myself of the greater warmth generated by the scriptorium being directly adjacent to the calefactory.

My assigned work also brought me closer to what was to lead to my eventual fall from Grace - reading, and through reading to a subversive, non-Benedictine questioning.

Added to the many daily offices we had to perform, we were required to spend at least two hours a day reading. We were instructed that reading was to help us meditate and through meditation to find an understanding of God and the sweetness of Heaven. I began with this intention, but as I studied, among other readings, Jerome, Ambrose, Josephus, as well as the Old and New Testaments, I discovered my concern was increasingly turned not to capturing the reflection of my soul but more simply enjoying for their own sake the stories of David and the Goliath, Samson and Delilah, John the Baptist and, of course, the many revelatory stories of Jesus to be found in the Gospels. In the Dialogues and the Lives of the Fathers I found my thoughts wandering from Benedictine contemplation to comparing William's character and his death to those of the martyrs and saints who had preceded him.

Perhaps it was my being totally immersed in the life of St. Sebastian, pierced with arrows, rescued, made whole again and then beaten to death, a mercilessly cruel fate that God seemed to reserve for those who loved Him most reverently, that the sudden appearance of Brother Thomas in my cell, a proscribed space, strictly reserved for silence and for solitude, startled me so.

"I am made to understand, that you were a close friend of the martyred boy, William," the apparition rasped at me in a horse whisper.

I could only nod, open mouthed, taken back as I was by his outlandish stature and visage, to say nothing of the unheard of entry into the sacred domain of a monk's cell.

Interpreting my silent response as adherence to the Rule, his great head wobbled from side to side and he offered me what he took for a smile, but which was projected more as a stretched rictus of pain.

"You may speak, my boy. We have the approval of Prior Elias."

"Yes. William," was all the answer I was able to summon.

"Ah, I see. The Prior told me as much. My dear brother. My poor dear brother, let me explain."

I was unaware at that moment, but my singular complicity in the story of St. William of Norwich had begun.

Moving William

It was on the week after Palm Sunday. Lauds had ended and Psalms had been sung. It was ink dark and still, an hour or so before the day begins to break and bird song captures the world. Six of us, who had not retired with the others to the dormitory, moved with Holy Purpose through the narrow stone passageway by the side of the Chapter House and emerged into the Monks' Cemetery.

There was no moon and the torch carried by the leading monk illuminated but a small circle of ground in front of him. I was the last in line and, although I was most familiar with the random scatter of white headstones set in the grass, still I found myself stumbling as my crutches caught up in the night-obscured holes and hollows.

"With care, Brother," cautioned Thomas, steadying me with a firm grip.

When we came to William's sarcophagus, the monks lit a number of candles and set them around so we could better gauge the task in hand. Thomas then took an iron wedge from a cloth bag and reaching up set it firmly under the heavy stone lid.

"Here, take this," Thomas said, passing me a wooden mallet. "I am too low down and besides, you have the strength in your arms more than any of us. Go, strike hard, Brother Joseph. Strike hard, strike true."

We were engaged in a Sacred Mission, but still I was reluctant to disturb my friend's rest. I hesitated a moment, looking for assurance from Thomas. He inclined his head and closed his eyes, whether in prayer or not to witness the damage I might do if I missed my mark, I know not. I made one crutch fast against the side of the sarcophagus, pulled back my right arm and swung the mallet. A painful vibration shot up my arm. The effort was rewarded by nothing but a dull echo from inside the burial chamber. The lid remained firmly in place. It required two further blows before the stones parted. The others came forward, lifted off the heavy lid and put it on the ground next to the open sarcophagus so that Thomas might stand on it.

The Holy Dwarf stepped up, set the candles along the rim, leaned as far as he could and stuck his globe-like head over to peer inside. He motioned for us to join him. No one moved. I could taste their apprehension, which I shared. We all gazed with awe as a sudden breeze guttered the candles on the open grave. Through the light-flecked tallow smoke I imagined William raising up, his winding sheet in tatters, the sunken flesh stretched across his face. I closed my eyes against the horror, but the image would not leave me. This was a William I did not want to see. Moreover, this was a William I did not want to dislodge the joyful, living, loving William I carried with me and wanted to carry with me.

"My Brothers," Thomas called, "please come forward and look upon the Saintly Child. There is no reason to fear. No, no reason to fear and every reason to celebrate for soon he will be rightfully crowned. Come, rise up and rejoice, my Brothers, at the Glorious Vision of our Holy Saint!"

There were visions aplenty in the cloister. Almost every night moans, shouts and weeping could be heard as my brother monks suffered the visions, omens, hallucinations, ecstasies of Divine Visitations. The Blessed Virgin or St. Benedict were the most welcome visitors, but there were also less propitious divinations, cloaked as Divine, but not sent by the Lord.

One such was visited upon Brother Allen, who woke the entire dormitory in the early morning with a howl of anguish so full of pain that it overwhelmed his vow of silence. Leaping up from his bed, he ran wild eyed but unseeing from bed to bed, accosting each monk in turn and demanding, "Have I had a vision? Have you had a vision? Did he have a vision to find out Eternity?" After a time he appeared to calm himself, began to mutter a prayer or incantation and then fainted insensible onto the floor. When he was finally brought to consciousness he could remember neither his ecstatic outburst nor the vision that had led to it. A week later he embraced his vision of Eternity. He was found dead in his cell, cold and stiff on his knees in prayer.

Thomas's visions were more comprehensible and served a more worthy purpose. It was soon after our last discussion about William, that Bishop Herbert de Losinga, the founder of the Church in Norwich, began to appear to Thomas in dreams to demand that rightful veneration be afforded the boy martyr.

He came for me in the scriptorium and reverting to sign indicated that I should follow him to Prior Elias's lodgings. When we arrived, Godwin was already there. The priest, who judging by his many chins, had put on additional rolls of fat, glowered when I entered the room, but upon seeing Thomas, his grim visage was lost to a thick-lipped smile of greeting.

"Welcome, my brothers," offered Prior Elias, who appeared drawn and unwell, his eyes cloudy, the skin on one side of his face flowing downward as melted tallow. "What reason, Brother Thomas, has compelled you to request this meeting with myself and our brother priest? Yes, yes," he added, unable to conceal impatience. "Please, you may speak."

Brother Thomas nervously shifted his weight from one leg to the other, pulled at the skirt of his diminutive cassock and cleared his throat.

"Reverend Prior," he began, "I have asked that Priest Godwin and Brother Joseph join me to hear the joyous news I bring you, for I have learned so much from them about the blessed life and death of the boy William that they are worthy of being witness to this joyous occasion."

161

He then proceeded to relate how, over a period of some weeks while he slept, he had been called upon by Bishop Herbert, who told him that a precious treasure was hidden in the cemetery, and a thief was preparing to steal it away, causing irreparable harm to his Church. However, if these Holy Relics were soon gathered and brought into the precincts, then William and the Church in Norwich would be celebrated throughout the kingdom and beyond the seas, just as the Jews who martyred him would be forever condemned and excoriated.

"I did not carry out his orders, awaiting a further revelation. He came once more and pressed me to do as he had bid. When again I demurred, the venerable man returned a third time, holding the hand of a small boy. He was in a rage at my disobedience. He told me that in doubting his commands I was unbelieving, just as my namesake had doubted the Lord Jesus Christ. Saying that, he grabbed hold of my arm and pressed his fingers deep into my flesh so that I would understand the truth of his message."

With this, Thomas rolled up the sleeve of his cassock to reveal a black blistered mark, which showed as a clear indentation of a fiery thumb. Prior Elias, who had been lolling in his chair, listening to Thomas with polite indifference, sat up straight and stared at the monk, fear and uncertainty in his eyes.

"Oh Glory!" ejaculated Godwin, rising with some effort from his seat and casting his arms upwards towards Heaven.

"The Martyred Boy himself then spoke. He ordered that a resting place should be made ready for him in the boys' choir in the Chapter House. As a boy he desired to rest among other boys. I was instructed to bring his momentous news to you, most respected Prior, and to our Bishop."

As Thomas presented his account, I could see the Prior becoming increasingly discomforted. A spasmodic twitching took hold of the fallen side of his face and a thin line of drool escaped from the corner of his mouth and fell onto his cassock. Perhaps this extreme reaction was not surprising, as he had been consistently sceptical about the claims for William's martyrdom and now he was hearing irrefutable proof that he had been grievously mistaken, and his mistake would put the Church and the cloister in mortal peril.

It was scarce two days after Thomas had brought the Good News that I found myself in the Monks' Cemetery looking at the grave of my departed friend.

The Chapter House

I was unable to resist joining Thomas and the others as they stood peering into the candle-lit sarcophagus. I prepared myself for the horror I had conjured, drew in a rasp of breath and thrust my face over the stone side. My first thought was one of relief. William was not there. After six years in the Monks' Cemetery my William had escaped, leaving behind, pushed into a far corner at the bottom of the tomb, a collection of mouldy rags out of which protruded a sharp scatter of bones, a hint of a brownish skull crowned with strands of hair and two sandals, one with a broken strap. I smiled, then gave out a spluttering gurgle of laughter. All the monks turned as one, alarm and confusion at play across their faces.

"Brother Joseph! Remember, silence, decorum. The Rule, Brother, remember the Rule," Thomas whispered harshly, ignoring the Rule.

"Brothers, we must be happy, we must rejoice" I said. "It is clear, can you not see that William has gone, that he has been called up to Heaven?"

This statement was greeted with shushing and hissing noises from my fellows. I said no more.

Turning to the Holy Task, they reached in and collected up the remains in a clean linen sheet and put them on a bier. By that time it was after Lauds, and the sky was beginning to lighten. We were joined in the cemetery by the rest of the cloister, and with much solemnity the bier was carried into the Chapter House where William was placed in a new sarcophagus that Prior Elias, remaining in his posture of grudging acquiescence to the import of Thomas's visions, ordered to be set in a grave level with the floor, as, he said, befit a person of lowly birth and scant importance. However, the diggers had failed to go deep enough and the stone tomb stood out well proud of the pavement, something which angered the Prior. Nonetheless, due of its weight, once in place it could not be moved without considerable effort, and the Prior was obliged to allow it to remain in its elevated position.

As I watched and listened to the ceremony of translation - the magnificent procession of fifty cassocked monks, the reverential chanting, the acrid plumes of tallow overlaid with the sweetness of beeswax and incense - a celebration that I had wished for since I was a novice, I was visited by a vivid, lifelike remembrance of my dear companion.

"Ah, Joseph, for what purpose such a solemn occasion? Look at those maddened monks! Ha! What a mad, holy lark it is! A truly holy, holy lark, Joseph!"

I put my jittering fingers to my lips to quiet the irreverent spectre from offering further inappropriate commentary on the proceedings being performed in his name and to his honour. I wanted to remind him of the Rule, but fright had stilled my crippled tongue and I could manage not even the faintest sound of protest.

"Don't look so miserable, Joseph. Smile my dearest friend, smile, for I am beyond the reach of misery and beyond the reach of care. Smile, Joseph, remember to smile." The ghostly shade gave a playful William wink and rising up towards the soaring vault of the ceiling, vanished amidst the candle smoke.

I resolved not to share this disconcerting vision with anyone. If believed, and I did not think they would when put against Thomas's more awe-inspiring visits from Bishop Herbert, my irreverent visitation, which I knew in my heart was a genuine visitation, would have only caused me to be mocked or denounced. More importantly, my story of a frivolous William may have detracted from the wonder of his Miraculous Victory.

The installation of William in the Chapter House was indeed such a victory, celebrated first by the monks and then a few days later by the pilgrims who came in great numbers seeking for the intercession of the Boy Martyr.

I recall one of the first, well recorded by Thomas, was Clercia, the wife of Gaufridus, the Lord of Mattishall. She came into the Chapter House on the arm of an esquire, a slight woman, each step stiff and uncertain and, by her pinched expression, exceedingly painful. Standing in front of the sarcophagus, she offered a quiet prayer and then bestowed a kiss upon the stone. Immediately the hurt left her face, replaced by a radiant smile and, waving away assistance, she walked from the chamber with firm purpose.

As the tales of miraculous cures circulated, so more sick and feeble persons thronged to William's sepulchre. Gout, the flux, blindness, dysentery, weakness of the limbs, dropsy, headache, deafness, sleeplessness, madness - nothing was thought to be outside his healing powers, including maladies affecting asses, cows, chickens, pigs, indeed any of God's creatures.

Within a few months, where the fabric of the tomb was not polished by constant stroking of needy hands and by fervent kisses, it was pitted, as the more desperate scraped off small pieces of stone to affect cures by mixing with water the holy powder so obtained. In ecstatic abandon, the wretched mob fouled the floor around the sepulchre with their muddy boots, bloody bandages, abandoned crutches and the slime of their hysterical spittle. My William would have been amused by this uncontrolled, unholy, holy clamour. Not so Thomas's William, who he said had come to him at night in a righteous fury to rail against the desecration of his tomb.

"We should cover his sarcophagus with this fine red cloth," Thomas said, holding up a richly woven fabric that flowed from his stunted arms unto the floor. "Candles as well. Holy martyrs demand candles. We will put a large candle made of the finest beeswax and set in a silver tray at the head of the tomb. Each day the pavement is to be scoured. It is essential that respect is shown, Joseph. Our love for the Blessed Martyr demands it."

Thomas's plans came to naught.

"You will immediately remove the candle and the covering, Brother Thomas," Prior Elias ordered, standing by the tomb, his features greyer and more troubled than I had before witnessed. "You are assuming too much. Such decisions about what is to be done in the Chapter House are my responsibility alone."

"I do this only out of the most devout intention, Brother Prior. I do this for the glory of our wondrous Martyr."

The Prior remained implacable and Thomas was obliged to remove the cloth and the candle.

"It is the man's envy or that of others who have always stood in the way of recognising our martyred son. Do you not mark how the Prior would not accept the evidence, conclusive though it was, that William was murdered by the Jews, and that he was loath to permit his removal to the cemetery until interest in the holy relics was voiced by the Cluniac Prior? Now when the visions vouchsafed to me confirm the boy as a holy martyr, the Prior continues his obstructive course. Although charity forbids me from harbouring anger or malice towards my prior, to whom I owe total obedience, I fear that he may be called upon to pay dearly for his denial of William."

Three months later Prior Elias was found dead in his lodgings. He was succeeded by Brother Richard de Ferrariis, someone who supported, with the appropriate fervour, William's cause. The red cloth and the candle were restored to the sepulchre. Never again was a voice raised in the cloister to question the Divine Revelation and Glory of St. William of Norwich.

Cripplegate

During my years in the Priory I often espied the malformed crone and the blind men William and I had forced our way by when first entering the Cathedral precincts. They soon become no more remarkable to me than the grass or the trees or, indeed, the gate where they congregated. I was prompted to think anew of the plight of those desperate mendicants once William's body had been translated to the Chapter House and miraculous cures began to multiply and pitiful souls afflicted with similar ailments and worse descended on the sepulchre seeking relief.

"Of course, Brother Joseph," the Prior said. "Your intentions are worthy of you. Moreover, as you know, we are enjoined by the Rule never to forsake charity. So, I give you leave to take a ministry to those wretched ones at the gate. If you are able, bring them to our Lord Jesus Christ. If they are willing, bring them to the healing power of our Blessed Martyr."

"They will not thank you," warned Brother Jerome, the novice master, who had been forced to give up his position because of failing sight. He had taken a special interest in me when I was a novice and continued to offer friendship and sage council.

"It may not even be safe for you. They are folk made desperate by their fate, Joseph."

"Why would the Prior give me his blessing if there was cause for concern?"

Jerome shrugged. "I cannot answer for another. All I can say to you is that charity and good intentions are not always sufficient to surmount the base nature that rules the hearts of men. Many will turn away. Others may put you to the test. Perhaps this is what the Prior intends, for we only discover the reality of our vocation and our love of God when that vocation and that love are tested at the limits of what we think we can bear."

Carrying the weight of Brother Jerome's dark forebodings, I went out early one cold winter morning to bring the Good News to those bereft of hope. I had to proceed with great care as my crutches were continually sliding away from me on the icy ground. When I finally arrived at the gate there were but three or four piles of filthy rags laid out not far from the guards' brazier. The Prior had ordered that when snow was on the ground the guards were not, as was their custom and their cruel diversion, to drive away the beggars.

"My friends," I called out. "Arise, I bring you tidings of joy and deliverance."

The rags did not stir, but the two guards warming themselves by the fire turned towards me. It was difficult to make out their faces, as both wore hooded cloaks.

"What brings you out here on this cold morning, brother monk?" asked one of them, squinting at me while scratching vigorously at his beard.

"I am here to do God's work among the unfortunates over there. I intend to bring them to St. William so to relieve their 'misery."

"He saying what?" inquired his companion. "I can't understand him, I can't."

"Some nonsense about God," the beard scratcher replied uncertainly.

"Wait just a moment now, Guid, it's that monk cripple with that knotted tongue. Of course, the monk cripple, that's him. Maybe he come out to visit with his relatives?"

The one called Guid laughed, spat into the snow and slapped the other on the back.

"Perhaps you should go after that boy saint's intervention," said the joke maker, " to straighten out your own tongue and your own bent limbs before you go soiling your delicate monk's hands on these woeful creatures."

As I told Brother Edgar when he made the same suggestion, I never thought of asking William for that which I was offering to the denizens of Cripplegate. This might appear curious, but I had never known any other way of being, and although when younger I had sometimes entertained dreams of being unencumbered by a shuddering body and a tangled tongue, I had long since put these childish dreams aside so as to live in the world. Besides, they were beggars. I was a Benedictine monk, a person of some consequence.

"Yes, Corin speaks the truth, Brother Cripple. Best you limp yourself back to the warmth of your cloister."

Their comments showed both the lack of compassion one expects from people whose job it is to deny entry, as well as how distant the guards were from life in the cloister, a place which even on a summer's day could be damp and rigidly cold.

At that moment a grime-swollen face emerged from one of the rag piles. Bending forward on my crutches to look more closely, I observed that its eye sockets were empty, the skin reddened and puckered.

"What say you?" the blind man asked in an angry voice, the rags flapping wildly and then recomposing themselves into a human figure as he struggled to rise.

"He wants to bring you to the Boy Saint, is what he be saying," the guard Corin offered mockingly.

"Come, Old Dudda, come and be you respectful now."

"What he saying?" repeated the blind man, turning his head towards the guards.

"I am here to offer you and your friends succour, to bring you hope."

Another collection of rags began to move and another blackened face framed by large hands grasping two sticks peered out at me. As he moved without standing, I knew it was the legless man.

"What does he bring for us?" asked the man. "Food, ale, a warm blanket?"

"Words is all he be bringing," answered Corin. "The monk cripple will bestow some holy words on your sorry self."

"Me, I want a warm blanket," muttered the legless man. "Why don't you have no warm blanket to be giving me?"

"No. I'm sorry, but I have something much better than a blanket, or food or ale. I want to bring you all to our Blessed St. William so you may be freed from your afflictions and made whole again."

The blind man and the legless man were now joined by the old woman with a disease-ravaged face who inhabited the last stack of rags. They crowded around me. The crone fingered my cassock. I pulled away and as I did the circle, at once curious and hostile, tightened.

"You wanting to make us whole, does you?" she said, grinning toothlessly. "You want to make me being young and fair, does you?"

Apparently she was the only one able to decipher my speech.

"A blanket that's me," the legless man repeated.

"He be wanting to give you back your eyes, Old Dudda," she said. "Remember when you had eyes? And you, Cedda, you'd get back your legs. Remember when you had legs?"

"Why would anyone do such a terrible thing? How would we be living then?" Old Dudda asked plaintively.

"Take the blanket and send him away!"

Cedda had pinned my crutches hard against his wheeled board. Old Dudda's head was swinging back and forth, his hands reaching for me. The old woman pushed her face so close to mine that I was forced to confront each oozing pustule. She grasped my cassock firmly in a claw hand.

"You want to being after saving us? Well then, save us from such talk, save us from your blasted, interfering saint. Now you had better be getting off quickly before Cedda figures that your monk's cassock would make do for his blanket."

I yanked the old woman's hand from my cassock and pushed Cedda's board so that he careened away, trying in vain to find purchase with his short sticks on the icy ground. I pivoted on my crutches and hurried back towards the Cathedral. As Brother Jerome predicted, my ministry to Cripplegate had been fruitless.

An Offer And A Warning

"It will be duly recorded, Joseph. It will be meticulously recorded. For his glory and the glory of our Cathedral, we must proclaim the good news of our dearest Martyred Boy. We must proclaim it wider and farther than our weak, mortal voice can carry the news. We will set down a mighty testament that will outlast our brief earthly-bound lives and that will reverberate as a mighty echo down through time until He returns in Glory. A testament to our blessed Saint William. A testament unveiling the profane, deadly perfidiousness of the Jew. Will you, my young friend, my good brother, assist me in this most holy endeavour?"

"I am but a scribe, Brother Thomas, not a person who weaves tales, holy tales or other tales. I write what is already written. A scribe is all I am."

With dainty step he moved the two paces across my cramped cell, where he should not have been, on tiptoes reached up and grasped me by the shoulder, which he should not have done. I was soon to learn that Brother Thomas, who professed, as of course he had to, that he lived strictly by the Rule, in truth lived in all practical matters by his own rules. A small hand squeezed my shoulder with a strength that belied the compressed stature of its owner. He cocked his head to one side and looked up at me with one of his most sincere lopsided smiles.

"Ah, my dear brother, do not concern yourself, I will be the weaver, the master weaver, if you will. While you, Joseph, you will provide the woollen yarn, the strong thread, at the very least a goodly proportion of the thread. You were his friend. You were with him in the house of his murderers. You know things, you have heard things that we are obliged to expose, both as a warning to our Christian brethren and to demonstrate the

173

terrible and glorious reality of the martyrdom that took place in that accursed house."

"I have my duties to perform. I have my work in the scriptorium. I have ..."

He swatted away my protests with a wave of his hand.

"How do you imagine I was able to enter your sanctum? Prior de Ferrariis. Yes, the Prior has sanctioned our task and to that end permitted me to intrude upon you to ask that you help me. I am sure you will not fail me, you will not fail the Church, you will not fail your beloved William - our beloved William."

Some five years after Thomas had come to the Priory William's relics had at last found their final and most exalted resting place in the Martyr's Chapel. The doubters and detractors had been vanquished. The first great battle of Thomas's crusade had been won. He was recruiting me as a foot soldier for the second battle. If I had known the fate of such soldiers in the Holy Land, I may not have been so ready to enlist. It was not as if I hadn't been warned.

"You must be on your guard concerning Brother Thomas," Brother Edgar cautioned me the following day, after I had explained what I was about to undertake. "I, together with some of the other brothers, believe that it is not for the love of Our Lord Jesus Christ, or even for William, but for his own preferment that he has become the Blessed Boy's most fervent champion."

"A saintly boy, Brother Edgar, William was a saintly boy. A martyred saint who suffered for the Faith. Why else would the Bishop and our late Prior have allowed his translation first to the Chapter House, then the High Altar and now to his own Martyr's Chapel, if they too did not believe in Thomas's visions and in William's sanctity?"

"My dear boy, you are touchingly naïve of how the world

174

moves and what moves the world. Politics and gold often clothe themselves in more seemly garments, or in this case, holy vestments. As for the translations; he was taken from the Chapter House because the constant entry and exit of pilgrims prevented us from performing our duties in that place. He was taken from the High Altar for the same cause. You witnessed this yourself. Did it not become impossible to process through the crush of pilgrims?"

"The devotion of the pilgrims and the miracles, you saw how the sick were cured, the lame were made whole, the weak strong. You cannot deny him, surely not."

"Do I deny William? I do not. He was a fine, an upright lad, I could see that. It is beyond doubt that he was cruelly used and murdered by the Jews because he was an innocent Christian child. Yes, Joseph, the lad was martyred. Yes, his relics have given miraculous cures to the faithful. What I am trying to tell you is that the matter is not a question of the child's Divine Calling, it is that in this affair Brother Thomas is both more and less then he appears. I repeat, be on your guard."

"I do not understand. More or less of what is Brother Thomas?"

He smiled and shook his head.

"So, what am I to fear, what am I to guard against?"

"A path, Joseph, a path that makes such grandiose promises about leading one into the light can too easily deliver you instead into Eternal Darkness."

"Eternal Darkness?"

"Yes, the Pit, Joseph, the Pit."

Not wanting to be offered yet another riddle in answer to a riddle, I resolved to ask no more. If, as Brother Edgar said, there was no question that William had been martyred, that he had been raised up to the Heavenly Place, I saw his doubts of

Thomas's probity as evidence not of the latter's failings, but of Edgar's resentment that Thomas had appointed himself to the position of William's sacrist and principle acolyte. I confronted him, pointing out that we were enjoined by St. Benedict not to be jealous or to entertain envy.

My erstwhile parent and now my brother stared at me in open-mouthed surprise. Anger then briefly traced across his broad face before he broke into a broken-toothed grin. He laughed silently, his heavy body shaking violently under his cassock.

"So bold, Joseph my boy. So bold, so pious, so Benedictine. You have travelled so far, we both have travelled so very far, that we would be sorely pressed to recognise the dishevelled, ranting anchorite and the frightened crippled half-Jew child who wandered together in the wilderness of Thorpe Wood. I will pray for you, my brother. I will pray that my suspicions about Brother Thomas prove to be unfounded. I will pray for your salvation and for his."

Brother Edgar's prayers proved not to be enough to protect me from my self-regarding folly.

Weaving

"It is the Greater Truth we must reveal, Joseph. To manifest that Truth we will have to probe more deeply than what may seem real to our earth-bound senses. That which is holy seeks instead for a transcendent reality, much in the manner of all the Angels and of all the Saints. So it will be in our telling of William's life, his martyrdom and his miracles."

What I recounted to Thomas about my years at Saddlegate proved too rooted in my narrow earth-bound senses to afford the transcendence demanded in the life of our saint. The Holy Dwarf was, therefore, to weave my story into a more vibrant tapestry worthy of the Heavenly Glory due to William.

"A saint must be proclaimed when, or preferably before, he enters into the world. This is why William's mother had her vision of the fish with twelve fins that bleed - the Disciples and the Stigmata of the Lord - that flew up to Heaven. This is why her father, the priest Wulward, on hearing the vision told her that she would bear a son who would attain the highest honour and be carried up and exalted in Heaven. This is why when as a small, innocent child his very touch broke the iron fetters of the penitent man."

"William never told me of these stories," I said. "He never boasted or put on airs. He was a simple boy, full of life, full of love and joy too. Always full of life is how I remember him."

"Humble? Would you say he was a humble child?"

"I would say that, yes a humble boy. He had a strong faith as well. Many were the times he told me about Jesus and the Holy Mother and the wonder and inner peace to be found in prayer."

"Humble and low born and close to God, as was our Saviour.

177

Do you not see? This was the reason that the Jews sought to sacrifice him as they had sacrificed Jesus, by mocking him, torturing him and finally crucifying him."

I knew from my own experience that the Jews in Saddlegate were capable of violence, which was why I believed, no not believed, I knew that upon discovering that William had aided my escape they fell into a rage and murdered him. My confidence in their guilt did not, however, extend to imagining Mordechai or Miriam or even the stern-beard Eleazar taking part in the outrages that Thomas described - binding William's head and body with ropes, strapping a teasel in his mouth, shaving his head, setting a crown of thorns upon him until he bled, fixing him to a cross, piercing his side with a lance and pouring boiling water over him to wash away the blood. I expressed these doubts to Thomas.

"Joseph, Joseph, can you hear yourself denying your friend, much as my namesake denied Jesus. Do you have to put your fingers into the nail holes, thrust your hand into the mortal wound on his side?"

"No, Brother Thomas, I would never ... I would never deny William. Never."

"So," he said, "how am I to receive what you are telling me? How do you know this did not happen? Do you have any proof that this did not happen?"

"No, I have no proof. But, where is the proof that it did happen in the way that you describe?"

"The visions, Joseph. He showed me, the small boy with Bishop Herbert showed me. His bleeding hands were held out in supplication and I was made to watch as he was brutally martyred, just as I have written it. Remember his violated body, Joseph? The body bore signs of torture and of divine suffering. Did you not see the wounds on his head, the wounds on this body, the teasel gag? How are we to account for these?"

It was impossible to argue against Brother Thomas's visions or the evidence of William's torn body.

Thomas put his quill down next to the parchment upon which he had been writing his account. A spot of ink spread out and soaked into the table top. I reached over with a rag to wipe the expanding stain so it did not soil Thomas's pages. After staring at the floating dust motes for some moments, he climbed down from the library bench and came around the table to where I sat. A shaft of sunlight coming through the narrow window illuminated his broad face, giving it at one moment an angelic mien, at the next a visage of demonic thunder.

"Joseph, listen closely to what I say," he rasped by my ear. "Do you believe in William's sanctity?"

"Of course. Yes, I believe. I have always believed."

"If so, then you must trust me with his life, with setting it all out with care and in the prescribed manner."

"I do not know what you mean, Brother Thomas."

"Have you not read St. Gregory of Tours? Recall if you will how he marks out the lives of the first saints and tells us that we must speak of the 'Life of the Fathers' because while we see a great diversity of virtues among them, there is but the one life of the body that sustains them in the world of men and the realm of God. Reflect on these words and you will understand how we are called to interpret the life and miracles of William."

It was then that I realised why many of the events described by Thomas were so familiar to me. Was it not St. Gregory of Langres who broke the bonds for the prisoner? I could not remember which saint it was, but the curative stone shavings that came from his tomb offered many miracles. Moreover, many of the cures ascribed to William, they too were to be found in the 'Life'.

When I asked how it was that William could replicate the experiences of such venerable saints, why his miracles were so similar to theirs, Thomas was incredulous.

"Do you not see the meaning here? Only one who is a true saint will be able to carry out the deeds of saints."

"But...," I began.

"I have tried to explain, Joseph," he said impatiently. "St. Gregory showed us the way of understanding, of celebrating saints and their lives. As St. Matthew said, 'By their fruits you will know them.' If that was sufficient for him and for the Holy Fathers, it is surely good enough for William, for me and for you."

When I hesitated, he grabbed hold of me, pinching my arm firmly.

"We must be resolute! We must stay strong or those who in their blindness and cupidity tried to keep the Heavenly Crown of Glorification from William will gather their forces. They will try to detract from his sanctity. They will cast slurs on his fame and persecute his memory by making light of him. When they have accomplished their cunning slanders and brought him low, they will turn their attention to those of us who most fervently championed his fame - the gabble-mouthed cripple and the Holy Dwarf. Yes, Joseph, I know full well by what name I am known by the Philistine babblers. Do you wish by your irresolution to let this happen to our William, to us?"

"No," I replied with suitable contriteness, "I do not want that to happen."

Henceforth, I stopped asking questions and proceeded with a full and assured heart in the task of assisting Brother Thomas in his, in our blessed endeavour.

Concerned that offering my fulsome assent to his visionary story of William's bloody and tragic death might not be enough to assuage Thomas, and wanting by every means possible to bind William's death irrevocably to the Jews, as well as binding myself to the side of the Angels, and deciding that it made little difference precisely how they killed him, I presented Thomas with a genuinely transformed, if not transformative, tale, suitably decorated and embellished, that in its first incarnation I had heard from Saul Ibn Abraham.

My poet protector had passed through the French City of Narbonne on his journey to England and remarked to me on the large number of Jews he had found residing in a community that had been there for hundreds of years.

"I discovered among them many famous scholars whose wisdom in interpreting scripture is influential in communities of Jews scattered far and wide in Christian lands."

Drawing on the idea of revealing a Greater Truth, I told Thomas that every year in that city a great meeting of these eminent scholars was held to decide in which country a Christian child would be sacrificed. I explained that the blood of an innocent had to be spilled in contempt of Christ in order that the Jews could some day return to Jerusalem. It was William's misfortune to live in the country and the city chosen for the year 1144. However, unbeknownst to them, the Jews' crime resulted not in a return to their homeland, but instead the creation of a holy martyr for Christ.

Thomas was delighted that I had joined him so completely in Divine Weaving.

My short-lived prevarication was put behind us, and in a spirit of brotherly harmony, the writing of William's life and miracles moved forward apace.

Messages

Thomas and I were still at work on the Book when I occasioned to discover a message left in my pallet. On a scrap of parchment wrapped around a flint, presumably to get my attention, someone had written, "Ask after the teeth." It made no sense. I thought this cryptic note might refer to Brother Jonathan Primo, who, during a meal had complained vocally, for which he had been severely admonished, about the losing of the last two teeth in his ancient mouth. When I inquired of that brother about his irretrievable loss, I received an extremely bad-tempered snarl, which convinced me that I had been the butt of an unseemly, unBenedictine jest. I was suitably chagrined and put the note out of mind.

On retiring a week later, I was again greeted by a sharp stab to my back. "Ask after the sandal." The message was written in the same hand. I decided not to give my tormentor the satisfaction of asking further questions in the cloister. In truth, even if I had wished, I was mystified as to whom I might address questions about sandals. All the brothers wore sandals.

The next missal, sent in an identical manner, came after another week had passed. "Ask as to where he journeys." It was at this point I became more intrigued and uneasy. The note leaver was either setting me a riddle, a cunning snare or both.

Teeth, sandals and journeys. Journeys, sandals, teeth. No matter how I tried to fit the pieces into an answer, into a discernible shape, neither came. My failure undoubtedly pricked the patience of my secretive correspondent, for yet another, and thankfully the last, flint was soon delivered. This time I found it before lying down, for, slow learner that I was, it took three painful lessons before I learned to examine my pallet each evening. "Ask after unholy theft."

I found myself increasingly preoccupied in my struggle to find the meaning of the four notes. When I should have been immersed in prayer or devotional reading or meditating, my thoughts wandered from praising God to theft, sandals, teeth and journeys. The daily offices lost their divine magic, my sleep was disturbed, my dreams captured, my peace of mind, so finely settled in the rituals of the cloister, lay broken and scattered.

I visited the Martyr's Chapel before the pilgrims came so I could ask William for guidance. Apparently, he was too engaged in providing pilgrims with curative gifts to help his old friend solve a frivolous riddle. I received no guidance.

"Are you quite well, Brother?" inquired Brother Edgar, as he accosted me outside the refectory. "I marked that most of your food was left on the plate and this is not the first time in recent weeks. I also mark that your face is drawn and your limbs more than usually agitated. Perhaps you need to pay a visit to Brother Castus in the infirmary."

I had not wanted to share my burden, believing that the riddle was intended for me alone and that the answer might in some way show up a failing of commitment to my vocation or expose me to ridicule or to sanction.

I looked to Edgar and saw the hurt of familial concern in his eyes. Realising that of all men he would not judge me, I proceeded to tell him what had transpired. He listened intently but said nothing for a full minute or two after I had finished my tale.

"I am sorry to learn that you have been tested so sorely, Joseph," he said solemnly, his bushy eyebrows drawn into a single caterpillar across his broad face. "I am also sorry I cannot put your mind at ease. However, I think you may find that our dear brother, the Holy Dwarf, holds the key to unlock this flinty conundrum."

"How so?" I asked.

"All I can tell you is that I have heard curious rumours concerning William's sacrist."

"What rumours are these? Why have I heard nothing?"

"I cannot answer for your lack of knowledge. Perhaps your ears are blessed with a virtuous drape that shields you from the common gossip of the cloister. To my shame, I carry no such protection. So, although I cannot prevent it reaching me, I can refuse to aid in its proliferation, thereby compounding the sin of gossip, which, as you know, only gives a chance to the Devil to sow the seeds of discord and uncertainty."

The next day, as I was on the point of unburdening myself to Thomas it came to me that he was one of the few monks given leave by the Prior to journey outside the confines of the Priory. What these journeys might have to do with teeth, sandals and theft remained a mystery, and so thinking he might at the very least have knowledge of one side of the nocturnal messages' four-sided riddle, I told him everything that had happened.

The response was startling. He dropped his quill, careless of the ink splattering on the half-finished page. His bulging eyes bulged more prominently and a look, at one moment of horror, in the next of anger, suffused his face.

"Monstrous!" he finally managed to say, his voice high pitched and strained. "Monstrous to spread such slander against a man of virtue, against a man of... I mean to say, if someone had not collected the teeth after he was removed from his resting place in the cemetery... I mean, they just lay there in the old tomb, Joseph, after we had lifted out and wrapped the sacred body in the linen, they lay there in the far corner abandoned, almost totally obscured in the burial dust. Only two small teeth, two very small teeth. Teeth destined to be forgotten, to be lost to the world. Who would benefit if they had been forgotten? I tell you no one would benefit, Joseph, no one at all."

I struggled to take in what Thomas appeared to be saying. Had this servant of the Son of God, this man who vowed to live in poverty, obedience and chastity, to forgo worldly possessions and follow the Divine Rule of St. Benedict, had this most devoted man, this man most championing of William's holy cause, had he purloined his saintly charge's very teeth? Had he then also stooped to rob a sandal? Teeth fallen from his dear mouth. A sandal fallen from his dear foot.

Thomas with a hesitant awkwardness rose from his bench across the table and came to sit next to me. His breathing was laboured and his hands picked nervously at the sleeves of his cassock. After a minute or two he managed to compose himself and in a softer, confiding tone said, "You see, Joseph, just this evening past William came to me in a wonderful vision and told me to set the teeth in holy water and give the water to Brother William so he might drink. You know of our unfortunate brother's terrible illness, do you not? I am told he is near death. Poor man! Well, I am now going to the infirmary to administer the healing liquid, which the blessed William said would bring Brother William back to health."

I was being graced, as the Bishop, the Prior, indeed the entire cloister had been before, by a Thomas vision. This one unsettled me more than the admission that the man with whom I worked so closely and had assumed was a friend, was, in fact, no more than a common thief of holy relics.

Brother Thomas hopped down and bandy-legged, rushed for the door.

"And the sandal?" I called after him, choking on my anger. "I take it that too you collected so it would not be lost?"

He stopped and spun around. Wrapped now in a regained calm, he smiled pityingly at me.

"You are too young and inexperienced to understand these matters, Joseph."

"What of the time you have spent outside the Priory walls? What of that? Are we not enjoined to only find salvation within the walls?"

"You surprise me. Recall what befell Prior Elias for his denial of William's purpose. Just as his eventual acquiescence, half meant as it was, did not shield him, so your friendship with William will not shield you, if you were foolish enough to mount a half-informed and ill-considered denunciation of his most humble servant and sacrist."

"I do not deny William, Brother Thomas. It is you. I will deny you for the theft of holy relics."

Further accusations died on my lips as a dainty open palm was thrust forcefully at my face.

"Imagine what the cloister would believe after all that has transpired, if your sudden uncertainty is made known. Yes, Joseph, they will say, despite any protestations you might offer, that you have altered your story and are now defending the Jew murderers. They will say that your conversion was an act of convenience, not of the heart. They will wonder if perhaps you continue to adhere to the Hebrew faith. We don't want that to happen, do we?"

With this threat hanging in the air, he rushed from the room.

Fear Invades The Cloister

The day after our encounter I was informed that Brother Thomas had left the cloister on an important errand. I was ordered back to my duties in the scriptorium. It was not the first time this had happened, but I was concerned that one of his mysterious trips had taken place immediately after I had been so sternly admonished for questioning the purpose of these trips, as well as the veracity of his visions. Nonetheless, even burdened with this concern, I failed to connect our bitter encounter with the events that began a few days later.

You have heard that it was said, An eye for an eye and a tooth for a tooth.

But I say to you, Do not resist one who is evil.

It was early winter and we were in the refectory at evening supper. As usual, we sat on long benches with our backs to the wall. At the far end of the room, the Prior and the more senior monks took their places at the high table.

But if any one strikes you on the right cheek,
Turn to him the other also;
And if any one would sue you and take your coat,
Let him have your cloak as well;

The meal was taken in silence, broken only by the rustling of mice, cockroaches and other vermin in the reeds spread thickly across the floor, the clank of knives and spoons against bowls, the slurping of monks and rising above those worldly noises, the high-pitched voice of the Reader, Brother Anselmo, regaling us with passages from the Gospels. Meal time was about feeding both the stomach and the soul. That evening we were fed pease porridge and black bread washed down with a passage from Matthew.

And if any one forces you to go one mile,
Go with him two miles.
Give to him who begs from you,
And do not refuse him who would borrow from you.

Sitting next to me was Brother Marus, who had recently joined us from the abbey in Bec. He was a slightly built, scholarly monk who carried an air of otherworldly detachment. This was something all were expected to cultivate, but none in the Priory could match the exemplary Brother Marus in this regard.

He had taken a few spoonfuls of the porridge when his head snapped forward violently and he started to choke and to gasp for breath. The monk sitting to his right leapt up and began pounding his fist against the back of the struggling man. The choking did not abate. Instead, poor Brother Marus's limp body slammed downward with great force, driving it and his head against the table. The noise made was as if a ripe melon had exploded on cobbles. Monks ducked and fell backwards off benches as bowls, knives and spoons were sent flying. I heard a bone crack. A pool of blood spread out from his damaged face, soaking into the table planks. By the time Brother Castus pushed his way through the tangle of frantic monks, Brother Marus was beyond his ministrations and truly and finally detached from this world.

When the uproar had subsided and the body carried away, we all removed to the High Altar, where prayers were offered for our departed brother.

At the Chapter House meeting the next day the Prior told us that Brother Castus diagnosed a sudden rupture of the heart. Few who had been close witness to the death credited this explanation. The view more widely held was that Brother Marus had been the victim of a dreadful poison. All manner of rumours then circulated as to what poison was used, who the likely poisoner might be and why the unfortunate brother had been dispatched in such a terrible way. As no answers of any kind were forthcoming, mealtimes became uneasy affairs with monks casting wary looks at their fellows and pointedly reluctant to be the first to sample the food.

Poisoning was not, however, the only source of mounting fear and unease within the cloister. Two days on from Brother Marus's death a scaffolding tower collapsed burying three workmen and a lay brother. Luck was with me as I had passed the very spot only seconds before. Luck was also with the four men, all of whom were pulled from the rubble suffering nothing more than broken bones, bruises and lacerations.

Thomas had still not returned when the third accident occurred. I was walking through the nave together with Brother Jerome and one of the new novices, whose name I cannot recall. He was a particularly handsome lad with a willing smile who had come to us just that day from the town of Thetford. On entering the cloister we heard a shout of alarm ring out from above. As one we looked up to see a large piece of masonry hurtling down towards us. I spun on my crutches, pushed with all my strength and leapt sideways. Brother Jerome also threw himself clear. The square-cut stone missed us by no more than a few digits. Our Thetford novice was not so fortunate. To this day I see his terror-widened eyes set in that handsome face, immediately before it was crushed beyond recognition.

Having undergone a series of close encounters with death, which certainly more than fulfilled St. Benedict's instruction to keep death before one's eyes each day, I had expected to receive comfort and reassurance from my brother monks. Instead I found myself the object of whispered accusations of having committed some heinous, sinful act and in doing so incurring God's displeasure. As Jonah, I was endangering all who sailed on the ship of the Norwich Priory and should be cast out before further misfortune descended upon the more virtuous members of the cloister.

"I have called the community together in council," intoned Prior de Ferrariis, "to consider the many misfortunes that have befallen us within the last days and so we may....".

"If you please, Brother Prior," spoke up Brother Lipius, a close confidante of Alexander, Godwin's son, "how then are we to understand Brother Joseph being present at the death of Brother Marus, a day later at the fallen scaffoldings and yesterday, once again, someone dies at his side?"

"The cripple is cursed!" a muffled voice called from out of the press of black-cassocked bodies.

"Jew!" another shouted.

"Brothers!," the Prior boomed. "You are to speak not in anger but rather in humble submission. I can see by your intemperate outbursts that what I have heard is true. Some among you have been spreading uncharitable calumnies against our dear, unfortunate brother, Joseph. Need I remind you of your vow to live your lives by the Rule? The Blessed St Benedict instructs us not to bear false witness, to practice charity, to help those in trouble, to console those in sorrow. When we are tested by adversity and ill fortune, such as in these last days we have been, salvation can be found only by strengthening our love and support for each other. If we let the Fallen One divide us, to direct our fears and uncertainty against our brothers in Christ, he will have been victorious and we will be forever lost."

"For whatever cause," interrupted Brother Lipius, "his being among us poses a danger to our house."

"Throw the Judas over the side!"

"Jew!"

"I will not tell you again, brothers," continued the Prior, raising his voice over the shouting, grumbling monks. "I forbid you to follow so blindly the faithless stirrings of your own hearts. Further, I have listened to more than enough and

190

order that you desist from disputing so insolently with me, your prior. You will obey me and do precisely what I decide should be done. Is that understood?"

His challenge was met by bowed heads and silence.

I was encouraged by the Prior's words, but they were heeded by few of the brothers. After the Chapter House meeting, the handful of monks who deemed to look my way, did so with unfriendly eyes. My erstwhile brothers either ignored me or feigned deafness when I tried to communicate. Under cover of darkness I was forced to endure one indignity after another. One night my crutches were taken from where I slept, on the following I discovered an eviscerated eel under my blanket, on the next, human faeces. I tried as best I could to observe Jesus's precept of not opposing evil and presenting my left cheek to be struck, but my Christian passivity, no matter how divinely inspired, seemed only to enflame enmity. The assaults continued. Even those whom I counted as firm friends, Edgar, Jerome and two or three others, kept me at a discrete distance.

In despair, I approached Brother Edgar to ask for his support and his counsel.

"I am sorry, Joseph, but I can do nothing. You will have to bear these calumnies until they run their course, as they assuredly will."

I hoped for so much more from my friend and mentor that I abandoned my customary Benedictine fortitude and lashed out angrily, calling him a coward, a blackguard, as well as a Judas Iscariot for his betrayal. My forthright attack was met first with surprise and then resignation. Without a sign or a word, Brother Edgar glared at me, then turned and walked away.

Since the time of my banishment to the room under the eves in Saddlegate, I had never felt more forsaken and alone in the world.

Flight

A week had passed, and Brother Thomas had not returned to the Priory. I attempted to discover where he had gone, but no one would tell me or for that, communicate with me on any subject, either verbally or with sign. I wondered if my threat to expose his unholy thieving had forced him to flee the Priory. As it transpired, I was both correct and mistaken.

A brother, whom I was unable to recognise under his closed hood, ducked as he entered the low door into the scriptorium. He bowed a silent greeting at the master, Brother John, and handed him a note. The old man glanced curiously at the visitor, but proceeded to read the note and then, when he had finished, bent his head in assent. The tall monk motioned to me and I followed him out into the walkway of the cloister. The day was brutally cold, the sky cloudless. The grass in the centre of the cloister was dusted with early winter snow. Monks could be seen passing in and out of the numerous openings that gave onto the walkway. As I breathed in this harmonious scene, its tranquillity was shattered by a cacophonous darkness of rooks that flew overhead, casting ill-omened shadows across the cloister. A shiver passed through me. I can remember this moment with particular clarity. It was to be my last in the Priory.

"Come now, Joseph," said the monk. "We are about to embark on an adventure, you and I."

The voice was curiously familiar, although I struggled to place it.

"Who are...".

"There is not much time," he said, pulling me so fiercely by the sleeve that it was all I could do to remain upright on my crutches.

I threw off his hand. I required no assistance to move at pace. Although my legs still danced to an unreliable drummer, my arms, now so stick thin and feeble, were then immensely strong, and when gripping my crutches I could propel myself forward faster than most men could walk.

I was suspicious of this stranger, but also sufficiently intrigued and so carried on with him around the walkway to the South Door of the Cathedral. I stopped abruptly as we reached the open doorway. Here, where I had first entered the Priory ten years previously, caution overcame my curiosity.

"Why do you hesitate? Please, my friend."

"As I'm sure you know, we are forbidden to leave these precincts without consent from the Prior. Further, why should I be going anywhere with a stranger who hides his face from me?"

"If I was to tell you that your safety, nay, your life depended on you accompanying me, would that persuade you? I see by your look that you continue to doubt me. Let me remind you of all that has happened close by to you in the last days, the terrible injuries and, worse told, the deaths. I can assure you these were not the result of ill fortune. They were carried out by design, Joseph."

After the incident of the falling masonry, I fleetingly harboured a suspicion that my proximity to disaster was not simple coincidence. I quickly dismissed such thoughts as unworthy. I was living in a Christian community, and, although my recent persecution was evidence that brotherly love was not always observed, murder was, I believed, a cardinal sin, too terrible for a monk even to contemplate.

I was fumbling with these thoughts when the stranger gently eased me through the door and with a hand on my elbow guided me to a thick clump of snow-bowed bushes near the high flint walls that enclosed the Cathedral grounds. Here, hidden from view, he lowered his hood and with a wide sweep of his arms divested himself of the monk's cassock. Standing in front of me now was a strongly-built man in a riding cloak and high boots. He wore a heavy black beard and long flowing hair. Observing my confusion he smiled broadly, then laughed.

"I see by the vacant expression on your twisted face that you fail to recognise your old friend?"

He was taller and broader than when I had last seen him, but his sparkling green eyes immediately gave to me the owner of the voice.

"Marcus?"

With two swift strides he closed the distance between us and embraced me. I froze in his hefty arms, so startled was I by the forgotten, prohibited touch.

"Please excuse me, Joseph, but seeing you once again, it comes to me how very much I have missed you. I am so overjoyed to see you alive and well. I feared I would not arrive in time to warn you of what is afoot. Yes, yes, I will explain, but first...".

He handed me a cloth bag containing trousers, a white linen shirt, a tunic, hose, a soft cap, together with a fur-lined cloak similar to the one he wore.

"Change into these, it is best there should be no report from the gate of a crippled monk leaving from this place. Do not forget to cover your tonsure with the cap. Don't stand there staring like a moonstruck coney, Joseph. Hurry now, before we miss our opportunity."

I did as he ordered. We had not long to wait for that opportunity to arrive. Some few minutes after I had shed my monk's trappings, a group of about a dozen pilgrims exited from the Cathedral. As was commonplace, among them were the sick, some carried on litters, the hobbling lame, the blind and those victim to unseen ailments. As they passed we slid out from our place of concealment and, unnoticed, joined their number. So it was that we were able to leave the environs of the Cathedral without note, and with the exception of the vile insults thrown at us by the cripples at the gate, without challenge.

Norwich
In The Year 1155

Marcus Redux

arcus led me hurriedly through the city streets, retracing almost to the cobble and rut the route William and I had followed ten years previously. It marked my first foray outside what I had assumed to be the safety of the Priory. Long isolation from the rudeness of popular life left me repelled and disoriented by the noise and dirt and fetid odours and the rumbling crowds. My regained friend guided me to a house close by the reeking waters of the Great Cockey, not far distant from Saddlegate, and adjacent to what Marcus said was a bathhouse.

I was still attempting to come to terms with what he had relayed to me outside the Cathedral and to arrange my senses from the onslaught of our hurried journey, when he ushered me into a large, low-ceilinged room. The two benches that it contained were coated in yellowish grime. Wooden bowls with remains of food were scattered across a filthy table, two legs of which were shorter on one side than the other, making the entire room appear to be on a slope. On the pounded dirt floor were four or five straw pallets, draped in blankets, their neatness at odds with the surrounding chaos. After having lived for so long in a place of strict discipline and cleanliness, such carelessly befouled disorder jolted my unworldly soul.

"I am sorry, Joseph, but this is the sole refuge in the city whose tenants I can depend on to offer you protection. At a good price, of course."

"What is this terrible place?"

"This, my gentle friend, is where live, when they are not plying their trade in the bathhouse, a number of women of my acquaintance"

"What trade would that be?"

"Do you recall the night in the dormitory when you awoke in tears telling us that you had a dream, a vision of St. Augustine? You called out, 'He's alive and with us, here in our quarters! He is miserable with our sinning! Arise! Arise!' "

"No, I do not remember such an event, Marcus. I must have been...but what does this tell me about the women or their trade?"

His face split in an uneasy grin. "Let's say it is a trade that your miserable St. Augustine said was desirable to have in order to prevent lust spreading in the world."

"Marcus," I shouted out, "please tell me you have not delivered me into the care of harlots!"

"These harlots are the most honest women you are ever likely to encounter. So do not judge them harshly. Besides, was the blessed St. Mary Magdalene not one of their number?"

I could trust that out of all his learning as a novice, Marcus had partially mastered the most salacious of texts.

"The Blessed Saint renounced her ways of sin to follow our Lord. These women who live here, if I understand you, have not."

He threw up his hands and laughed, "I yield, Brother Joseph, to your superior learning."

"That victory affords me no comfort, Marcus. This place gives me no comfort. Could you not find a more salubrious, less scandalous place of refuge?"

"Given time, perhaps. For the moment, however, when I explain why I came for you, you will be content to be anywhere but where you were. Sit. Go on, Joseph, you will not be much soiled. Sit while I tell you an unsettling tale."

With fastidious reluctance I sat down gingerly on one of the grimy benches. Marcus sat next to me.

"During the week now gone, my Uncle Simon, who I've told you of before, has entertained a number of clerical guests at his manor. The priest, Godwin, and his son, together with a curious dwarf, who wore the garment of a monk. I was not there when they first arrived, so only overheard the conversation when they learned that attempts to put you out of the way had misfired. They were most agitated when the groom brought the news, so agitated that they took little notice of me where I sat in the gallery above the long room."

"I am a person of scant import, Marcus. For what cause would these men, men who are my brothers in Christ, want to, as you say, 'put me out of the way'?"

"I am afraid I cannot give you an answer to that question, Joseph. They did not discuss reasons, only the various means that had failed and their new scheme."

"Which was?"

"Again, I am not sure, only that they instructed the groom to tell their confederate in the Priory, whom I gathered was one of the servants there, to ensure on his life that the next accident was a success. Oh yes, one further comment was made. It seems that your demise was important, not only to silence you, but also to dissuade others from coming forward. Who these 'others' were or what your death would dissuade them from, that was not spoken of."

I did not need to learn more from Marcus. The pieces of the puzzle had all been joined. As I am now, I was doubly then - a fool, a fool for not having seen that which was so obvious.

"This is why you came for me?"

"Oh, yes, of course, Joseph. You know of my great fondness for you. Or," he said with a bearded pout of mock sadness, "have you forgotten your Marcus?"

The spectacle of this huge, manly man attempting to affect the grimace of a babe caused me to forget the prohibition against boisterous laughter.

"I have not forgotten you, Marcus," I said, smiling up at my knight errant. "Even after all this time I have not forgotten you. We were children then, playing as children do. I am now a monk, a vocation that demands I give myself to Christ and put aside childish things and temptations of the flesh. If you had read more deeply from St. Augustine, you would know that."

"Didn't he say that love is the beauty of the soul?"

"Love of God, Marcus, not worldly love. 'For as I became a youth, I longed to be satisfied with worldly things, and I dared to grow wild in a succession of various and shadowy loves. I became corrupt in thy eyes, yet I was still pleasing to my own eyes -- and eager to please the eyes of men.'"

"Well, my fine scholar, it is clear we two have taken different paths. Is it not curious then that you who have embraced St. Augustine and I who have put him out to death sit here together in this house where abide those who are so fully in the world of the flesh."

"So speaks the Devil, Marcus. So speaks the Devil."

Three Strumpets

Three loud-spoken, red-rouged, disorderly women burst into the house. They brought with them a blasting aroma of rose petals and musk. The first of them, a black-haired woman with hips so wide she was obliged to enter the door at a judicious angle, grinned when she saw me, walked over and, without a word of greeting, snatched the wool cap from my head.

"Oh, look, ladies, we have our own tonsure head!" she cackled. "Ain't he the very horse's pips, if I ever seen 'em? And you know me, I seen plenty."

"Cerinda," Marcus said with a mocking seriousness, "I would ask you to treat your guest with the kindness of dignity. He is a poor, humble monk with no knowledge of the world outside the Cathedral walls and even less the acquaintance of your ungodly domain."

"Unlike some of them others then, them other men of God," laughed a second woman, whose name was Ermyntrude.

"Poor child," cooed the third, a skinny, redheaded harridan. "He looks close scared to death."

Since entering the cloister, the only women I had seen were those who came to the Cathedral to attend Mass or to ask for William's curative intercession. As was expected, all these women were, as were the Jewesses in Saddlegate, demurely clad. This was not something that could be said of my new companions. Upon entering the room, the three furies who milled around inspecting me had thrown off their cloaks to exhibit thin shifts revealing more of the female form than I desired to imagine. They did not wear hats, veils, wimples or hoods and their long, uncovered hair, a thing I understood to be permitted only in the privacy of a bed chamber, was yet a further provocative shock.

"What name do our holy man go with, Sir?" asked Ermyntrude, looking to Marcus.

Having to be spoken to through an interlocutor was a commonplace when people first looked upon my twisted face and the contorted dance of my crippled limbs. In a strange manner, I had almost come to depend on this unkindness from strangers. I had also come to rebel against the assumptions of simplemindedness informing such treatment, by trying to be forcefully outspoken. However, my tongue-mangled words often resulted in this tactic simply reinforcing those initial assumptions.

"I am called Brother Joseph," I said, with all the force and clarity I could call upon.

"Oh glory! It speaks," shrilled the red head. "At least I guess that's what its doin'. Is that what he's doin', Sir?"

"Bro-ther Jo-seph," I repeated. "Bro-ther Jo-seph."

"He is called Brother Joseph," repeated Marcus. "We best now call him Joseph, plain Joseph. Does that meet with approval, Brother?"

"If it must," I replied, cast down in my heart.

I pulled Marcus to one side, out of the hearing of the painted grotesques who, laughing wide-mouthed, whirled about, acting out a demonic dance in the centre of the room.

"Am I to assume by this that I am to have to abandon my calling, Marcus, that I will not be returning to my life in the Priory? I have been almost ten years there, since a boy. It is all I know. Without the cloister I will be lost to myself and to God and to William as well. A life without these is little more than ashes."

Marcus, adopting a look of genuine concern, said softly, "My dearest Joseph, it is not you who are abandoning your calling, but your calling that is abandoning you. It is, of course, possible that after a time you may be able to resume, but for the moment it would be a thing far too perilous to contemplate. Whatever it is that the priest and the dwarf desire to hide, it must be something of great import for these men, who have taken the exacting path marked out by St Benedict, to have you murdered. Further, I believe, albeit I have no proof, that there are others in the cloister who share their fear of being discovered and would in consequence assist them in finding ways of silencing you."

It was sometime later that I discovered Marcus's suspicions were well founded. In addition to the purloined teeth, Thomas had taken the sandal, Godwin had removed the teasel gag from William's dead mouth and three of the monks who had helped translate the body from the cemetery had also gathered relics - a foot bone, a scrap of cloth from the winding sheet and some hair. I did not know what the monks did with their stolen relics, but Godwin sold curing draughts of teasel-dipped water to those for whom a pilgrimage to the shrine was either too arduous or not sufficient to effect the sought-for relief.

"For how long you be expecting us to keep this cripple monk of yours hid?" called out Cerinda.

"I cannot say," Marcus answered. "Until the danger has passed. Not before."

The wide-hipped woman raised a questioning eyebrow.

"I am telling you, woman, I do not know. Here, take this. You keep Joseph safe from discovery and more will follow."

He drew a weighty leather purse from the waist of his trousers and spilled out three coins, which he dropped one by one into the women's outstretched hands.

Falling From Grace

"**S**o our little monk, what is we now to do with you?" Cerinda asked.

Before I was delivered to the House of Strumpets I was a Benedictine monk, a soul joyful in the love of my Saviour, my entire being at perfect repose with that love. I was content that the rest of my days would be measured out in the comforting rhythm of prayer, meditation, reading and Holy Offices, together with visits to speak my day and my heart to William. It was not to be. As the days of my unholy exile passed, one by one the onioned layers of my avowed monkish identity were peeled away. It began in a very pointed and painful manner soon after Marcus had left me alone with my new guardians.

The three women circled as if carrion birds, studying me, while I, their wounded rabbit, stared at the floor.

"The tonsure!" cried out Ermyntrude, as if she had made a miraculous find. "If we must keep him hid, then the tonsure must be gone."

The others muttered their assent. The red head, who was called with appropriate purpose, Swetelove, shuffled over to the corner of the room, bent down and picked up a small cloth bag, out of which she pulled a long-bladed knife. Licking her thumb, she ran it along the knife edge and then smiled at her compatriots.

"No, not that!" I pleaded, twisting away and throwing my hands up to cover the long-sought-after symbol of my calling.

My resistance proved of no consequence.

"If you struggle so, little monk," said Cerinda, "there is no accounting for what may occur. The losing of an ear, may-haps?"

I attempted to heed her demand, but my convulsed body would not cooperate. Swetelove gripped my head tightly between her powerful hands, Ermyntrude took hold of my shoulders, as Cerinda wielded the dull blade. She was quick but neither gentle nor remorseful for her lack of gentleness. The secular transformation took no more than a few minutes before I was left hairless and bloodied.

Cerinda stood back to admire her butchery. The others released their hold of me. I wiped a trembling hand across the top of my head. The hand came away covered in blood. I screamed out in anguished fury and buried my head in my hands. I must have presented a pathetic sight, but one the three women greeted not with sympathy or reassurance, but rather with howls of triumphant derision. The rigours of their profession did not encourage softness of the heart.

Accustomed to a room crowded with other sleepers, sharing nighttimes with five women, two additional harpies having joined us early in the morning, proved to be surprisingly easy. I placed my pallet in a far corner and immediately closed my eyes so I might not look upon their preparations. As it happened, without the monks' snoring and their vision-induced screaming and shouting, I slept more soundly then I had ever done in the dormitory.

Because they plied their trade in the bathhouse, the women bathed each day, as well as lavishly anointing themselves with pungent oils and strong scent. It was for this that my initiation into the non-cloistered world took a worrisome turn a few days later. The women decided that I could only meet the demands of their delicate noses by bathing. I explained that I always washed my face and hands before each meal and before prayers and that I had taken a bath as recently as a month before. Surely, I told them, that was sufficient.

"A month?" Swetelove exclaimed, "Why little man, it is a marvel your stink is not worse still. A real holy stink! Now, don't you be going on so with that wide stare and twitched up face. A touch of water never did no one... Oh no, it ain't the water, is it?"

"Ha! Ha!" screamed Cerinda, "Not the water, Sweetness, no not the damned water at all. It's us, it is. He don't want us seeing on his monk's little secret, do he? Keep it hidden, even from themselves, they do. Well, them kinda secrets ain't nothing to us."

"Think we ain't seen such secrets afore?" asked Malot, having no more than sixteen years, the youngest and most fresh-faced and most comely among the five whores.

"True, that be," added Swetelove, throwing back her long red hair. "Monk's secrets, priest's secrets, merchants' secrets, knights' secrets, a goodly number of them secrets have passed through our hands."

"And in and out and through other places as well," Cerinda howled in delight at both her wit and being witness to my spiralling discomfort. "Curious to tell, with all of 'em secrets, some bigger than others, as is the way, they is all just about the same. So, you tell me, if every man is carrying the same secret, what the hell kinda secret be that? No bloody secret at all, that's what it be. So, you be coming along now without giving us no cripple's fussing."

They moved towards me, smoothing their designs with silken words and calm assurances. I backed away, and as I did I tasked them by saying that their ablutions and heady perfumes might cleanse their bodies, but that they could never cleanse them of their sins.

"Reckon, I do, that it be too far gone for me to be fretting on my sinning, Brother," Swetelove declared. "I reckon you be just near too far gone backwards and all."

As she spoke, something struck me in the small of my knees. I fell, my crutches flying. Before I reached the floor

I was caught from behind, my legs too were captured and I found myself completely upended, lifted, helpless as if a spitted bullock and carried out from the house by the four laughing whores. Within a few moments they had transported me to the neighbouring bathhouse.

Flesh In The World Of The Devil

It was not in a deep cave or below the earth, as I had imagined it would be. I did not see torture being inflicted nor hear the wailing of the damned. No matter, as I was thrust across the threshold into the bathhouse, excepting the sweet, pungent bathhouse perfume being redolent of Paradise, although I realised immediately it could be nothing more than a deception of the Fallen One, I was convinced I had been delivered by Satan's Whorish Imps to the very depths of Gehenna.

We entered an immense, red tile floored room, the far reaches of which were obscured by steam-filled air. The source of this interior fog bank were two great cauldrons of water set over high-flamed fires. They were attended by men wearing only thin breeches and wooden clogs. Their bare chests dripped with rivulets of perspiration. A number of lank-haired women in damp garments that clung lewdly to their bodies carried buckets of heated water to what appeared to be large barrels on either side of the room. Some of the barrels were positioned behind partially drawn curtains. It was to one of these that I was carried, fear and wonder having quieted my purposeful resistance. Only my body's everyday consciousness-defying spasmodic twists and shudders remained to be attended to by my captors.

"No harm now coming to you, Joseph," cooed Cerinda, as they closed the curtains and set me down on a raised pallet at the side of the barrel. "Don't you go on struggling so. You be doing yourself an injury if you don't quiet yourself."

"You wanna be taming them wild rollin' eyes, Joseph," Malot said, reaching over to stroke my head.

They had begun to remove my clothing, and so a desperate

purpose reignited my resistance. I managed to fling off one of them, but was quickly pinned hard to the bed by Cerinda, who raising her skirts, climbed astride me, her heavy legs gripping my sides, her ample posterior on my chest and her breasts, thankfully still encased in clothing, pushed softly into my face so I could scare find my breath.

Shrieking with hysterical abandon at the desperate futility of my efforts to escape, the four malevolent whores proceeded to strip me naked. As my trousers came away, their licentious bawling ceased abruptly.

Even in the roasting throes of despair, I knew too well what was to follow. And it did.

"Oh," one said quietly, "what does you have there, little monk? I ain't never seen the like, I ain't."

"Like the others when they rise up from sleeping, but if I ain't mistaken this one is still abed."

"Once I seen this," observed Ermyntrude in a reflectively knowledgable tone, "a Jew I been having in London had a similar, but never seen or heard of such hanging on a good Christian monk. Never have. Curious it is."

An enticingly soft hand encircled me. Another joined. For what seemed a timeless moment, my body settled into total, unfamiliar repose, as if, completely divorced from my reason, it was making its own assessment of a new discovery. The moment passed. A decision had been made.

"Not so little now. Oh look, you ragged, scale-backed whores. Look to our pious one!" cried out Cerinda, turning around from her perch on my chest to peer back at my mounting shame.

My constant twitching jerks now took on an added and most urgent quavering. It mortifies me to tell, although the first time at the hands of a woman, or in this instance I believe it was women, this was not of itself an unfamiliar occurrence. Despite my fervent prayers that God grant me a sober heart and a watchful mind, while I slept the Devil refused to rest. It had happened too on other occasions, the details of which I mean to guard as secret and carry to the grave.

"So quick, the Jew cock of the monk!" crowed Swetelove.

"So generous too! He flows on, he do," joined one of the others.

"And yet he looks unhappy," Malot said, with a rare hint of compassion in her voice. "Oh, our sad little monk."

"Not at all of any use that," Cerinda said harshly, staring down and addressing herself directly to me. "Whatever you be, Jew cripple or cripple monk or even cripple Jew monk, you be a man like other men and that's the end of it. So best you stop worrying so at what is not there for changing."

Albeit an unlettered whore, Cerinda showed herself to be a rough-speaking sage as well. That thought came to me much later. At that moment I had no time for lofty reflection. As one trial had come to an end, another was upon me.

Cerinda climbed off me, but before I was able to move or cover my nakedness, many hands lifted me up and plunged me down into the barrel of water. In the cloister, bathing was a cold, solitary and carefully modest affair. Modesty demanded no part of your body being visible to others lest it inflame passions to which all flesh is prone. Cold water was yet another means to defeat those selfsame passions.

None of this held in the bathhouse. Hardly had I been embraced by the warmth of the water, than I was also being embraced by the nakedness of Swetelove. She was joined moments later by Malot. There was no room remaining in the barrel for Cerinda and Ermyntrude, so they called out words of derision and encouragement from the barrel's edge where they stood watching, their bare arms and breasts exposed.

Notwithstanding the shock, confusion, shame, fear and, most importantly, a desperate concern for the future of my immortal soul, that day, there in His Hellish Domain, caressed by warm water and a copiousness of accommodatingly soft flesh, I gave in to temptation. I gave in a number of times. I gave in with the abandon of the newly converted. I gave in until the whores themselves gave in. I gave in out of exhaustion. They gave in because the bathhouse keeper, an immense, perspiring mountain, pushed his bulk through the curtains and in a spluttering rage ordered them to attend the paying clients.

With the Devil in the ascendant, another, and probably the most substantial layer of my identity as a Benedictine monk, was peeled, or better said, stripped away.

No Way Back

I was lost to God. Completely lost. I prayed to be given back chastity and continence, so that I might return to Him. Nonetheless, when I recalled what happened in the bathhouse and imagined the possibility of further encounters, I could only repeat the words of St Augustine and pray, "but not yet." With visions of flesh, quite specific visions of quite specific flesh, plunging me into hellish torment, I could find no path back to the calm island of Faith. It was then that Marcus returned with dire intelligence that sealed off forever any hopes of rediscovering the path or retracing my steps upon it.

Apparently his three coins were not enough for the whores. They demanded I labour for my keep by cleaning the house. I held that this was not something suitable for a man of God. They all howled wickedly. One tweaked my chin, another made to grab for my manhood, while a third ran her hand across my shaved head, pointing out that I was a monk no longer. I was, they said, just a common sinner, like other sinners and if I knew what was in my best interests, I would do precisely what they asked of me or else. They would not expand on what 'else' might mean. Not wanting to find out - their flagrantly-mad behaviour both enticed and frightened me, the latter always getting the upper hand - I set to. I was scrubbing down their filthy table, when Marcus came swaggering in through the door.

"What is this?" he demanded indignantly. "Have you become servant to those damnable, scabrous whores? He looked about. "They are not here?"

I dropped the sodden rag and pointed, indicating they were in the bathhouse.

"Yes. Good. For what I have to tell you, better that the whores don't hear of it, albeit as things are in this terrible death pit of a city, they will learn of it soon enough."

"What news can be of such import, Marcus?"

"Well, let's see," he said, appearing uneasy, something I did not associate with the always gathered, Noble Marcus. "Please, Joseph, sit. Now, ah, I am much grieved to have to tell you that your friend, the man you told me was both your mother and your father, that is Brother Edgar, is dead."

My first reaction was a numbing disbelief. A great many thoughts assailed me, most only half-formed before being overridden by the next. Years with Ederick in Thorpe Wood tumbled through, the harshness, the beatings gone, only tenderness and love remaining. His joyousness of greeting when I appeared at the South Door of the Cathedral seeking sanctuary. The kindness and love he offered as a friend, confidant and moral guide during my time in the cloister. Less welcome, but regrettably the most poignant, was the remembrance of our last encounter when I had stung him with poisonous insults and he turned his back on me.

I screamed in torment at my loss and then wept, all remembrances drowned by grief. It was the last time I was to allow myself the luxury of tears.

"Joseph!" Marcus called, lifting my wildly writhing body from the floor. He held me tightly in his strong arms, whispering endearments until, after what felt an age, I relaxed into softer twitching and less racking gasps.

"I am sorry, Joseph, but I am afraid there is worse yet to tell."

I halted my crying, readying myself for the next blow. When it came, it was so unbelievable that there was nothing to do but laugh at the absurdity.

"They, at the Cathedral that is, they are saying you are the

213

one responsible for his death. I know, yes, I know, if it were not so serious an accusation, I too would join in laughter. But in truth, there is no jest intended. They mean to find you and return you for trial by ordeal, the same trial they desired to impose on the Jews for the murdering of William."

"How did he, I mean Edgar, how did he come to die?"

"I do not know. I have heard only that his body was discovered and it is said that you have fled from the Priory because you had a hand in his murder. They say that the two incidents occurring at the same moment cannot be coincidence. They ask why else did you flee if not for having committed some unspeakable act."

"Why in the name of Our Blessed Saviour would I want to kill Brother Edgar? It was well known by all that he was my sponsor, my dearest friend. Why, Marcus, why? It makes no sense."

"I concur, Joseph, there is no sense to it. Even if they claim to have sworn witnesses, there is, as you say, no sense at all."

"How is that possible? There can be no witnesses if there was nothing to witness."

"I believe it was St William's brother, the monk Richard and two others. They tell as how they were witness to a disagreement between you and Brother Edgar some few days before he died and you disappeared. Do they lie?"

"No," I replied slowly, "Indeed, they do not lie. I had taken Brother Edgar to task for not standing by me, as he should have done, when others in the cloister turned against me, calling me a Jonah and worse, blaming me for the accidents that you informed me were the handiwork of Godwin and Brother Thomas, aided by your uncle. None of this could move me to the murder of anyone, especially a person as dear to me as Brother Edgar."

"It is curious, is it not, that you stand to be undone, not by the plots to murder you, but by circumstances unrelated to those plots."

"You will forgive me, Marcus if I can find no comfort in such a thought."

He offered a knowing smile. "No comfort indeed. I fear, my friend, that it may not be ere long before you may find little comfort here in this place, for as we speak the story of murder in the Priory travels throughout Norwich. Soon the whores will hear of it and they and their confederates among the city's thieves, cutpurses and cutthroats may see in it more to gain by giving you up to the Sheriff than providing refuge. Further, they may reason your being here puts them in greater jeopardy of the law."

It was not enough that my closest friend was dead and I accused of his murder, I was going to be denied shelter from the coming storm even in a squalid abode inhabited by whores.

Marcus came over to where I sat head down, half dazed and put a warm, thick arm across my shoulder.

"Don't despair my sweet friend," he said, squeezing my hand. "Without fail I will return for you this evening and under the concealing shroud of darkness I will carry you to a place of greater safety."

Taken

The evening was drawing in when I heard someone at the door. Thinking it was Marcus, I rose from the bench and took up my crutches in preparation for flight. It was not Marcus. Instead, wide-beamed Cerinda, followed by Malot and behind her four rough-hewn men burst into the room.

"There he be!" Cerinda shouted. "There be the monk."

Apparently the news from the Cathedral had reached the whores more rapidly than Marcus had imagined. They in turn had no hesitation in putting me on the block. Why not? Their favours were in the market, their sympathy, assuming they had any for me, was not. Nonetheless, as in my cloistered, non-worldly self I imagined intimacy to carry with it something more, their treachery wounded deeply.

Startled and fearful, I stumbled backwards, overturning one of the benches. The single taper set upon the table gave off more smoke than illumination, distorting the advancing figures into devilish creatures whose faces and bodies melted and then reformed and melted again as they advanced towards me. I had seen their like many times before. I cried out hoping that I would thereby awake from the familiar nightmare vision and find myself back in the safety of the dormitory. There was no such easy release. These demons were corporal beings, not phantoms to be banished upon waking.

"Be there easy, lad," the closest one, a slightly built, rat-faced man, said. "There ain't nothing to be feared of."

"Come now, Joseph," the comely Malot called to me from somewhere behind the men. "No one wants to do you no harm."

"Who are these men?" I cried out to the two whores, who

216

had been joined by Swetelove and Ermyntrude. "What do they want of me?"

I well knew the answers, but as one does in such hard-pressed circumstances, I blurted out the questions so as to tell them I was possessed of reason and even of choice. The effect was precisely contrary to those weak-hearted expectations.

"You stinking, lying strumpet," raged one of the gang, a fat man with a raw, puckered burn covering half his face. "You told us as how this one was a monk from the Priory, the one they been after finding."

"Truth, he be that monk," replied Cerinda indignantly. " Like I been after telling you, we was paid to hide him. Shaved his head and all, we did. It's him, and no doubt. Swear it on my mother's heart, I do."

"First off, if you ever knowed a mother, and of that I be doubtful, you'd be selling her whole, never you mind the old woman's heart. Second off, this be no monk as I'd ever seen. By what he does appear and what he be spitting out, he be no more than a crippled simpleton you after trying to pass us as something more."

"She's saying true," piped up Swetelove. "When that gentleman brought him here, he had the monk's tonsure, wooden cross too hanging round his neck."

"He do talk strange," added Ermyntrude, "but I venture as how he ain't so simple in his head as he sounds to be."

The fat man, obviously the leader of the gang, looked from one woman to the other, trying to fathom out whether he'd been caught in a web spun by a collective of mendacious whores.

"If you all been lying, you full well know what's down for you, make no mistake on it. Hear me?"

Cerinda boldly strode up to him, looked him straight in the

eyes, then turned her head and spat full at his feet.

"You hear me, you black-faced pig fucker," she said quietly. "You ...".

Her words were drowned out by the uproarious laughter from the three other men. The fat man's jaw dropped. Recovering, his face hardened and he made as if to strike Cerinda. She held her ground, glaring at him. After a long moment his arm faltered, then dropped to his side. He smiled coldly at the brazen whore and then turned away to appraise me once more.

"Faith, but you be a rough-tongued whore," he said. "Go on then, Creedal, take him down. Let us waste no more time on this. We'll soon see if he be who these dumb strumpets say."

Rat Face grinned a rat-faced grin and lunged for me. I swung my crutch as hard as I could. It caught him on the side of his head. Stunned, he dropped to the floor, blood flowing copiously from his mouth. The three others stared down at their fallen comrade and stopped where they were. The injured man groaned.

"Poor old Creedal, can't even catch himself an idiot cripple," laughed one.

The fat man gestured to the others and while Rat Face struggled to regain his feet, they came at me from three sides. The whores crowded behind them, urging them on with catcalls and vile epithets calling into question their paternity, courage and manliness.

I put my back to the wall and lashed out with my crutch. I managed to hit one, but the other two soon bundled me over. Once off my feet I was helpless.

Now standing over me, Creedal fetched me a hard boot to the ribs.

"Wait on that," Cerinda shouted, pulling at the man's arm. "You said as how he wouldn't be hurt or nothing like that."

218

"And you said as how he would be easy meat," replied the fat man. "Damned monk, if that who he be, carries a sharp purpose in them sticks. Ain't that right, Creedal?"

In answer, and with greater venom, Rat Face booted me again.

"Enough of that," said the fat man. "We is going to deliver him in one, not carve him."

His words offered little comfort.

I was trussed up in rope and carried roughly from the house. None of the whores either glanced my way or said anything to me as I passed. I wanted to believe this was out of embarrassment, but more likely it was disinterest. Trade is trade.

Thorpe Wood
In The Year 1155

Return To Thorpe Wood

The cloth bag was lifted from my head and I found myself stood shivering in the deep snow of Thorpe Wood, gazing up into the face of, after the shoat-devouring boar, my most abiding childhood horror. The Beggar Maker was changed and not for the better. The loose left sleeve of his tattered coat evidenced a lost arm. His scarred face was more deeply lined and haggard, and his once long dark hair had turned a deathly white. Not anchored to his head by a hat, it swirled in tangled wisps around his head in the gusting wind. A Pale Rider without his ghostly mount.

I was taken back to being that terrified child, crumpled on the ground while only Ederick, my dear Ederick, now, if God is truly just, with the angels, stood between me and a cruel life of begging, all in order to fill the pockets of that fearsome band of outlaws and their more fearsome leader. It was only then, in the moment of remembrance, that I realised the fat man and his confederates had brought me to the exact place in the Wood where Ederick and I had lived those many years since. The trees had grown and a few rude huts had been constructed, but it was unmistakably our patch of woodland. Even the shelter was still there, just visible if you had the knowing eye to pick it out from the thick vegetation.

"A most sorry piece of baggage you've brought me, Jep," he said to the fat man. "You come out here bringing me a tale of a murderous, renegade monk, do you? Well, my well-fleshed friend, he does not have the air nor does he give the impression of being a man of the cloister, or if he was, one equipped for violent deeds. Look at the state of him. Hanging between his crutches, twitching and shaking with the palsy. Murder? Surely not murder. Not this one."

He had not connected me with the crippled child seen years

since. I could not decide if his lack of recognition was to my advantage or my disadvantage. Either way, it probably counted for little to a man whose vocation left scant room for human sentiment.

His appearance had changed, but the ice blue eyes and soft, cultured voice were the same, as were the terror they engendered. Short on worldly experience, I presumed brutes to speak as brutes, knights as knights. First with Thomas and now with Bertram, I was discovering this presumption to be ill founded.

Jep, the fat man, so authoritative and confident down in the city, was cowed and uncertain in front of Bertram. Perhaps this terrifying wraith haunted his nightmares too. Perhaps he had witnessed him inflicting unspeakable horrors on his victims. Perhaps this witness fed his dreams, whether sleeping or waking.

"The whores," Jep said, nervously shifting his weight from one foot to the other, "they said as how he be the one the monks be after finding. They all sweared blind, they did. That's how it were. You saying yes, boys?"

Bertram gave them a questioning stare. The men, not meeting his eyes, nodded their agreement.

"Told us how they shaved off the tonsure," said Jep. "And look you here now."

He reached over and roughly pulled the wool cap from my head.

"See them cuts and them sores where the blade been. Shaved, just as the whores told it."

Bertram surveyed my damaged pate. He did not seem convinced.

"Whores say you? Whores would swear day was night if they could turn a coin for it. You know that well enough, don't you, Jep?"

Before he could reply, Bertram turned to me. "What do you say?" he asked. "Are you the murderous monk they seek? Did you strike down your brother monk? Did you?"

I shook my head vigorously and rolled up my eyes and gave him my most convincing idiot's grin, joined with a lolling tongue and side-of-the-mouth string of drool.

"He be lying!" shouted Jep, pulling me to him, his burned face touching mine. "You be lying blue as woad! You tell him so, go on!"

I smiled at him with all the joyous simplicity I could gather. This enraged him still more and he shoved me roughly away. I let go of my crutches, although I could well have resisted, and fell back laughing, as the dim fool I was, into the snow. No one moved to help me up. I continued to laugh and to splutter.

"I tell you, he now be playing at us. He was all fight and fury when we first found him. Not all that dumb show he now be doing. Not a bit of it. Look at Creedal's face. Caught him hard with that crutch. Hit Jessop too. Not no soft, grinning fool then he weren't. And it weren't only them whores who are after saying the monk they been looking for were a cripple. Heard that from others as well. Going all over the city, it were. A crippled monk was what they say. And look what we got, a cripple."

"Cripples are not difficult to find. Norwich is a city overrun with cripples. No, I reckon as those whores have guyed you badly, Jep. Now the question is what we do with a worthless cripple. We hardly have food or shelter enough for ourselves and our Hebrew Guests we got waiting."

Jews? I wanted to ask, but held back. I did not wish to give myself away as someone with reason.

"Let me send Creedal or one of them others back down," Jep begged. "Go to the monks and ask. Tell 'em we got us, maybe got us, the one they be looking for. Tell 'em how he looks. There

223

be profit in it if we got the right one. If not, well, you knows what."

In the event Bertram did not know 'what?' Jep drew a filthy thumb across his equally filthy throat.

So, I was well caught between the monk's trial by ordeal and the Pale Rider's knife. Playacting had gained me nothing but a modicum of time. My fate appeared to be sealed.

Jews In The Wood

All that I had experienced, all I had learned, all my travails in the world had failed to reward me with wisdom, virtue or moral courage. It had all amounted to nothing. I had come full circle, back to Ederick's crude lean-to in the snow where, leaving aside birth and abandonment, my journey had first begun. Bertram's men pushed me through the low entry of my old home to keep company with their 'Hebrew Guests' until the snow let up and one of their number could go down to Norwich to confirm whether or not I was the monk sought for murder and, if by happenstance I was, how much I might be worth to them.

I stood on unsteady legs in the smoke-filled darkness listening for phantoms of the animal-skin-clad, ranting, father-mother Ederick and his ill-formed foundling. My imagination, usually so productive of purposeful visions, could conjure no phantoms of any variety. I was greeted instead by the sound of pain and lamentation. As my eyes became adjusted to the gloom, I made out the source. On the far side of the hut were two figures, one lying, the other on its knees. Their forms were dimly illuminated by a small fire that was producing more smoke than heat. I probed the floor with my crutches and moved slowly towards them.

Mordechai lay covered in a thin blanket. His eyes had sunk deep into his almost fleshless face. The bony skull that remained carried random grey tufts of what had once been a luxuriant beard. He was dying. His moans were weak affairs indicative of waning strength. Miriam, dressed in a torn gown, knelt by his side, rocking back and forth while softly keening. Every few minutes her praying slowed so she could reach out and swab at his forehead with a damp rag.

At last I had come face to face with two Jews who had no doubt had a hand in William's barbarous sacrifice in Saddlegate. Standing over them, I reached into myself for the anger and hatred I had taken pleasure in harbouring for so long. No matter how hard I tried to raise up that anger and that hatred, nothing came. Looking down at the pitiful scene at my feet, at two people who had treated me with kindness, the well of blame and resentment went stone dry.

Miriam, her eyes dulled and continuing to rock back and forth, glanced up without wonder or concern as I approached. It was as if, after an unexplained absence of more than ten years, I had been expected. Whatever had happened to bring her and Mordechai to that frightful place had numbed her ability for surprise. For her anything was possible.

"Mordechai," she said, each word formed with immense effort, "it is Joseph come, come to see you. Ah, the Lord He, He is merciful. Mordechai, look, please look, he is right here standing, standing beside you. You remember little Joseph, do you not? He was, he was with us, yes, in the house only the other day. Our dear, our dear little Joseph. Joseph. Mordechai?"

At first I thought she was attempting to revive her companion's spirits, but quickly I realised that she was in truth visiting a long-vanished past.

With great effort, the dying man rolled his head to the side so he was facing me. A spark of life flickered in his deep-set eyes, but lasted only a few seconds before it gave out. His eyes then closed, and he appeared to fall into a deep sleep. Under the blanket his chest rose and fell imperceptibly.

"You must, must forgive him, Joseph. He is so very weary. So weary from ... You will see, after resting, then he will be feel much improved, much improved. Will you not, Mordechai?"

In the world she was looking out upon, Mordechai was only in need of sleep. Because of where she had chosen to go and her jagged speech, it took some time before I could retrieve enough pieces to put together a story of what had befallen them.

They, together with a man named Samuel, who despite my protestations she insisted I knew, had set out to visit her sister who lived away on the coast in Yarmouth. Not far out of Norwich, where the high road passed through thick woodland, they had been set upon by the robbers who demanded treasure. Samuel and Mordechai told them that they carried no treasure. Samuel was cut down where he stood. The men then attacked her and Mordechai, tearing their clothing from them in search of valuables. When Mordechai tried to protect her, he was beaten senseless. Having found little of value besides their garments, Bertram decided to carry the Jews back to his camp and had then sent word to their co-religionists in the city, saying that if they wanted to see the two alive they would deliver a ransom of 10 marks, a substantial sum to find, even for the Jews. Almost a week had passed and nothing had been heard from the Norwich Jews. In the meantime, Mordechai was nearing his end and Miriam had gone mad.

After a time, one of the guards brought us a bowl of cold pease porridge along with a flagon of water.

"Eat," he ordered sharply. "No one goin' to be paying for dead Jews, they ain't or for that, a dead crippled monk neither If that what you be."

Miriam tried to feed Mordechai, but the old man was insensible to her efforts. He spat out the few morsels that managed to pass his lips.

"You must eat," I told her. "You cannot help him if you don't eat."

She smiled wanly, shook her head, not at me but at some invisible presence and stared off into the middle distance. Still holding the bowl, she once again took up her keening and rocking.

There was nothing to be done, so I pried the bowl from her fingers, retreated to the other side of the lean-to and ate the porridge. It was hardly manna, but I had eaten worse.

Deathbed Stories

The robbers had not bothered to keep up our old lean–to in a sound condition. Drips of melted snow came through the split thatch and draughts of cold wind blew in through the many cracks in the rough wattle and daub walls. Nonetheless, slumped near to the fading embers of the fire, I managed to slip into fitful sleep, albeit one in which I was assailed by the blood-soaked childhood demons that had haunted me so brutally following my last confrontation with Bertram those many years past.

"Joseph," an unsteady voice called to me.

I awoke with a start, thankful for being freed from the torment of my nightmare.

"Joseph? Is that you? In truth, you?"

I was being measured by Mordechai, his sunken eyes reflected in the glow of the fire that our captors had rekindled while I slept. I immediately discounted kindness as a motive. Rather, they had come with more wood because neither frozen-to-death nor starved-to-death hostages would serve their purpose.

I reached across Miriam's sleeping body to pick up the flagon.

"Yes, it is I, Joseph, Mordechai. Will you not take some water?"

With effort he shook his head.

"A dead man has no need of water. I require only peace of mind to ease my journey."

There was nothing to be gained from arguing with him.

"Did the monks treat you well, Joseph? Better than your own people treated you? We did not treat you well, did we?"

"How did you know?" I asked, incredulous.

I had assumed that the Jews knew nothing and cared less about what had happened to me.

"How did we know?" he said. "When you are prisoners in a hostile land, you survive only if you seek out any intelligence that might shield you from harm. At times, of course, as life unfolds its mystery, even the correct intelligence will not serve to protect you."

"And William?"

"Your friend? The tanner's boy?"

"Why was he …? Why was …? Why did you…?"

At this, Mordechai was racked with coughing and for some minutes following he did not speak. Then, as if seeing me for the first time, he repeated.

"Did the monks treat you…?"

"Yes, most of them were good to me."

"I am pleased for that. Pleased."

"What about William?" I insisted. "Why did…?"

He either could not or did not want to hear the question.

"Joseph, I am a most fortunate man that you have come to me, even if you are a phantom. Are you, Joseph? A phantom?"

"No, I am flesh and blood, as you are."

"That's precisely what I would expect a phantom to say."

"I am …".

"Phantom or no, there is something that has been sitting heavy upon my heart for many years. I should have spoken before, but did not have the courage to do so. Now, blessed be the Lord, I am beyond fear, and with no fear there can be no need for courage."

I assumed he was going to tell me what had happened to William. Why they had murdered him. How they had murdered him. He didn't. Instead he told me a story about myself.

Some years before Saul delivered me to Saddlegate, Eleazar's wife, his first wife, and their baby son, together with two of her cousins, had left Norwich to visit his kinfolk in Beccles, a town two days' ride away to the South. No one had returned, and word came that they had never reached Beccles. It was assumed that they had been waylaid on the road, much as had happened to Mordechai and Miriam. Such depredations were not uncommon in those lawless years.

"We never spoke of it, but I knew my brother, and I am convinced that the loss of his wife and child was always with him. To believe that you were that child would have been a painful rebuke to all the hopes he had for his son, the memory he held of his wife's purity and, of course, for himself as a father."

Just as he found it impossible to entertain the idea that I might be his son, it was hurtful for me to recollect my tart, harshly-spoken encounters with Eleazar as if he were my father. If I were able to choose, either Ederick or Saul would be preferable as paternal shepherds for the lost lamb that I was.

Nonetheless, Mordechai's revelation did at least allow me to re-imagine my abandonment in Thorpe Wood. Instead of being rejected and left to die by an uncaring mother, I can see a young woman struggling across a field of knee-deep snow to escape murderous brigands and secreting a wrapped child out of the path of harm, trusting in her merciful God for his salvation. In this new story I was loved, as I had always wanted to be. A mother's love, even a dead mother's love, more than balanced the scales against a denying, and now dead, father's enmity.

On the edge of losing his life, Mordechai had given me the life I had never been able to imagine. It was at that moment, holding close to that new life that I began to imagine, no not

231

imagine, to know with a clear-eyed certainty, that Bertram had more to answer for than my childhood terrors and my current predicament.

Not My Concern

"I wager the one whom you seek is in here, Nephew," said Bertram to someone behind him as he entered the lean-to holding a spluttering torch above his head.

A large figure loomed up at his shoulder, the face obscured by a cloak and the indifferent light.

I had been in the Wood for two or more days. Three of us shared our confinement, but the others' presence made few ripples in the pond. I was utterly alone. Mordechai never replied to my continued enquiries about William, instead he had lapsed into an internal dialogue of incoherent mumbling while drifting in and out of consciousness. When not asleep or staring empty-eyed into the void, Miriam spoke to me in quite a normal manner, asking how I was faring, whether I was being diligent in studying Torah with Rabbi Nathan, who I did not know, and making other commonplace observations, all of which evinced that she was no longer a hostage in Thorpe Wood but had returned to a safer time and place. Neither Mordechai nor Miriam took notice of the new arrivals.

"I do believe you have won the wager, Uncle. Looking upon him it is difficult to credit, but from what I have learned, that pathetic issue is the very man, the very monk, sought by the Prior, indeed the whole of the Priory, for the foul murder of a brother monk."

I was of the opinion that it was impossible to be in the grip of fear and hope in equal measure and at the same moment. It was not. At that moment, fear was tight-drawn company to the words, hope to the voice speaking the words. I was hearing Marcus, but immediately dismissed that notion as a product of desperation. After all, Bertram had called him 'nephew' and the other returned with 'uncle'. A Norman of lordly birth kin to the Beggar Maker was not likely or indeed possible. Fear triumphed. Hope was banished.

"Mark that, will you," Bertram laughed, looking at me, "a cripple monk, not the cripple fool you meant for me to take you for. More fool am I to be so easily fooled. How much gold did you say they offer for his capture and return?"

His mysterious companion stepped into the torch light. Hope victorious! It was Marcus. I was at such a complete loss, that if I had had the words, I would not have then been able to find them.

"They did not let on more than allowing it to be a goodly sum," Marcus said, appraising me with the cold eye of a stranger. "I trust they will be generous. From what I hear, which is of common enough talk in the streets, the monks are all afire to find this renegade, of whom it is said he was at one time a Jew."

"A cripple Jew monk!" Bertram burst out. "What tales you do bring, Nephew. What tales. I would ask for a retelling of how you unlocked the guarded secret of where in the Wood we dwell. And more, that we hold the so-urgently-sought-after outlaw monk."

"As I recounted, Uncle, I learned all from your man, Creedal, who I came upon by happenstance at the house of the harlots sited near to the Cockey."

"I note you share the predilections of my esteemed brother Simon for the company of whores. A weakness our older brother, your father, also shared."

"And you do not share the same weakness, Uncle?"

"I remain curious," replied Bertram, ignoring the other's question, "as to why Creedal was so free in the telling to you so dangerous a secret. Dangerous, that is, to his continued ownership of an injudiciously wagging tongue."

"Oh, he was not so free," admitted Marcus, smiling in the remembering, "At first meeting, that is. But, just as there are no secrets that whores won't trade for coin, so it is with men such as Creedal. Always a price. Easier to strike that bargain when in his cups, and the sum offered enabled him to purchase the favours of the flesh."

"Did the loquacious Creedal part with any further confidences?"

"Of the Jews?" asked Marcus.

"Of the Jews, indeed."

"Yes, Uncle. He told of visiting the Jews who live nearby on the matter of a ransom, if that is of what you speak."

"Precisely," answered Bertram. "The Hebrew brethren have shown considerably greater reluctance to part with their treasure to secure the freedom of those two Jews lying there than Creedal has done to part with confidences as to my affairs. Perchance, this is the reason he has not yet returned."

"Perchance," echoed Marcus, with innocent mien.

In truth, Creedal had not returned to Thorpe Wood because, unless as ghosts, dead men do not travel well, if at all.

After Bertram retired, Marcus told me that when he had come for me, the whores made out that, against their most vigorous efforts to protect me, I had been taken off by ruffians. Poor Creedal had the misfortune of arriving just as the whores were spinning their yarn to my friend. Before he expired, the robber, who unaccustomed as he was to the finer points of bathing, had imbibed an excessive amount of bath water, unburdened himself of all the many secrets that were weighing upon him.

"I was aware that Bertram was an outlaw, but I had only met him once and that was when as a child he paid a visit to my father. I was never able to learn exactly what led him into such a life. My father refused to speak of it or of Bertram. My other uncle, Simon, has been similarly reluctant."

"Curious to tell," I said, "it was but a few paces from where we are that as a very young boy I also saw Bertram. Begging was his purpose for me. Said I was by nature made for it. If not for Brother Edgar, then Ederick, who, at peril of death, stood him down, I fear to think what would have become of me. Now, Marcus, once more I am compelled to ask that same question. What is to become of me? Will you not take me from here?"

"Have patience, Joseph, before long I will find a way."

"Please, Marcus, before word reaches here as to what really happened to Creedal and we are both placed in danger."

"What of those Jews?" he asked, gesturing to where the two silent figures lay.

I glanced over at Mordechai and Miriam. I thought of William, murdered and violated, lying alone among the fallen leaves. The scales swung against them.

"The Jews are not my concern."

The Truth Will Set You Free

Jesus said that the Truth will set you free. However, first you must discover God's Truth and then you must embrace it. The Carpenter did not set an easy task. And what of the worldly, day-to-day truths? If only they could set you free as well, I might have enjoyed a more contented life. You see, a good lie, a comforting lie, a convenient lie, a lie that if not known as a lie to he who lives and dies with it, is as good as not being burdened with the truth. At times it is much better than being so burdened. As it fell out, the truth that I continue to carry, that most terrible truth, has shackled me in chains for more than eighty years. Worse to relate, it was forced upon me by one for whom truth was at best an inconvenient irrelevance, as was I.

"I will take him back to the Priory," offered Marcus. "I am known to them. They will not question me too closely."

"You will return to me with what they pay for the capture of this dangerous murderer?" asked Bertram, casting a sardonic grin in my direction.

"Do you doubt me?"

"Do I have reason not to doubt you, Nephew? Does the same blood not flow through you as through me and through my noble younger brother, your uncle."

"What am I to take from that remark? I know my uncle to be unbending and oft times cruel, but have you perchance treated with or had some commerce with him to cause you to besmirch his name and mine by a spurious equation of blood?"

"Spurious equation, Nephew?" Bertram laughed, his scar rippling as a purple viper's tail wrapped round his neck. "When I relate the nature of our 'commerce', as you choose to name it, I will leave it to you to decide on the spuriousness or not of the equation."

237

He paused. Picking up a stout branch, with his one good arm he stirred the fire. A cloud of sparks rose up and danced, red pinpricks against the darkness. Further away on the other side of the clearing three or four of his gang sat hunched over a separate fire. Bertram may have been an outlaw, but he was also a Norman of high birth who resisted too-familiar contact with his lowborn Saxon ruffians.

"Some years since it was that I had dealings with my brother. Apparently, it had come to his ears that I was engaged in a certain trade that would service his requirements."

"Of which trade do you speak?" asked Marcus.

"You have no doubt heard what some choose to call me?"

"An outlaw," returned Marcus. "A highwayman, a despoiler of women, a thief, a…".

"Enough!" Bertram called out angrily.

Across the way, heads turned in our direction. Bertram stared into the fire.

"No one has dared address me as such to my face, but at a safe distance, when out of my hearing, I know that I am called the Maker of Beggars."

"Of course," Marcus said, hesitantly, "the Beggar Maker. I have heard the like. What pray, has this to do with my uncle?"

"Well, on occasion the process of transformation, of changing, can go awry and we are left not with a child fit for the street, but one fit only for the grave. The meaning is clear, Nephew?"

Marcus studied the ground at his feet and nodded.

"Well," continued the Beggar Maker, his voice as heavy as the surrounding night, "your esteemed uncle desired me to deposit the body of, shall we call it an 'unsuccessful transformation', one with quite particular wounds, not in an unmarked grave, as was my practice, but rather where the body would be easily found by those passing. I expressed my doubts as to the wisdom of this. I explained that my success as one who transformed children and my ability in avoiding the executioner's axe, relied on there being no bodies, so no evidence. You cannot accuse a man without there being at least some evidence. He said that I need not concern myself, as the blame would not fall upon me. When I pressed him further, he said the less I knew the better it would be for me and for him. So, hand on my heart, black as the heart may seem to some, hand on my black heart I waited until there was an unfortunate accident before delivering the body requested. You might view me as an evil man, and that may indeed be the case, but I do not set out with the intention of murdering young children. An accident, it was no more than an accident."

"You speak of a boy?" Marcus asked, throwing a pained look at me. "The one found nearby? This would be little William murdered by the Jews?

Bertram fixed a baleful eye on Marcus. He held out his one hand, palm upturned, as if in supplication.

"So," he replied with a half smile, "Perhaps then I should be called rather 'The Saint Maker'. It lies better on the tongue than Beggar Maker, does it not?"

Bertram waited, but Marcus did not reply.

"Yes, I see. My brother never upheld his part of the bargain. He refused payment. He complained that I had killed the wrong child. He had stipulated only the body of a child. How was I to know the child was kin to a close confidant of his? Further, even this served to be to his advantage. The priest became the principal voice in stirring the mob against the Jews, as well as their principal accuser in the Synod. Oh yes, Nephew, how could it escape my notice that fixing blame on the Jews for murder was from the beginning my brother's objective? It was common gossip that he owed more than he could find to repay his debt to the old Jew. When the Bishop had refused to take action and the Sheriff moved quickly to protect the Jews it appeared that his plans had been thwarted. It mattered little, however, for the church acquired its saint, the priest and his family gained in the reflected glory, and even brother Simon prospered as he was later able to murder the Hebrew usurer with impunity."

My poor dear William, 'no more than an accident'. How he must have suffered. But he did not suffer at the hands of the Jews. It was Bertram, who but for my brave Ederick would have ensnared me as one of his beggars, perhaps even murdered me to provide the body demanded by Simon de Novers. He did not kill by accident. He killed to order. William! Joseph! A fool indeed. So full of blind hatred for my own people. Yes, my own people. They treated me harshly, but not so harshly that they deserved to be hounded, to be killed, to have their property robbed from them or put to the torch.

Fool I was. Fool I have remained.

Out Of The Woods

Bertram eventually agreed to allow Marcus to take me back to Norwich so that I could be handed over to the Priory monks. To ensure that his nephew made good on his word to return with the thirty pieces of silver, he insisted that Jep accompany us.

"What about the Jews?" I asked Marcus. "We cannot abandon them here."

"I was made to understand that they were not your concern?"

"They were not. Now they are."

"I see," he said. "What I fail to see is how we will persuade Bertram to part with them while he awaits the ransom. We are fortunate that he has given me leave to take you away."

"If we do not help them, they will die. Mordechai is already on the edge and Miriam will no doubt follow ere long."

"Put this from your thoughts Joseph. The fact that you know that William was not murdered by the Jews, does not give you responsibility for the welfare of these pitiful souls. They are captive here through no fault of yours."

I continued to plead with him, but to no avail. The next day we left the camp without Miriam and Mordechai.

I sat perched on Marcus's horse, my ever-quivering arms around his waist. Jep walked to the side. Snow was falling, as it had each time I arrived or left out from Thorpe Wood.

After about an hour Marcus stopped.

"Something amiss?" inquired Jep, looking up.

"It is nothing," replied Marcus, dismounting. "I must relieve myself."

He began to walk away.

"And you, crippled one?" asked the fat robber, turning to me, "I wonder whether you be for the noose or whether you be for the axe? You have a best guess?"

He never heard my reply. Marcus cut him down with a single sword thrust through the back. He was looking at me, his eyes wide and uncomprehending as blood dripped and then gushed from his mouth, staining the snow.

"What would you have me do?" Marcus said, seeing the look of fear struggling for purchase with the spasms that wracked my face and body. "You did know it had to be done, didn't you? Better here before he realises we do not make for the city."

He climbed back on the horse, but instead of continuing down toward the river, he started to retrace our journey back towards Bertram's camp.

"Not a word, Joseph. Do not utter a word."

When we were near enough to hear the robbers talking to each other, Marcus got off and with me clinging to its back, led the horse to a dense stand of line-thin birch below the camp. We waited there until dark, and when we could no longer hear voices Marcus left me and went off up the slope. Half an hour later he returned with Miriam slung over his shoulder. Her hands and feet were bound and she was gagged. Finger to his lips, he motioned me to be quiet.

The snow had begun to fall more heavily, but we did not stop moving until well away from the camp. Marcus built a fire in the lee of a large boulder. It was only then that he freed Miriam.

"Mordechai! Mordechai!" she screamed, looking about her in terror.

"Calm yourself, woman," Marcus said, putting a restraining hand on her shoulder.

"Miriam, it is Joseph," I said. "You are safe now."

She stared at me wild-eyed, with no hint of recognition.

"Mordechai!" she wailed again and again, while pulling at her grey, straggling hair.

I gave Marcus a questioning look.

"I could not bring him out, Joseph. He was dying, almost dead from the way he looked. It was difficult enough getting her from the hut without alarming Bertram and his men. I tried to reason with her, but she did not want to leave him and so I had no choice but to tie her."

Miriam continued to cry out until we were forced to gag her once more and to tie her up so she would not run off into the night.

Marcus and I settled in our capes near to the fire. The snow had stopped falling, the sky was almost white with stars and a large crescent moon had risen from behind the tree line. The night noises of the wood were muffled by the thick snow. The only sounds to be heard, besides Miriam's sobs and the twig snap of the fire, were the piercing cries of woodland owls.

"Was it difficult to learn what truly befell your friend? An accident, as Bertram would have it, an accident, mind you, not the martyrdom of a saint."

"Accident, Marcus? How can what your uncle did be called an accident? William died while he was being purposely mutilated. Mutilated, Marcus, or as your uncle called it, to save his shame, 'transformed'. Transformed from life to death, Marcus. That is murder without doubt or discussion. You ask is it difficult for me. Yes, difficult indeed. Beyond rage, it tears at my heart, Marcus. I loathe to imagine what he suffered at the hands of those men. Nonetheless, as shown by the many miracles he has worked, he did not need the Jews. He did not need them at all. Jews or no Jews, William was forever marked out as a saint, and for me that is what he always will be."

"You are a loyal friend, Joseph, loyal beyond the grave. It is to your credit. Now try to sleep. Tomorrow we have far to travel."

At first light we set off, Marcus leading the horse carrying me and Miriam.

"The snow will have covered our tracks," said Marcus, "but we best make haste in the event they are clever enough to pick up our trail from here."

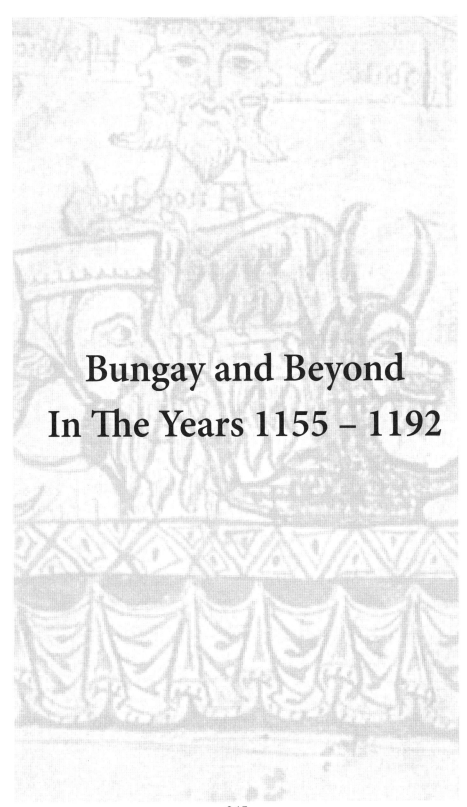

Bungay and Beyond
In The Years 1155 – 1192

Journeys To Freedom

Once we came down the hill from Thorpe Wood to the river the snow had stopped falling and the way, although thick with snow, was at least flat and so became somewhat easier for travel. Miriam sat sideways on the horse, slumped limp against me, while I did the best my cold and spasmed limbs would allow to keep her from falling. Marcus, who had to wade through the snow while leading the horse, continued to glance over his shoulder, to ensure we were not being pursued, as we followed the course of the river southwards. Near to Norwich, we passed water mills, fish weirs and tanneries, all made idle by steep-ridged coverings of snow and ice. Our journey's landscape was hardly differentiated, encased as it was in a shroud of white. Few people were to be seen.

It was a most difficult passage, each day pushing through deep snow and at night having to search for shelter and food. On the first evening we were welcomed at a manor house of a family known to Marcus. The other two or three stops were at churches where we were taken in when Marcus explained he was taking two sickly pilgrims to Bury St. Edmunds.

Thankfully, the extreme conditions we faced gave me no time to dwell on what I had learned about William and about myself.

"When we arrive in Bungay," Marcus said on our fourth and last day out from Norwich, "I will tell the Jews there how I came upon two sorely distressed Jews on the road near to their town. They are not to know of your monastic sojourn or that you are sought by the Priory for high crimes. To them you will be a kinsman, a poor cripple who cannot speak, and you must not even attempt it. The woman is so addled she will not disabuse them of this."

It was as Marcus had predicted. We were taken in, with many questions being asked, but with no answers able to be offered, at least none that made sense coming from Miriam. Given the few Jews who had settled in the region, almost of all of whom originally came from Rouen, it was no surprise that she was well known in Bungay, being related in some way to a number of the people there.

Although my duplicitous behaviour should have denied me, fortune smiled upon me in Bungay. Saul Ibn Abraham happened to be there, passing through the town on his never-ending poetic journey, delivering verse to one unappreciative stone-eared Jewish community after another. What was not so propitious for him was that my old mentor, friend and protector had recently lost his sight.

"If I were a good Christian," he laughed, "I would make pilgrimage to Norwich and pray to their new boy saint we are supposed to have made for them, for which they should give us thanks, instead of murder and riot."

I did not tell him what had happened to me, and he did not know of my friendship with William or that I had fled from Saddlegate. My arriving in company with Miriam strengthened the perception that I had not strayed from the Norwich Jews.

"But, Joseph," Saul continued, "I am blessed, thanks be to God, for my hearing remains and I am able still to listen to the music of the words. If only others could hear that same music, my life in this accursed country would be more worthwhile, as would theirs."

Music of words or no, going blind posed many challenges for a wandering Jew poet. As fate decreed, I was to offer a solution to his most immediate need and he for mine.

"Joseph," Saul confessed, "I have been in this cold and inhospitable land far too many years. Old age is working into my bones, and I yearn, before I become too old to feel the

247

warmth of the southern sun and smell the heady fragrances of my youth. It is time for this blind poet to go home. I know you are crippled, but you are young and you are strong and I think not adverse to adventure. Would you be my eyes, Joseph? I can promise you that adventure and a world of Jews as you could never find either here or in your earthbound dreaming."

And so it was that some days later, with a weighty purse filled with gold coin provided by Marcus, Saul Ibn Abraham and I, Joseph of Norwich, set out on an epic journey which took us through France and the kingdoms of Spain to the golden city of Toledo, a city where I was to spend the next forty years and discover how to become, praise be to God, the Jew that I was born to be.

After that length of time and a full life enriched by learning, to say nothing of Saul's youthful fragrances and the ever warming sun, one day, I felt the chill breath of Death upon me. Knowing beyond doubt that I was soon to die, I longed to find rest in the place of my birth and more, for where I had found my greatest love and because of it, committed my greatest folly. Shortly thereafter I began to make my way back to the city of Norwich. As it happened, however, Death, a cruel jester, apparently decided to turn his face away. Instead of the longed-for release, I have been burdened with many more years of painful remorse and slow decay in this unfriendly place. No matter, if, as it seems likely, my end is finally so near, I will meet it close by my dearest friend, my sainted William.

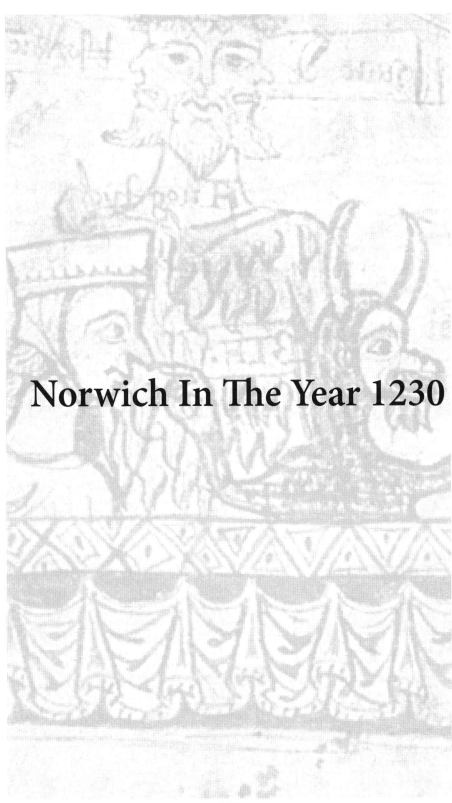

Norwich In The Year 1230

For Christ And St. William

The Franciscan stares at me expectantly, but I let my head fall to my chest and tell him nothing. After all, I am exhausted and there is nothing of real consequence to tell.

The door to the street opens and two women and a small child enter, followed by another Franciscan friar. As they approach the bench, I recognise both women.

"Joseph," one called Hannah says, raising her voice as people will do to the aged and infirm, and then enunciating each word as if they existed apart, rather than being joined together in a sentence. "I am relieved to see you are safe. We saw everyone running from the house where you live and then men breaking in and ransacking. How did you manage to escape?"

I shrug. "The Holy One, Blessed is He, saw my travail and sent his emissaries, two angels in the guise of young boys to rescue me. They brought me here."

"What does the old man say?" asks the other, whose name I cannot recall.

"Something about the Holy One and angels, but that's all I can understand. Poor old man," she says, putting a finger to the side of her head.

Experience, scholarly knowledge and perhaps a touch of wisdom amount to nothing when encased in an ancient, crippled body. So, Joseph the Fool.

The women and children that were here when I first arrived come back into the room and are greeted with embraces and tears.

"You are all welcome to take refuge with us," says the first friar, "until the storm has passed. We trust in God that this will be but a short while."

There is a loud clamour just outside and suddenly the door flies open and men push their way inside.

"Stop!" shouts one of the friars, holding up a large wooden crucifix to the advancing mob. "These people are under the protection of the Order of the Blessed Saint Francis!"

"Aside, Friar," yells the foremost, a heavyset man brandishing a thick wooden club. This is none of your affair."

The two friars place themselves between us and the mob.

"Why you want to protect murderers of Our Lord Jesus Christ?" someone calls out.

"You supposed to serve Christ," another adds. "Not the Jews."

"These women and these children and this crippled old man, they did not kill Jesus," replies a friar. "Surely you people must see that."

"What about our Saint William?" the heavyset man asks. "You not going to stand there and tell us it weren't the Jews that murdered him?"

"And cut that boy. Jews done that, right enough."

"Stand aside, friar. Stand aside."

No one moves. The children begin to whimper, as do the women. I too am frightened but refuse to bend or break. I must accept that the long earth-bound journey of my soul is nearing its end. I pray.

"For Christ and St. William," someone in the mob bellows.

I lift my eyes to the mountains -- from where will my help come?
My help will come from the Lord, Maker of heaven and earth.

The cry is taken up by many voices, "For Christ and St. William! For Christ and St. William!"

I shrink back against the wall, unable to finish my prayer. The mob surges, the friars are knocked aside. Clubs and rakes and scythes and flaming brands. A woman is thrown down in front of me. Screams. A chorus of screams. A club. Another.

"For Christ and St. William!"

A searing pain in the side of my head.

"For Christ and St. William!"

* * *

Out of the depths I call to You, O Lord.

I can no longer hear the groans, the crying, the screams. Only my ragged breath remains, echoing softly against the damp walls of what I imagine is a well. I feel no bodily pain. To be precise, I cannot feel anything except the parched dryness of my lips and throat. The rest of my wasted body has flown from me, leaving only perforating thoughts and distant memories.

I must have been the last one. Through the haze of darkened glass I remember hands pulling at my clothing, a sharp pain in my shoulder as I was thrown to the ground and then being dragged by my feet. A rag carrying the stench of pitch had been bound across my face. When I shouted at the mob, I received in reply low curses together with a stiff boot to my side. There followed a sense of weightlessness, cool air rushing by and then the breath being crushed from me as I landed on something pliant, squirming and warm. Voices rose from beneath me, the pained and frightened wailing of children, others calling out in prayer, all struggling for life ebbing away, life no longer in their grasp.

For almost a hundred years I have conceived many deaths and prayed that a soft death would be visited upon me, not this death now before me, one that was never there in my darkest moments. So here I lie on a tangle of corpses, Joseph the Fool, finally called to account, not for loving too well, but for chaining that love to a hatred that has consumed so many Jews before and is now consuming him. Justice for a fool.

Truly a fool. A fool dying a foul and unholy death. Not washed, not dressed in the tachrichim, not wrapped in a white shroud and lowered and returned to the clean earth. There will be no "Blessed are You, Lord our God, King of the universe, the True Judge." No "This is for the good," for how can such a response be given for such an abominable end for me and the poor innocents below.

The bodies beneath me have ceased their moving, the moans are silenced. The once warm flesh beneath me now feels waxy, damp and cold. I am doomed to spend my last moments buried in this Hell, but I refuse to leave my last thoughts buried here with me. I prefer to have those thoughts fly up to recall the vibrant times, the better times, even the difficult times, I have experienced during my long journey. As William said, other people can attempt to impose indignities upon you, but they are only real indignities if you swallow them down and permit them to have dominion over you. Although a fool, that I refuse to allow.

Hear, O Israel, the Lord is our God, the Lord is One.

Afterword
Norwich 19th of March, 2013

The remains of 17 people suspected to have been killed under 13th Century religious persecution, have been given a Jewish ceremonial burial in Norwich.

The bones, which include the remains of 11 children, were found piled in a well during survey work ahead of the city's Chapelfield development in 2004.

Historical evidence has indicated the remains are of Jewish descent so they have been buried on sacred land.

About 100 people from a number of faiths attended the historic event.

Clive Roffe, Norwich representative on the Board of Deputies of British Jews, said the service was emotional.

"To bury 17 people at once had to be an emotional experience for all those who attended, no matter what their faith.

"The wider Jewish community is delighted we've been able to do this and after more than 800 years since they died it's a very fitting end."

"The people we buried today had a sad and brutal ending to their lives, so at least these souls are now at peace."

BBC News Norfolk

Sources

The sole primary source of William's story is the virtually contemporary hagiography, *The Life and Passion of William of Norwich by Thomas of Monmouth*. It is made up of seven short books which were written between about 1150 and 1173. It was originally translated from Latin in 1896. It has recently (2014) been retranslated with a new introduction by Miri Rubin. Unfortunately, this new edition came out after I finished the novel and so I was unable to avail myself of either the fresh translation or the superbly magisterial and comprehensive introduction. There is no better account, not only of Thomas's work, but also of the historical context and the terrible legacy of the case of William of Norwich. Rubin also cites the most significant scholarly articles on the subject.

On the Benedictines, beside Thomas's account, I found Julie Kerr's excellent *Life in the Medieval Cloister* particularly useful. Among other books that proved helpful were:

Ian Atherton, Eric Fernie, Christopher Harper-Bill and Hassell Smith, eds., *Norwich Cathedral: Church, City and Diocese, 1096-1996*.

Ronald C. Finucane, *Miracles and Pilgrims. Popular Beliefs in Medieval England.*

Ruth Mazo Karras, *Common Women. Prostitution and Sexuality in Medieval England.*

V.D. Lipman, *The Jews of Medieval Norwich.*

Irina Metzler, *Disability in Medieval Europe. Thinking about Physical Impairment during the high Middle Ages, c.1100-1400.*

Ivan G. Marcus, *Rituals of Childhood: Jewish Acculturation in Medieval Europe.*

Carole Rawcliff and Richard Wilson, eds. *Medieval Norwich.*

Miri Rubin, *Gentiles Tales. The Narrative Assault on Late Medieval Jews.*

Israel Jacob Yuval, *Two Nations in Your Womb: Perceptions of Jews and Christians in Late Antiquity and the Middle Ages.*

The Cover. The cover shows a cartoon doodle from an Exchequer Roll of 1233 held in the National Archives. All the figures are of prominent Jews who lived in Norwich